LILIES

that

FESTER

Marion Ansell

MENTOR

This Edition first published 2000 by

Mentor Books
43 Furze Road
Sandyford Industrial Estate, Dublin 18
Ireland
Tel. (00353 1) 295 2112/3   Fax. (00353 1) 295 2114
e-mail: admin@mentorbooks.ie
www.mentorbooks.ie

ISBN: 1-84210-018-1

Editing and Layout by Mentor Books
Cover Design: Slatter-Anderson
Printed in Ireland by ColourBooks Ltd.

1 3 5 7 9 10 8 6 4 2

ABOUT THE AUTHOR

A late starter, Marion Ansell began writing after emerging unscathed from a serious car accident. Her first foray into writing was a volume of street poetry retelling her wide experiences of weddings, funerals and parties. Further encouragement by her coterie of friends and acquaintances then led her to write her first novel, *Lilies that Fester.*

Marion merrily declares she is forty-nine going on eighteen. She lives in decadent splendour in Cambridge with her devoted husband, Matthew, and Belladonna, her black cat.

To Leslie Read who taught me the art of yarn-spinning, and to Evelyn May Read, deceased, who used to shake her umbrella at the schoolteachers who didn't understand lateral thinking.

The summer's flower is to the summer sweet,
Though to itself it only live and die,
But if that flower with base infection meet,
The basest weed outbraves his dignity:
For sweetest things turn sourest by their deeds;
Lilies that fester smell far worse than weeds.

William Shakespeare
1564–1616

Contents

Prologue

The man was alone. He lay in complete darkness, paralysed arms neatly arranged over his chest and crossed at the wrists like those of a dead knight. The man was still alive. He had his hearing and his sense of smell but he couldn't speak or see. He was well aware of where he had been put and why, so he allowed a small frisson of self-congratulation to skitter through his mind. It was a relief that he hadn't lost his memory or his powers of analysis. His sightless eyes glittered with rage. He was grateful for the small mercy that he could hear what was going on around him outside his prison. The greatest concern of the mute man was the fact that he was unable to move a muscle – except his eyelids which blinked rapidly as hot tears ran their course down into his ears and on into his tangled blond hair. His tears were a salty cocktail of injustice, rage, self-pity and fear. Despite the pitch darkness and the paralysis in his limbs he knew he was surrounded closely by four walls, entombed. He was sure that he was alone in the building now.

His self-bestowed omnipotence had blinded him, he had thought himself invincible, all-knowing. He had underestimated badly. He had made a grave mistake and now he was paying for it.

There was a very familiar smell in the confined space round him. He recognised it as the cloying stench of decaying flowers – lilies, lots of them. He inhaled again. These lilies stank. Although sightless he knew they were limp and dying, turning to mulch. The once-proud heads shrivelled and brown.

He lay in total darkness on a bed of dead and dying flowers, unable to move. Somewhere in the background he could hear a heart-wrenching torch song being sung with a hopeless passion. He wondered if his enhanced sense of smell was compensation for the loss of other vital senses because mingling with the nauseating perfume of rotting flowers he could detect another insidious drier back note. He concentrated very hard, painfully summoning the vestige of his faltering brain-power. Then he had the answer – smoke.

He could smell burning.

1

Dinner at Eight

The dinner party was the ideal occasion on which to take stock of progress. The individual counselling sessions were all concluded and by gathering the women to share their experiences and hopes, she presumed they'd be relieved to meet others with similar scars. She thought of them as her 'optimistic leper colony', four women who'd shed the chrysalis of dead guilt. They would meet to chew over their problems, make a meal of the past and spit out the unpalatable, rejecting what was too rich to swallow. By coffee and mints she was convinced they'd each go their separate ways bearing a semblance of wholeness.

Letti was a good listener, a qualified and respected counsellor. She'd earned her colours in a hospital in her homeland that was little more than an asylum, before graduating to one of London's most elegant private nut-houses where burned-out rock legends and bejewelled humpty-dumpty heiresses, all the king's whoreses and some of the king's men were put back together again. The quartet of murderesses she'd invited to dine had all done their time at Her Majesty's pleasure while receiving the varying amounts of drugs and direction. Letti had spent the requisite hours with them and superficially they were as patched up and clean as possible except that Letti was a perfectionist and she liked a bit of extra-curricular, a little 'cowboy work'. The dinner party was the final farewell, the goodbye kiss and pat on the bottom to a quartet of naughty girls who'd stood in the corner long enough.

Letti was five-foot-two-eyes-of-grey and forty-eight. She was lean and plain until she smiled. She had a penchant for multicoloured hand-knits which brightened her basic collection of bat-like flowing black garments. She was a retro-hippie, a small foreigner with bright beady eyes and brighter accessories, the most brilliant of which was her brain. Arriving in England a naive student, she'd been through the emotional mill. A succession of dusky airmen, an idealistic carpenter who'd dumped her to carve out a simple life from a Donegal hillside, a sprinkling of beautiful but flawed junkies, an alcoholic mechanic and a few regrettable one-night stands represented the collective fabric of her love life including Charles on whom she'd burnt her fingers the most, yet she still hadn't considered herself as having ever truly been in love. Letti knew about men; an ectopic pregnancy and the loss of an ovary had taught her the measure of pain. She was well armed to listen, soothe and counsel, having emerged from a great deal of soul-searching and self-healing and at last she was enjoying a relationship with 'Mr Right'.

Mr Right had similarly spent a large part of his early life abroad travelling with his parents, a secretive child in a Force's family. She suspected he'd had an introverted childhood. He was awkward when talking about himself at length but this was the perfect foil for her profession. At the end of the day Letti found a refreshing clarity in not having to listen to rambling diatribes on past insecurities and intricate hang-ups, so he suited her. He'd shown little inclination to move into her minimalist apartment, bringing with him all the accoutrements of modern man from woks to boxer shorts. She wasn't particularly into ironing and he looked as if he was a bit of a stickler for creases in all the right places. On balance he seemed quite capable of looking after his own domestic arrangements but nevertheless Letti harboured a master plan, her dream for the future. She had it filed neatly at the back of her mind in readiness for the appearance of the right man – husband material.

Her previous serious romantic involvement had been with Charles the academic whose qualities had almost fitted the profile she had mapped out as perfect for the role but her learned lover was already spoken for having a subservient wife tucked away in Europe. This was very convenient from Letti's point of view but firmly ruled him out of the running as a long-term consort.

This latest Mr Right happily carried no such baggage. It was early days yet and although so far he had shown little interest in shacking up with Letti, there was definite hope. On several occasions he'd quite comfortably engaged in tentative conversation concerning their possible relocation to Letti's homeland in the distant hazy future somewhere along the path of true love. For the moment Letti had to be satisfied with this. It was enough basic structure for her to embellish with harmless and comforting fantasies and it got her through the tough working day in a career with which she was becoming increasingly jaded and frustrated.

Until her prince came along Letti's prudent utilisation of her inherited family assets together with her razor-sharp brain and voracious appetite for hard graft had provided wealth, style and satisfaction. The added quotient of love had somehow unbalanced the arrangement. Mr Right provided a relaxed and pleasing aspect hitherto missing in Letti's life.

She had the excellent sense to take it slowly, play it by ear and not push him into an engagement. 'Softly, softly, catchee monkey' was the premise by which she had begun working at this relationship. It had to work, she was going to make it work. Letti knew she was no great beauty but this man had already declared his love. She rather fancied ditching her career and becoming a country wife. She wanted to pick up the threads with her brothers if they were still alive. She could afford to be patient but not too patient. Being a keen observer she couldn't help but clock up every little plus-point. He would bring her gifts: usually books, sometimes jewellery, often fine wine. Letti had built up both a valuable and interesting library and a plentiful cache of wine. It definitely wouldn't be a dry dinner party. While selecting which wine should accompany which course she allowed herself the delicious luxury of thinking about Mr Right.

He saw her every couple of weeks, worked in computers and travelled. He was tall and blond and hid guileless brown eyes behind tortoiseshell glasses. Without his glasses his eyes were stunning, brown as dark toffee but with a glint of blue which Letti could occasionally glimpse if the light was exactly right. He was definitely the more beautiful partner of the two of them but he said Letti's mind was the sexiest and most attractively complex thing about her. He also said he loved her. All these

endearments Letti stored up in her mind's bottom
drawer. She was absolutely sure this one was
honourable, sure to the point of resting on her
laurels but every couple of weeks was not quite
enough for Letti's liking. She considered discussing
the subject with her guests tonight. They were all
worldly women, too worldly perhaps. Letti
resolved to see how the conversation progressed
before she had her say. She expected there would be
a lot of demons to exorcise this evening.

Mr Right was called Jon and he called her
Honeybunny – ridiculous really because a less
fluffy woman would be hard to find. Letti was
angular not fluffy, all geometric haircut and black
garments, all cheekbones and incisive brain. The
secret cherished nickname 'Honeybunny'
appealed to her alter ego. In one of her early-hours
journeys into self-analysis she yearned to be a
dewy-lipped nubile platinum-blonde and with not
a lot between the ears. The girls in the hairdressing
salon or the bland nymphets who doled out her
lasagne in the hospital canteen were to be secretly
envied – no problems, no responsibilities other
than the decision about which wine bar to frequent
on a Friday evening and whether they had a hole
in their tights – bliss!

Letti/Honeybunny mulled over her role in life
as she laid her stark black ash dining table with
plain silver cutlery and pristine white china. It
would be an attractive meal, visually pleasing,

easily digestible with little extravagances, treats to tempt women, especially women who had consumed quite a few institutional meals. She paused and admired the oval dishes bearing halved avocados and crab meat drizzled with vinaigrette. White linen napkins and square Bohemian glasses flanked each setting. On the lacquered Japanese side table five sharp fruit knives glittered beside a deep crystal bowl of peaches and apricots. On a black octagonal plate, a small stilton sweated in a coulis of port which shone blood red in the candlelight.

Having set the stage Letti looked forward to gathering together her four patients, or clients as she preferred to think of them. After all, the service she provided was not unlike that of the envied hairdresser, using her skills to improve the client's perception of herself and then sending her off to face the world outwardly attractive, that is until the client tries to do her own self-styling in the future – a little more difficult without the security of a professional touch.

Letti eased a Jacques Brel CD into the player enjoying the clear factual lyrics. Clipped accounts of love, life and loss – reflective but not consistently sad, realist music for real women, women with optimism. As Brel sang a harsh docklands shanty about wanton wenches and randy Dutch sailors the intercom buzzed the arrival of Elizabeth.

2

Fitou and Fratricide

Elizabeth's prison pallor was at odds with her big-boned generous-bodied country-girl air. She wore her mousy hair in a bob and her pain in her eyes. Like a camouflage suit she wore mismatched florals, no jewellery, little make-up and her heart on her sleeve. This heart had been bared so frequently to Letti that Elizabeth felt her counsellor knew all there was to know about 'Before'.

Before the incident Elizabeth had helped run teagardens with her mother in a pretty village where nothing much happened. She was determined to return to the same village and brazen out the inevitable gossip and whispers. She longed for the poppy-studded barley fields, the scent of over-ripe plums, birdsong, familiar cottages and favourite walks. She needed to go back, recapture and re-create after the interminable grey incarceration in the impersonal concrete city. Even this lovely monochrome and linear apartment of Letti's was of little comfort. The waxen lilies reminded her of funerals. Funerals reminded her of her brother. Memories of her brother reminded her that she could never ever go back and find peace, but now she was no longer alone and she was willing to try.

After her release Elizabeth had been found a placement in a big brash coffee bar. Her tea-garden skills had been put to good use but the ugly steel equipment and the irritating hiss of the espresso machine jarred her senses and depressed her almost beyond endurance. The clientele were stressed and rushed, too busy to make anything but minimal conversation. She slapped sandwiches onto plates and crockery onto tables like a robot, not noticing those who were not noticing her. Floral china, walnut cake and chapel-going folk with time to chatter seemed a million miles away and yet against all odds one afternoon James ordered a cappuccino and engaged her in the first worthwhile conversation since her release.

James had persevered. Being a sales representative limited his visits to once a week but over the months he'd waited for her to discard her uniform and her mistrust and now he'd proposed. Although she was a tall woman Elizabeth felt feminine and less clumsy beside James who was six feet tall and favoured soft corduroy jackets and quiet evenings in her tiny bed-sit where they wove dreams of setting up home together in a small village, having two children, working and playing together – maybe even embarking on a new teagarden venture.

Letti ushered Elizabeth into her home, divested her of a couple of patchwork layers and offered her a glass of Fitou, a dish of black olives and a warm welcome.

Elizabeth gravitated towards the huge vase of white lilies, a breath of nature to gaze at and admire, a talking point albeit funereal. Elizabeth preferred spring cowslips, summer poppies, the natural harvest of the countryside, scarce nowadays but free for gathering by little girls in the 1950s, those painful years when 'It' happened. Even hot-house lilies reminded her.

While they waited for the remaining three guests to arrive Letti coaxed Elizabeth to recount a tale she'd heard many times before, a simple wistful children's story but without a happy ending. Elizabeth sank into a leather armchair, curled her legs beneath her, contemplated the glass of wine, glowing richly red in the candlelight and embarked on the story of her bête noire – the tale of the big bad wolf . . .

'It was advisable to prepare for the long and exciting journey by wearing our best wellingtons and gathering emergency supplies which amounted to a bottle of cola 'borrowed' from Marjorie's dad's shop in the village, a selection of banana and golden syrup sandwiches and a sherbet fountain to ensure we wouldn't starve.

'My dolls pram although second-hand was the largest and so we took that, transporting a favourite toy apiece – my well-worn teddy bear and Marjorie's kaleidoscope. I put a knitted doll's hat on Willum, our cat, but he wouldn't stay in the pram. My brother Philip couldn't come either because he was too young but mainly because he was a boy, so he busied himself sulkily scraping a grave for his newly deceased pet newt lying in state in a matchbox. Philip's pets were always dying so we had made a wonderful animals' graveyard amongst the nasturtiums by the whitewashed wall of the outside lavatory. Mum was at the chapel doing the flowers and Dad didn't mind what we did as long as we didn't tread on his beans.

'As we trundled the dolls pram out of the shady lane and into the spring sunshine Willum raised his head and surveyed us with his usual feline disinterest until we got some distance away. He was a nervous cat who bolted whenever Philip came into his presence and on seeing me depart ran off somewhere to hide. Willum then was our only witness as we embarked on our annual search for bluebells in the nearby woods.

'We took turns to push the pram. Marjorie was

plump but pretty in a red velvet dress which looked a treat with her wellingtons. She was my best friend because she drank up my horrible lukewarm school milk for me as well as her own. I was prime decision maker of our duo because I was the taller and my granddad was the first in the village to own a car which made up for the outside lavatory in village status.

'Our first stop was the spindlewood tree halfway down Millers Road where we picked the shiny cerise buds to keep in our jewellery boxes until they shrivelled and dried. There were elm trees then, crowned with rooks' nests and if you parted the hedge you could find clusters of mushrooms if it was early enough in the morning. The sun was high and sparkles of moisture bejewelled the cobwebs on the hedgerows which we shook to disturb little brown spiders.

'Along the verges to the bottom of the hill were white violets and tall grasses, cuckoo-pints and cowslips. We crouched often, adding to our posies which were limp and warm by the time we reached the Woods Road.

'"My daddy knows the farmer so it's perfectly allowed for us to be here," I announced as Marjorie struggled with the spelling and the meaning of PROHIBITED ACCESS on the weatherbeaten sign.

'Past this point were ploughed fields of young green corn and deep ditches either side of the farm track. Occasionally we stooped and searched for fossils and bits of broken blue-and-white china and the luckiest found opaque glass marbles from cast-aside ginger beer bottles – a legacy of a bygone age. Pausing for a sherbet session Marjorie casually wiped her hands on the red velvet dress. I jealously thought her stupid not to have worn corduroy dungarees like me. Marjorie was a beautiful and cherubic child. I would have done anything for her.

'At the entrance to the woods we left the pram and I jumped the ditch at the gap, pulling Marjorie with me. Then I held the barbed wire apart so that she could squeeze through. There was a tuft of coarse grey fur caught on the barbed wire. I thought someone had been very careless in not holding the barbed wire apart for their poor dog. One last heave and we were in the woods. The earth had a damp toadstool scent. Shafts of April sunlight filtered through the gaps in the treetops highlighting a thick carpet of bluebells which we energetically harvested in sticky fragrant armfuls.

'We waded in deeper kicking at brambles and squealing as we discovered rare and prized wood-orchis, a startling pink amid the common bluebells. A fat speckled thrush eyed us beadily as we emerged into the clearing which marked the halfway point. The old rotten log was still there. Brushing away a shower of ebony earwigs we sat and devoured our sandwiches squabbling over whose had the most ketchup. Marjorie drank the most cola because she said fat people needed more liquid. So very soon she trotted off to squat behind the biggest tree and I entered that half-world state of daydreams, composing songs and inventing friends, where even adults can lose ten minutes or half an hour with no recollection of passing time.

'A wood pigeon's call disturbed my reverie. I could still see the edge of Marjorie's dress, a bright contrast to the dark tree trunk. I crept up to her and yelled "Boo!" leaping around the tree and grasping a handful of her red dress which to my amazement was simply a torn fragment of the whole, about ten inches square, caught up in the undergrowth.

'The woods are still there but they seem less of a forest. The spindlewood tree, the cowslips and the white violets are now flattened by a pavement. The lane is now a road, the mushroom meadow houses an immaculate residential estate and disease claimed the elm trees. I wonder where the crows roost now? Nobody ever found Marjorie.

'I returned to the woods much later when Philip was old enough to protect me but all we found, ugly in a carpet of bluebells, was a rusty upturned dolls pram and an empty cola bottle.

'Years later as an adult I returned to the scene again accompanied by my brother Philip who was still endeavouring to protect me from childhood fears and memories. We had trudged down Millers Road in silence and plodded along cart tracks until pausing dejectedly at the edge of the woods. Philip leaned against a tree, lit a cigarette, exhaled and completely out of the blue began his confession.

'He said he was furious at being left behind that day, enraged at being considered too young to participate in our all-girls adventure. Unseen he had followed us and while I'd sat lost in dreams he'd watched Marjorie go some distance into the woods. He followed her and invited her to explore the old well in the ramshackle farmyard on the edge of the woods. He said he'd bribed her with chocolate and told her there was a toad at the bottom of the well and if you leaned over and cupped your hands it would hop into them. Lovely trusting Marjorie did as she was told and Philip had pushed her in, spitefully and impulsively, before hauling back the rusty metal cover and obliterating all evidence of his irrational deed.'

Elizabeth curled deeper into the comfort of Letti's armchair and drained her glass. A warm flush, the combined result of the wine and her anger, thawed her pallor. She became more animated, more anguished and her story became enlivened, related in less of a monotone. Letti replenished her glass and receded into the shadows. She'd heard it all before in instalments but never told as lucidly as this and knew better than to interrupt. Elizabeth, knuckles white, gripped her glass and resumed her tale.

'Philip said he was horrified and amazed at getting away with it. The police had gone along the abduction route instead of seriously looking for her body. Popular theory in the village post office pointed accusatory meddling fingers at tinkers, teddyboys, poachers, paedophiliac uncles, dodgy travelling salesmen and a former schoolmaster, all resulting in a dead end, an unresolved case. Philip added that the entrance to the well was completely concealed, so flush to the ground and protected by nettles as to be considered unapproachable. Few of us children knew of its existence.

'I neither remembered the well nor believed his confession. I couldn't grasp the fact that some twenty years after the event my own brother, as if discussing the weather, would casually admit to killing my best friend as calmly as offering me a cigarette. He said all kids shove and push each other when jealous and at seven years old death was an abstract idea to a child and he fully expected his victim to emerge from the depths of the well, chastened at having been taught a lesson for leaving him out of that day's arrangements.

'I don't know what I felt – shock, fury, disbelief? Whatever I did feel I have no recollection of fearing Philip. I asked him to show me where he'd taken Marjorie and impulsively ended her life on that idyllic spring day. Without hesitation he shrugged and nodded as if relieved at unburdening himself and we trudged towards the old farmyard in uncomfortable silence.

'It was a sad graveyard of mouldering haystacks, rusting implements and ramshackle sheds. He remembered exactly where to go and, forcing a path through the nettles and blackberry brambles, lifted a crumbling sheet of corrugated iron to reveal the dank opening. Ding dong bell, pussy's in the well, my mind chanted silently. Philip broke down, kneeling and bursting into tears – shocking adult tears – at the enormity of what he'd done. Twenty years of guilt and remorse poured down his angelic face, the face of a brother I no longer knew. Then with his back to me he called down into the shaft telling Marjorie how sorry he was, but how pleased he felt at finally confessing although it meant that now her best friend Elizabeth would have to join her as his secret was out.

'The secret was out all right and I saw red. The red rust on the makeshift well-cover, the remembered-red of Marjorie's velvet dress and the shocking violent red of my brother's blood as I stuck my car keys into the side of his beautiful neck. He turned and stared at me before toppling forward and downwards, his look of surprise, then puzzlement, then regret locked with my own blank stupefied gaze. It seemed as if he was suspended for a moment in time and then down he tumbled without a sound until he crashed into Marjorie's bones, unmoved and untouched except by insects and mud-dwelling creatures for the last twenty years.

'Impulsiveness, spite and the burning desire for

revenge must be a family trait, I thought as I covered the well once more and crunched my way back through the nettles and brambles like an automaton, a zombie, shaking my head in denial. As carefully as I'd tidied up the well entrance I tidied away the act I'd just committed into a deep and secret compartment of my mind which, in the future, after I'd been punished for avenging my best friend, you, Letti would patiently probe to unlock my story and put me back together again.

'Deep in this reverie, this adult daydream, I parted the brambles and emerged with blood on my hands to meet the rheumy horrified gaze of a grizzled farmhand who looked as if he'd rather not have witnessed the whole episode. As he shambled off to call whatever was the equivalent of the village bobby I sat on a pile of old sacking to ponder on the probability that when they found Marjorie down there too they'd naturally and wrongly deduce that it had been me who killed her and not Philip – the big, bad and now very dead wolf.'

3

Avocado, Crab Meat
and Champagne Perry

Georgia and Penny arrived together at the apartment building although they hadn't met before.

Penny was an extremely well-preserved fifty-something, favouring divoré velvet, Thai silk shirts, heady perfume and sheer hosiery. Her energy was boundless, HRT came as standard and her libido knew no limits. She choreographed three jobs to finance her lifestyle, cruelly curbed since the exit of her last husband. She drove a red cabriolet in the exact shade of the varnish on her immaculate toenails.

On this occasion she had elected to take the train to Letti's gathering, her intention being to get 'absolutely rat-arsed' should it be required of her to recount the sordid little interlude in her past which she'd already dismissed as a 'nine-year hiccup'.

Penny saw the nine vanished years of her life spent doing time for the disposal of Perry as an inconvenience and a jolly good chance to slim and 'get in touch with herself'. Nothing got Penny down, not even Champagne Perry as she'd so adoringly christened him when they were an item and he'd enjoyed the practice of dribbling Krug into her navel before lapping it up like an obedient slavering puppy. Actually if Penny cared to reflect he did have spaniel's eyes. He was a heavy man, heavy on the compliments, heavy-handed with her brandy decanter and fast approaching the silver anniversary of a very heavyweight marriage. Penny didn't give a damn if his stale, Danish pastry of a spouse wouldn't be his smorgasbord. At that time Penny certainly would. She flung herself into the affair, spread herself wantonly for the taking on her oyster satin sheets and offered her all, minus her heart, as the ultimate doggie treat to spaniel-eyed Champagne Perry. Too bad it all turned into a dog's dinner.

'I'm Georgia, as in midnight train to,' said the black-haired female in heavy mascara who'd arrived simultaneously for dinner at eight.

'Shit! We're late – Hi, I'm Penny as in Lane,' answered Penny, squinting at the minuscule sparkly timepiece spanning her tanned wrist. 'Lovely to meet another of Letti's projects. I gather all we've got in common besides our hostess is incarceration.'

'Mmm, I've only just got out. Hanging around in that shithole for what I consider a crime of passion hasn't done a lot for my looks or my bank balance, hence the stripey suntan. How come you look so wonderful?' Georgia enquired.

Penny laughed in sympathy. 'The tan's as fake as the low-life I disposed of. It doesn't matter what colour you are sweetie, we're all sisters under the skin.'

God! thought Georgia, she's got balls.

Penny secretly thanked the same God for blessing her with her current arty, wealthy lover, Jeremy, the epitome of executive elegance – and probably married judging by his long absences – but so generous and obligingly suitably unavailable.

Penny too had a master plan. She wanted a husband, preferably not someone else's but pinching someone else's was not out of the question should a suitable candidate come along. First wives were disposable. Before Champagne Perry she'd had a penchant for solitary evenings spent gently immersed in aromatheraputic bubblebath while waiting patiently for her next husband to materialise. Thoughts of Perry had put her off bathtime. Nowadays she preferred showers.

Jeremy, the tall part-time escort with his hand-painted silk waistcoats and handmade shoes, appealed to her sense of style and her sensuality and seemed an ideal candidate for sharing a shower and the rest of her life for that matter. He had great potential. After the pig's earhole of a relationship with Perry she was going to keep all possible suitors at arm's length this time until she was absolutely sure. Jeremy was unavailable tonight which made the prospect of a free meal in elegant surroundings, a bit of in-depth girl-talk and one final free counselling session all rather attractive.

The door opened. 'Oh good! You're both here. Come in.'

Letti drew Penny and Georgia into her haven, a den mother greeting a doyenne of style and a denizen of the underworld. Georgia was the black queen and Penny the white, visually different but invisibly bound in a complicated web of mutual insanity.

Letti introduced Georgia and Penny to Elizabeth who having purged herself of the tale of the big bad wolf and drained her second glass was feeling uncustomarily mellow. The hostess seated her guests and passed around a crisp dry white wine, applied more dressing to the avocados and urged her guests to eat and enjoy. The empty chair was intended for Angela who was working late in the print studio of a department store, no doubt putting to good use her knowledge of the typography she'd elected to study while serving her sentence for ridding herself of the man who betrayed her.

As the wine flowed the women engaged in small talk which soon evolved into in-depth conversation and then flowered into soul-baring. Elizabeth who'd had the privilege of the one-to-one session prior to the others' arrival was content to observe. Penny, she thought, exuded style and confidence from every pore but Georgia was a different species. She bore an aura of secret sorrow, a veiled bruised look around the eyes, her lips taut and ready to spit out a biting self-protective backlash to anyone who threatened her. Elizabeth had seen the look before in prison, worn like a badge. It meant that at some stage in her life Georgia had been systematically beaten.

She hid behind the thick eye make-up – a public masque, a veneer of confidence for a wounded and private woman. She sat hunched and ashamed of her body, a study in burgundy velvet, wearing purple or black lipstick, difficult to define by candlelight but shocking on her pinched white face. Elizabeth recalled the overripe blackberries, the purple sloeberries of her country past and decided that Georgia brought to mind bruised wild fruit. You could almost see her bleeding – fermenting in hidden anger. Deadly nightshade, belladonna.

However it was Penny whom Letti invited to entertain. 'Tell us your story, Penny, share with us what happened to your Champagne Perry.' Penny soiled her napkin with a scarlet pout, cast aside a breadstick as if it were a gauntlet and addressed her audience.

'Perry was a saturnine and dark man, a petulant lover, greedy and overbearing. He sported a ridiculous sixties hairstyle and resembled a corpulent abbot. He had no money to speak of, it was all hers – the desiccated Nordic wife's. His cut-glass accent belied his limited means which were compensated for by his magnetism and silver tongue, the latter of which he employed to greatest effect in my bedroom. Now that I've met Jeremy, all these years later – my lovely leonine lover who hasn't a devious bone in his body – I can look at Perry's treatment of me objectively.

'In the beginning he was just the ticket. I knew he was married and it was a civilised arrangement, but as always with this type of setup eventually one begins to want more. I thought it was going to be Perry who clung. He chipped away at my independence and moved in within weeks – well from Friday to Tuesday on a regular basis – telling his wife he was on a business mission in Prague or some suitable excuse. He was a big wheel in the business travel sector, or so he said.

'I began to enjoy waking up, sated and warm,

with his big hairy belly against my back and the prospect of an acrobatic bit of morning delight followed by Earl Grey and an apricot Danish. When the cellulite's beginning to burgeon, my sweeties, it's a boon to have a fleshy man, it makes one feel so slender. I felt like bloody Tinkerbell, he made me feel so youthful, lithe and wicked!

'The nickname "Champagne Perry" suited him, he was a master of the excuse and as he bored with the novelty of me he'd make intricate arrangements and flamboyant promises and then he wouldn't show. Oh, the plans we made. The times we were to be dining in France, for example, and the subterfuge I'd have to create at the office in order to dash home to shimmy into something sexy, grab my francs, spritz on the perfume, sling the curling tongs into an overnight bag only to be met at the ferry with an apologetic cancellation due to "urgent business" or family dramas.

'I had three jobs you know. I held a minor but vital position with local government. On Saturdays I shop-sat at my friend Cassandra's boutique. We operated a barter system – she paid me in designer goodies in lieu of my services. Like the shirt? That's two Saturdays' worth! Then a couple of evenings each week I was a greeter in a restaurant, a marvellous source of men, rather like getting a preview of Harrods' sale. One's actually paid to chat them up!

'One evening, Perry fancied attending a

champagne tasting, so again I embroidered an excuse to leg it home, threw on the velvet and diamonds, tore to the assignation grasping the fifty pound double ticket, courtesy of my credit card as usual, only to be given the message that he'd been urgently called to Prague – or Paris or Penge or some such fictitious hive of industry he'd quote at one of us if he chose to be gracing the other with his presence. I can't recall the destination but the following weekend, Cassandra pityingly broke it to me that she'd seen Perry swanning past her weekend retreat in Norfolk with the desiccated Dane on his arm.

'I began to feel sorry for Helga or Britt or whatever her name was, until he took it upon himself to confess to her. I was stigmatised, branded the scarlet harlot. It was portrayed to her that I did all the running, had pitched myself at her defenceless husband and he, poor weak victim, had reluctantly surrendered.

'She took to sweeping into Cassandra's shop draped in the skins of dead animals and buying stuff by the rail. I wasn't amused. He owed me the best part of two thousand quid if I cared to tot up all the taxi fares and little financial loans I used to press upon him to finance our extravagant lifestyle in case she examined his cheque book. Cassandra could hardly ban her, she spent a fortune. I felt like packing in the job which I presume was the object of her visits but I stood my ground, endured the superior appraisals and unspoken scorn of Mrs Champagne Perry. But it got worse. She began pitching up with her daughters and her daughters' daughters, whole damned designer buggys full. I'm surprised she didn't cart the bloody cat in!

'Then they started the double act, closing ranks, writing joint letters accusing me of interfering in their marriage and threatening to sue me for stalking! Yes, I made the odd malicious phone call, one does. I knew it was over, but he was so persuasive, so outwardly dedicated that I had fallen in love. That's not at all like me but I yearned to spend Sunday afternoons at the garden centre. I desperately didn't want to be the spare woman at every wake and wedding. I knew I was the darling of every social function but it's infuriating leaving alone and going off into the sunset to a hot water bottle and a mug of hot chocolate for one. Methinks I protested too much about marriage; in times past of course I was dying to be a wife again. I longed for company under the double duvet so I, an intelligent woman of all these years, believed his crap and as he tried to back off I began to miss the bastard.

'After one grey solo Sunday – they're different somehow from Saturdays aren't they? – as I sat reading one of his one hundred and three lying love letters, all promising to leave her, Perry rang and said he'd quite like a reconciliation for old times' sake. She must have had her period.

Naturally, in seconds I put the champers in to chill, ironed the bronze silk teddie and as he turned his key and lumbered into my hallway, clutching a gaudy petrol station bouquet, I was all over him like a rash.

'Despite my noble decision to forget him, his expansive charm and his petulant hard-done-by helpless husband demeanour, I beckoned him upstairs to my, by now, almost overflowing Victorian bathtub. Golden ylang-ylang scented bubbles slid sensuously down the sturdy cream sides, turning the silver tray bearing the obligatory bottle of champagne and its prematurely ejaculated cork into a celebratory island. Playful now he knew he was out of the woods, and singing 'Bend me, shape me, any way you want me!' he generously took the tap end position and sank into the depths, his mat of chest hair floating on the surface, his belly and the instant promise rapidly gathering interest against it, hidden in the warm, musky depths.

'I straddled him and the floor was awash. He turned to survey the flood, revealing a neat possessive Danish marital love-bite on his fat neck. It only takes a tiny thing to turn love into hatred. Irritating habits, a misplaced criticism, a jarring mispronounced word. It was only a small bite mark but to me it was a message – a statement of ownership from his long-standing number one squeeze: Vampira staking her claim. I remember well the arc of my gesture as I reached for the heavy bottle of champagne and with the scarlet fingertips of my other hand, gently tilted Champagne Perry's head back between the taps. I settled fittingly onto his dick in the warm silky water and teased the rim of the bottle provocatively between his lips in a languid oral salute that caused him to raise his Bluebeard chin in order to gulp my offering in customary greedy manner. And then I put both hands around the base of the bottle and shoved with all the accumulated anger and resentment of the past months. Wedged beneath me he fought in vain, eyes wide, his erection diminishing. Down he went beneath the bubbles, his full lips clamped around the bottle neck, eyes bulging like a landed fish. I didn't save the whale.

'Of course Vampira commandeered his funeral arrangements. I was locked out of sight by then – doing porridge and dreaming of deluxe muesli. Had I been allowed a say in the proceedings I'd have had the organist play "Bend me, shape me!" as the oversized coffin, laden with garage-bought floral tributes was lowered into the earth. The golden inscription on the black marble headstone would have borne a fitting tribute – here lies Champagne Perry who died on the job, his favourite tipple in his gob.'

Georgia, who'd been mesmerised by Penny's confession and had posed motionless, an uneaten forkful of crab meat poised in midair, banged down the fork and clapped. 'Brilliant, babe, the bastard deserved it!'

Elizabeth, who sat eyes on the serviette she'd subconsciously been twisting throughout, quietly said, 'All we did was try and put the record straight, even the score, see justice done. I don't feel like a killer. James doesn't really believe what I did to my brother. I tried telling him but he thinks I've been away recovering from a nervous breakdown. That's why he's so gentle with me and compassionate and understanding of the fact that I'm not quite on the same wavelength as him at times.'

Letti reassured her. She said it was an absolute necessity to keep something of oneself back in a relationship – how much should be entirely up to the individual. It was an essential defence against the angst of future rejection.

Letti knew only too well that if you give everything and then he goes, you forget who you were before you knew him. She said many women turn themselves into a clone of their man, stealing characteristics, adopting a similar accent, a duplicate phraseology. In moulding themselves to please there is a refusal to acknowledge faults. She added that they even make up the most ridiculous excuses for errant partners to cover unexplained absences, excuses often so elaborate that they believe them too. In so doing the huge effort to please generates contempt as often as not from their object of worship.

'You must be true to yourselves. Don't just be the other half. Retain your own ideas and ideals, hang on to your own character traits, likes and dislikes, hobbies and friends. Individuality and strategy are your most potent weapons if the mating game is a war – and I've seen nothing to refute this. To keep the spark going, keep secrets!' My personal ethos is – once a story's told, it can't help but grow old.'

As she cleared the debris of the entrée Letti invited Penny into the kitchen to select the wine for the next course. Penny followed and offered to help with the food, but Letti, highly organised, waved her to a window seat in the no-nonsense navy and red kitchen which resembled the rather smart galley of a yacht on which Penny had enjoyed a passionate interlude in the more successful earlier years of her career – the pre-Perry years.

Letti carved succulent pinkish lamb from the bone and tipped steaming minted mangetout into a bone china vegetable dish. She firmly plonked the lid over the contents for all the world as if she was putting the lid on Penny's past misdemeanour. It was a simple no-nonsense gesture, symbolising 'Enough!' and suggesting too much good life had been squandered fretting over the demise of Champagne Perry.

'That was then and this is now,' said Letti. 'Tell me something sunny, something sparkling and uplifting. Tell me about Jeremy.'

Penny gathered her thoughts as Letti popped her head around the dining room door and gave Georgia permission to smoke between courses. She suggested Elizabeth tell Georgia all about her adorable James, the cappuccino-drinking sales representative who had lightened considerably Elizabeth's life in the coffee bar. Letti smiled as the brace of wounded creatures did her bidding, unwinding in a haze of good wine and cigarette smoke. In the background Bob Dylan's lyrical poetry at odds with his deadpan delivery lifted the reflective mood a notch or two towards optimism.

Letti returned to the kitchen where Penny was basting the carved lamb with its own juices. The scent of mint and rosemary permeated the room. Lifting a ceramic goblet brimming with claret and passing the same to Letti, Penny proposed a toast.

'To Jeremy, my soul mate, saviour and splendid shag, who's not around much because he's probably married like all the others. But this time I'm doing the choreography. I'm keeping it all in perspective. Neither depending nor spending! He's wealthy, artistic, gorgeous and occasional, by which I mean we have what I tried to have with Perry. We have an arrangement. Fortuitously, this new model turns up on time, never ever mentions that four letter word, wife. And he brings me lilies.

Bloody great arums, nature's ultimate in style. If I didn't believe in God I'd have sworn Conran designed the lily.'

Letti smiled. Why do most men presume females prefer roses? she pondered. Sweet, fragile, delicate and quick to fade. She reflected on the vast bouquet of creamy lilies in the other room. Her Jon too had bothered to study her tastes and send with sincere regrets those piquantly green-scented blooms to cheer her in the fortnight's absence his extravagant workload had forced on her. Penny's statement broke her reverie.

'I will not be lied to!' she said. 'Jeremy knows this. I tried to tell him about the Perry-in-the-bath sequence but he seemed to barely register the facts so I led him to believe I worked in Hong Kong for a few years. He doesn't question it and prefers merely to refer to the past as my "Little Chinese Puzzle". My silly little civil service position could just as well have been performed over there so it's plausible.'

Penny continued by stating that she herself would, after the Perry incident, lie to whom she chose and as often as she pleased but that it was her men who she would not allow to deceive her. Jeremy explained his time away from her as 'difficult circumstances that can't be helped'.

'That sort of explanation suits me. I will not hear domestic details, I just don't want to know!' Penny was becoming quite aggressive.

'You might one day trust again,' soothed Letti. 'After a succession of abortive relationships I have. The carpenter was wooden, the artist drew a blank and the mechanic had a screw loose,' she chuckled. 'And as for the academic, well, he had a lot to learn!' Letti's guest was treated to a rare and dazzling smile that so altered her serious and plain demeanour.

Penny, with a peal of laughter lifted the platter of lamb and pulled the skewer from it as instructed. Sacrificial lamb, she thought, as the pink juices pooled. A poor little lamb that's lost its way, reflected Letti, referring to her ex-patient and not dinner, which she proceeded to bear into the dining room. Penny followed in her wake carrying vegetables, two handmaidens joining two ladies-in-waiting and not an Emperor Rat in sight. On this occasion Letti's Jon, Penny's Jeremy, and Elizabeth's James all had other commitments. None of the women seemed to be losing any sleep at the prospect of time to themselves. All seemed quite secure in their new relationships.

Letti wanted to hear Georgia share her story with the others. She was also eager to find out all about who was helping Georgia emerge from her own particular nightmare.

4

Lamb, Slaughter and Minted Mangetout

Letti served the main course, offering garlic butter and rowan jelly while Penny poured the wine. The three ex-prisoners appreciated Letti's bacchanalian generosity. Apart from the occasional mug of under-the-counter home-brewed potato and parsnip fermentation, they'd had a dry time drink-wise while inside. However, some of the mind-altering drugs administered at various stages of their subsequent treatments weren't at all bad.

'Come, Georgia, will you tell us your story?' asked Letti.

'Pump up the volume, Dylan's too folksy. Get me in the mood with a blast of Meatloaf and I'll tell all, but it isn't pretty, I warn you!' came the reply.

Letti obliged and to a background of the mighty metallic rendition of 'Paradise by the Dashboard Light' Georgia extinguished her cigarette – the tip stained with a purple kiss – slowly chewed a piece of lamb while she gathered her thoughts, shuddered and then began.

'I tried to reform an alcoholic. He used to beat me for any reason. Sometimes a mere glance at him in what he considered a "funny way" was enough to set him off. He was a paranoid schizophrenic. They were always locking him up for GBH and not bothering to investigate and treat him. He was worse every time they let him out.

'I'm a visual person. I fell purely for his looks and the side of him that was charismatic, charming and as kind as a big old bear but when he turned, you could literally see the transformation in his eyes. I'd be confronted by a raving deluded stranger with unfathomable depths of violence and irrational cruelty. Always afterwards he'd be sorry, hardly remembering his actions. There would be an immense high where he'd take me out on the town with him, flaunt me, treat me royally and then make love to me afterwards with as much gentleness as he was capable of. Then suddenly he'd metamorphose into a bully again.'

Georgia paused, swallowed her drink and looked earnestly around the table.

'Don't ask, people invariably do. They ask if I

enjoyed the violence. Apparently there's a small proportion of masochistic females whose penchant for a good thrashing has done more damage to the battered women of the world than any act of physical violence ever will. No, I didn't enjoy his treatment of me.

'In the early days I enjoyed the challenge of trying to turn an essentially bad boy into a paragon. It's impossible. What he was suffering from was an illness. I didn't know at the time. We were like Bonnie and Clyde, every day was an adventure until the excitement wore off. God knows how I managed to hold down a job through it all!

'Once I came home in the afternoon to find him in our bed with a blonde. Do they have more fun, Penny? This one didn't.' Penny didn't answer for fear of stopping Georgia's flow. Georgia ate more food and continued.

'By the expression of horror on her face the girl in bed with him was unaware of our cohabitation. He'd slung my few cosmetics into a drawer. The unspeakable house we or rather I was renting was shabby with large sombre furniture. It looked a typically bloke's place. I couldn't be bothered to put my stamp on it. There was no point in collecting ornaments or decent glassware. When he was at his worst he'd smash, trample or tear whatever of mine was within reach – records, tapes, books, nothing was sacred. I kept only three treasures and I'd secreted them high and to the back of the smoked-glass cabinet where the booze was kept. He only had eyes for the spirits and never noticed the trio of precious objects which had moved with me wherever I had made a home.

'There was a blue glass jar holding two peacock feathers resembling a pair of exotic turquoise and jade eyes – passive company, my imaginary friend. Second was the German bisque doll, my grandmother's, still wearing a yellowed family christening robe. Shake her and she rattled – cold porcelain, rosebud lips, blank eyes, substitute for a dead baby. Third and last the multifaceted paperweight – a fascinating source of beauty promising a rainbow. I'd weighed it often in my hands, staring into its chameleon colours for as long as it took to unravel each problem.

'These were my three precious trophies, my one concession to designer living, and even these pleasing items had to be hidden from view. Otherwise the house was a tip. Trying to make something of him took up all my energy so I neglected the housework. You can't make a silk purse out of a sow's ear!'

Uncannily Meatloaf had got to the point where he was singing about not being able to find gold at the bottom of a cereal box. Letti was the only one who related the music to the situation. The others were engrossed, but Letti was an observer by trade.

'As I entered the bedroom he sat up with a

vibrator in his tattooed fist while next to him the startled girl shrank into my pillow. In moments I weighed up the situation. I was beginning to learn cunning, take on some of his characteristics, the very thing Letti has warned us against.

'Yes, I weighed up the situation with all the skills of a warfare strategist. To complain would mean a thrashing, to ignore would generate more contempt. He already referred to me as "the slave" in front of his cronies, the drinking and gambling buddies, "the bet set".

'I smiled and introduced myself. "Hi! I'm Georgia, the not-very-common-law wife. Do stay and join us for a drink. What'll it be, gin and tonic, ice and lemon?" I whirled on my heels and was back in moments with a tray bearing the remainder of my few cut-crystal tumblers that hadn't been smashed. Three slivers of lemon bobbed merrily in the stiff contents. I reflected that the other prize lemon was me, but ploughed on with the charade and served them both with an exaggerated flourish. Then I left the room to lock myself in the lavatory, cowering with my drink.

'I could hear the commotion, his husky laughter, a manic Muttley. Her squealing in shock and professing never to see him again, predictably taking my side. Sisters in surprise. I wasn't surprised, I knew his tricks. I emerged from my sanctuary in time to see her in the hallway clambering into her knickers, her unfinished drink cast aside on the telephone stand as she hysterically phoned for a cab.

'After her departure I braced myself and entered our bedroom where he congratulated me, took my hand in his great gnarled paw and pumped my arm up and down. In his monosyllabic way he grunted, "One up to you, babe. She was a lousy lay anyway".

'Sometimes he'd be gone for days, it would be a battle of wits on his return. Once in a flaming August when he was supposed to be off for a day finding building work, he didn't return for a fortnight. And then there he was, larger than life, looking as if he'd been on a supreme alcoholic marathon. Blinking in the sunlight he said drowsily, "Sorry babe, fog delayed return" and I, for once scoring a point, took from the oven in perfect timing his two eggs, four rashers, mushrooms and fried bread. I'd anticipated to the minute his homecoming, calculating when the pubs would open and how much cash he'd have on him. Touché.

'Often, after those nightclubs which had yet to ban him threw him out, he'd roll home in the early hours with selected inebriated satellites. Sycophantic clowns whom he'd lead into the bedroom, shattering my sleep and my privacy. They'd sit on the bed playing cards. The men would leer and he'd order me to get up and cater for them. I'd try to make something out of nothing

– omelettes, bacon sandwiches or whatever was in the fridge. There was never much to eat, he gave me no regular housekeeping money. I should think he ate a kebab for supper every single night during the time we spent in that house. He liked kebabs.

'We were waiting at the counter of a kebab house once, the Turk turned to slice the doner and Bruno, that was his name – I rarely say it because it feels like a curse, bad luck – Bruno spat into the bowl of shredded cabbage that lay on the bar. This was to sabotage everyone else's supper. Only I saw what he'd done but as he turned to smirk at me, to force me to acknowledge his deviousness, the Turk swiftly took up a forkful of the same cabbage, dumped it beneath the meat in Bruno's pitta bread and wrapped the whole in paper. By the time Bruno turned back to him, the Turk was nonchalantly squeezing a lemon over the complete, undesirable offering. The Turk said something in his own tongue as he sold Bruno the meal. "He's saying have a nice day," said Bruno. No he isn't, I thought. He's saying eat your own spit, you gobby, filthy son of a whore.

'So, he wasn't always so clever, but mainly he was and if I competed too much in the sick game that was our parody of a relationship he would be swift to teach me a lesson. I remember, on a hot summer night . . .'

Extraordinary! thought Letti. At that very same moment Meatloaf in the background was growling about a girl giving her heart to the wolf with red roses on a hot summer night. Little wonder Georgia has such an affinity with the music; Bruno seemed as though he had molten heavy metal running through his veins. Letti returned her attention to Georgia and her tale . . .

'On a hot summer night Bruno would pin me down with one great paw, naked and face downward on the bed, while with the other he'd reach up and pluck gross harvest spiders from the coving and put them between my shoulder blades, wheezing that husky laugh, enjoying my terror as I shuddered and screamed as the insects ran over me. I didn't suffer from arachnaphobia then. I do now. The neighbours had long since stopped reacting to my noise, calling the police or offering sanctuary. They daren't.

'He had lots of women. Once I found a red six-inch stiletto-heeled shoe casually lying on the back window shelf of my car and dirty marks on the roof lining, caused no doubt by some illicit acrobatics. On being confronted with the tart's shoe, he simply said, "I thought it was yours." I would find half a phone number hidden behind the tongue of his boot and the other half scrawled on a cigarette packet. I'd put them together and what would I get? A nurse or a secretary or a barmaid. All nice girls, all innocent of his wiles. After I'd dialled and listened to how they couldn't live without him I'd invariably end up comforting them. I lost count of the times I'd advise them to have a good cry, make a cup of tea and forget him. Tea and sympathy. They'd even knock on the door.

'I don't know why I didn't start a fan club for him. It was like living with a Messiah. He had an aura, albeit black, and a following. Ordinary folk would grovel and send drinks over to him in whichever pub he chose to favour, until he was barred and their profits took a sharp downturn. Wherever he went the underworld in-crowd followed. He was the pie-eyed piper; a drug I couldn't kick. I was enthralled with evil. I became blanched and bony, my career went down the pan.

'I say he was like a drug. I never used, never experimented but if he was rolling a joint and I wouldn't join in – I didn't smoke then – he would cram a wad of dope into my mouth and with one hand pinching my chin like a vice, would clamp the other hand around my head, pushing my jaws together and forcing my mouth shut until I swallowed the vile muddy cannabis. Then he'd roll around the floor to Pink Floyd, a grown man finding the merest thing amusing. All I got was a dull ache in the top of my skull, bloodshot eyes and bewilderment, plus the obligatory kicking if I dared not to join in. I smoke like a chimney now. He taught me how. It was preferable to being force-fed.'

Letti offered more vegetables, topped up the wine glasses and asked Georgia, who by this stage was taut-lipped, her eyes glittering with remembered fury, if she'd rather not continue. Letti believed in going straight to the source of the pain. She wasn't one to pussy-foot around the edge of a problem but she was beginning to wonder if getting the women together for this final sharing of stories was quite such a good idea.

She scanned the faces around her table and was pleased to see genuine emotion, animation, the spark of life that had been completely missing on their faces during the early counselling sessions. In fact there was more sharing, more information willingly pouring from these wounded creatures than she'd ever heard individually. A problem shared is a problem halved. They were delighted to meet each other, to discover like-souls who'd been to hell and back. They were no longer outcasts, freaks. In a bizarre way they were enjoying themselves at Letti's dysfunctional dinner party.

Georgia said she'd be more than happy to continue, and as Meatloaf sang of the unlikely scenario of a Miss America marrying Mr Right she continued recounting her antithesis to a love story, her version of a flawed romance with an unhappy ending.

'Our association limped on – it was hardly a romance. In a misguided effort to bond with Bruno I became pregnant. Rough handling and my love affair with Scotch whisky resulted in the first scan revealing a pitiful scrap of dead cells.

'I was lectured to by my doctor who didn't for one moment believe my excuses for the spectacular bruising that blossomed on my body at regular intervals. I was neatly vacuumed out and dispatched back "home" clutching a prescription for six months supply of contraceptive pills. I was relieved.

'Whatever I'd lost I'd gained in strength and resolve. Perhaps my unhealthy obsession with Bruno had been surgically cleansed from me at the same time as the D and C or whatever they call a necessary abortion. Bruno suddenly didn't appear so handsome. Never one for sparkling repartee, his sparse grasp of the English language now irritated me. I now found his particular brand of gypsy barbarism pedantic. My demigod had become half sharp. The magnetic field was broken, the aura dimmed.

'I'd called the foetus Luke. For three months I'd inwardly spoken to him, while kicking through the leaves during my walks to work, promising him a rosy future, just the two of us. I had decided to go it alone. I felt no pain at the loss of Luke – I shrugged it off, I'd endured worse – only a conviction that he'd been created for a purpose. His death underscored the futility of my existence, the dangerous, deluded world I inhabited with Bruno.

'Shortly after the miscarriage I awoke on a

snowy December morning, turned and looked at the beast in slumber, observed the gap in his gums where he'd lost two teeth in a brawl, noted the laughable attempt at designer stubble, the amateur tattoos. He looked like some great pile of debris after a storm and he stank like a brewery. I extricated myself from under the dead weight of his log of an arm, his careless embrace, took a cold shower, drank two cups of black coffee laced with Scotch and got the hell out of it, my few bits of clothing and my three treasures, the peacock feathers, the paperweight and my grandmother's doll, hastily secured in a black bin-bag. I didn't stop to say goodbye.'

'Brave, very brave, sweetie!' lauded Penny.

'Thanks,' answered Georgia. Then added, 'May I have a whisky between courses, Letti? I've brought my own.'

Georgia produced a hip flask. Letti told her to put it away and said that as Angela was due soon wouldn't it be a great idea to delay dessert and have a liqueur or a stiff spirit at this point in the proceedings as she had an idea they'd all need a drink if they were going to be treated to the finale of Georgia's tale. All agreed.

Actually Letti quite fancied getting drunk. This was out of business hours. They were no longer her clients and she was trying not to brood on the fact that Jon was not going to be around for a while, a good enough case for hitting the schnapps. She played a little guessing game, matching the tipple to the character of each guest. She was dead right. For Georgia she poured a malt whisky, Elizabeth requested sweet bland floral Cointreau, while Penny went for the cognac. Elizabeth helped clear away the remains of the main course and the waning candles were replaced. As Queen sang 'Death on Two Legs' the women closed ranks, drew in their chairs closer around the table, clinked their shot glasses and were all ears.

5

Boiled Egg and Broken Fingers

Georgia had secured a captive audience. Initially strangers to each other, the guests had bonded.

Letti believed the power of good food, sympathetic company and strong drink by far outweighed Valium, Prozac and the like for subduing demons and lowering defences enough to let truth emerge – truth that was shocking, abnormal, disturbing but nevertheless unabridged reality. She knew she'd tapped into a mine of mercurial emotion and that this revolutionary bit of homework was unorthodox but she was the conductor, the catalyst. She held the reins and she was pleased with progress so far and was damned if she was going to play it by the book. She'd broken no confidentialities. All her ex-clients were willing after-hours participants in this flawed fairytale.

Letti wondered who set the benchmark of normality, the plumbline by whose standards insanity versus sanity was measured. On balance she found these dinner guests preferable company to the bookish intellectuals with whom she worked. Life is a one-off, she mused, and death too for that matter and here was living evidence that human behavioural patterns didn't run to the master plan.

'Okay Georgia,' she encouraged, 'we'll have something stronger and give the main course a chance to get down while we wait for Angela to arrive.' Letti wasn't quite sure whether she meant the potency of the alcohol or the strength of Georgia's closing chapter. She suspected she was referring to the latter.

'Mama, just killed a man,' wailed Freddie Mercury delighted to get it off his chest.

Know how you feel, thought Georgia as she took up the thread and like Sleeping Beauty's stepmother applied her recollective powers, numbed in prison, to the spinning of an intricate tapestry. A tapestry so multi-layered and fragile that the judge, had he been privileged to hear her now that she was lucid, would have deemed her worthy of exoneration.

'I walked away into the snow which soon erased my footprints – the only trace I left behind me. It took six years to build a new life, a new me.

The journey from Bruno was in turn masochistic, methodical, cleansing and finally triumphant. Along the way I shed people, places and possessions through a maze of bedsits, musty rooms with mismatched furnishings, sallow halls reeking of damp carpet, ethnic cooking and perpetual disappointment.

'I clocked up the years and cleaned up my act. Eventually I found a new home miles away from Bruno. A glossy snow-white haven with charcoal carpets, a cooker and a bed – the basics. I felt as if I was barely functioning even then. A creature washed up on a smooth beach after a storm, encrusted with the limpets of broken dreams, the clinging tendrils of memory – an empty shell, fragile but washed clean.

'I was very pleased with myself at building a nest again. This was Home Sweet Home – all mine, not to be disturbed. The pleasing stark emptiness was relieved by my three talismans, hauled lovingly from countless cardboard boxes each time I'd upped sticks and set up camp feeling by some sixth sense that Bruno was closing the gap, searching for his stooge.

'I loved weekends, especially Sundays. I'd secure the doors, draw up my drawbridge and not speak to a soul for two days. I would sit cross-legged in the middle of my grey carpet, pick up the paperweight and watch its rainbow prism playing on the ceiling while in my lap I cradled

Grandmother's porcelain doll. As I rocked her she rattled comfortingly. The peacock feathers, their outer fronds resembling eyelashes, their dark velvety centres a pair of black eyes observing me from the safety of the blue glass jar.

'I stared into the doll's blank eyes and thought of Luke who would have been six years old, at school. He had been my last chance. I would never now have a child. I'd been celibate ever since Bruno. His overt maleness repulsed me. Now all men repulsed me. I wouldn't be caught again.

'I tried in the beginning to bear the gropings of one-night stands, just for a bit of human warmth. I might as well have been a corpse for all they got out of it. There must be a lot of blokes around with a taste for necrophilia. I gave up, I couldn't stand to be touched. I'd flinch even if some well-meaning hand was raised in caress. I wanted to share my bed with nobody.

'I was civil enough to colleagues at the latest job I'd found but that's as far as it went. I was terrified of revealing too much about myself in case it led to him tracking me down. No pity please girls, I'm telling you how it was. My solitude was of my own making, I chose anonymity, it wasn't forced upon me. People did try but they soon got the message, read from my expression that the blinds were drawn. I was an island and stronger for being so.

'It took ages before I dared express an opinion without looking over my shoulder for derision, laughter, mockery. Yes, he'd put me down but I wouldn't stay where I'd been put. I staggered to my feet, licked my wounds and walked tall. I didn't need love from others but I learned to love myself. It was wonderful to know that never again would I be forced to cook Sunday lunch with broken fingers and a broken heart or have to face his sadistic withdrawal symptoms after the pubs shut their doors on him. Isolation brought insulation. If you've got nothing then you've got nothing to lose.

'I had a new life. I knew I was home and dry because I arranged delivery of the Sunday newspapers, the yardstick by which I measured permanent residency and peace of mind. My Sunday newspapers, big wordy ones with an arts review that he would have shredded in the frustrated resentment indicative of the shame of the illiterate.

'Even then, sitting safely on my floor six years later, bad memories lasered my tranquillity. My thoughts of newspapers triggered a realistic replay in my mind's eye. I recalled a Sunday morning when we were shacked up in squalor, Bruno pacing the rented room, like a caged grizzly bear, willing The Three Musketeers, or The Duke's Arms or whichever hostelry still welcomed him, to open. It didn't matter where, as long as they held a licence to purvey liquor and did a "late 'un" after hours. Me cowering with a fresh boiled egg and the

Sunday papers spread before me on the floor. The prospect of a solitary, peaceful breakfast must have caused the shadow of a smile to touch my lips. He caught me smiling and turned on me the full force of his paranoia. His toleration was nil. He simply could not grasp the concept of a person enjoying their own company and their chosen pleasures. It was because he couldn't bear himself, hated his own company. He was a reflection of the misplaced admiration of others, his charisma an illusion.

'Challenging my ability to just quietly be, he acted swiftly. I remember clearly the sensations. The crunch of the delicate egg cup, the shell and my fingers as he ground my hand and my breakfast with it into the newspaper, squashed my enthusiasm under a brutal boot. How yellow the spoiled yolk upon the Sunday arts review. Girl With Broken Breakfast on a Sunday. Naive art.

'You see, my mind was already diverting my pain as well as my thoughts and reactions along taboo wavelengths, bypassing the normal channels of acceptable behaviour. I should have noticed the signs when I served that blonde in my bed with her gin and tonic, ice and a slice. Why didn't I notice I was becoming a little unravelled? "Not too tightly wrapped" describes it well, out of key – off kilter.

'As I sat in my haven, enjoying the luxury of the newspapers and thinking of that Sunday, bloody Sunday six years earlier, I congratulated myself on how far I'd come, how clever I was to have

extricated myself from the mess that was my life
with Bruno. I boiled myself an egg and toasted
nursery-style brown soldiers by way of celebration
to lay the ghost. Like a Japanese tea ceremony I
laid my breakfast banquet before me. This time I
was the master of ceremonies, no longer the
geisha.

'My doorbell rang twice. I jumped – I still did.
It was only ever a charity collector, a salesperson.
It wasn't Bruno's prolonged, insistent blast of a
ring. It was a polite request for admittance, two
timid short trills, a feminine ring. Ever cautious –
an old dog knowing all the tricks – I saw, through
the impenetrable hardware of my security system,
a stylish redhead. She wore the fixed smile of the
desperate saleswoman and, being in what seemed
to be about the eighth month of pregnancy, looked
shattered. I softened. I fancied an inane discussion
on cosmetics or basketware or plasticware or
whatever her wares. I'd shunned company for
long enough and after all she was a woman. I
unhooked the chain.

'Bruno elbowed his way past his convincing
partner in crime. The crime of finally finding me.
He strutted into my sanctuary, invading my
personal space, reeking of beer and revelling in his
achievement, his animal cunning. The redhead
fled, her usefulness no longer relevant. As he
swaggered around my room, drinking in every
detail, in his warped way assessing me and what

I'd scraped together, attempting to know me again, to reclaim ownership of his chattel, I tested my reaction. Six years on I quite frankly felt invincible, incandescent with rage. I hid it well. I was a candidate for another Oscar, the first being the one I'd awarded myself for technical brilliance during the 'Serving of drinks in bed to Bruno and that poor cow' incident.

'Not a conversationalist Bruno didn't say a lot. "Foundya bitch!" was his battlecry as he snatched up my grandmother's doll and smashed her at my feet. My doll, my mother's doll, and in her turn, my grandmother's doll. Eighty years of bringing pleasure to three generations of little girls who didn't have much was destroyed in seconds. Out of the disfigured head rolled a glittering trio of sovereigns, squirrelled away in a bygone age by my grandmother. The only rational thought my brain could produce was that at last I knew the source of the mysterious rattle.

'He who never dropped his guard, he who never put a big cruel boot wrong dropped to his knees in his greed. He snatched up the prize – sovereigns, a gypsy's bounty. "Look nice in a ring," he chuckled horribly, huskily, as he claimed them.

'Speaking his language, so there would be absolutely no doubt whatsoever of my intentions, "Gotcha!" I countered as I swung the lead crystal paperweight, casting another exquisite rainbow across the ceiling. I reacted with the desperate, final resource of adrenalin possessed solely of the cornered fox, the weakened prey, the tortured kitten. His skull where the heavy prism sought purchase split neatly. I'd employed the same sort of well-placed tap one gives to open a boiled egg. I stepped back and watched Bruno's blood and brains seeping through his cranium, scribbling a random design – a bloody Jackson Pollock – across my pristine arts review. Crimson Yolk on a Charcoal Carpet. The paperweight sparkled. From their turquoise jar the peacock feathers watched and were my only witnesses. On the caved-in remains of the doll's disfigured head the rosebud lips pursed in an eternal smile.'

In Letti's dining room the background music stopped abruptly. Elkie Brooks had reached her anguished crescendo – unloved, unsteady and sodden with lilac wine. Silence descended over the dinner table. In the aftermath of Georgia's tale the guests found themselves reflecting on their own personal experiences.

Elizabeth collected the dregs of her Cointreau with her little finger and thoughtfully licked the sweet crystals. The taste transported her back to the final sherbet session with Marjorie. Sweet Marjorie of the dulcet voice and innocent dimples. Image of a child that would never grow old – sweet Marjorie, sweet revenge.

The fact that Elizabeth bore no remorse for

neatly plugging her car keys into her brother's jugular vein and then watching impassively as he toppled down the well was a constant source of surprise to her. The moments it took to commit the act were etched indelibly in her mind's eye. The kill. She likened those moments to a white flash of sparkling energy, a starburst of rage. Electric ecstasy on overload. Being normally a gentle brown mouse, she treasured the experience with a confused blend of pride and guilt.

In the Sunday school nativity play while Marjorie of the rosy cheeks and beatific expression was the chosen one, the madonna, Elizabeth was relegated to the role of third shepherd on the left or innkeeper's wife. Always the bridesmaid never the bride – wallflower as opposed to rose. Now at least she'd had her moment of glory. In a blinding surge of passion, in that short out-of-control period, the insignificant shepherd became the avenging angel. She made the decision, acted upon it and paid a terrible price. They shut her away and now she was back, returned to the society that collectively had pitied her malfunction, her disability, integrated her into their midst in a mundane job but steered clear – until tonight.

Wherever Elizabeth went there was always a couple of yards of space around her, an invisible perimeter fence which normal folk didn't cross. There were plenty of forced smiles and vague invitations to the cinema, tea, shopping, but nothing definite. She was an oddity – until tonight. Tonight she'd become a founder member of an exclusive club, a coven of women who empathised, who'd also visited that white-hot forbidden place where you could bloody well do it if you liked, if you were cross enough. Take one step outside of your nice restricted self, aim and strike.

Oh yes, she'd been a very naughty girl but now, after spilling the blood and then spilling the beans to Letti, she was a fully paid-up member of the elite. She wouldn't do it again, but if by some remote circumstance of bad luck a similar situation arose, if she was pushed, she had the capability.

'Another Cointreau, Elizabeth?' offered Letti. 'You look as if you've solved a riddle – found the answer to the mystery of life, or is it death?'

Elizabeth nodded and smiled to herself.

Penny too had been considering 'disposal'. She was much too ladylike to mention murder. As the warm brandy bit the back of her throat she considered the love bite that had been on Champagne Perry's neck and she mulled over the reasoning behind her act of violence. Yes it was over the top but he'd inflicted an impressive catalogue of small cruelties, the sum of which had wounded her deeply, possibly scarring her for life. All the false promises, the let-downs, had chipped away at her equilibrium and that one silly little love bite – the Viking wife's marital mark – had tipped the scales and unbalanced her. The calculated branding of Perry, designed to niggle, had opened a can of worms and proved to be the last straw, the giddy limit. She knew her limits now, hers too lay just outside the borderline. It was better than sex.

She relived the jolting high, the Yes! Yes! Yes! Disposing of Perry had been a lovely wanton release. She'd bent the rules, rewritten them. 'Bend me, shape me,' she hummed to herself. She thought of the incident as culling rather than killing – ridding womankind of a glut of predatory greed. It was her duty to save Perry from himself, to deliver him from temptation, thus ensuring no further heartbreak for her and whichever gullible subsequent victim he may have progressed to after he'd sucked her dry – physically, emotionally and financially.

Yes, she'd championed mistresses everywhere and it had given her 'the buzz'. During the execution she'd felt positively orgiastic if she cared to dwell on it, which she did – often.

Jeremy was a delightful and considerate lover, the ideal replacement and the opposite of Perry, physically and visually, but sometimes she needed that extra push to tip her over the mountain top where Jeremy had hauled and cajoled her and she teetered, panting and flushed. All she had to do was resurrect the Perry obliteration scenario in her mind. At the desperate thrust of the champagne bottle down his gullet a delicious frisson never failed to shock her into 'getting there'. One little action replay and Penny was home and dry – or wet if one cared to split hairs – pubic hairs if one chose to be absolutely technically correct.

All this Penny had kept to herself during the silent reflection. Now a throaty laugh escaped as she accepted Letti's brandy decanter and filled the delicate balloon with a good slug. Tossing it back in a salute to herself she sat like a big golden well-groomed cat with a Cheshire grin directed at her peers.

'Death over dinner and a belting great ballad beats the hell out of sex and drugs and rock'n'roll,' summed up Penny as she turned to Georgia. 'Slaying that bloated dragon was better than nookie, girls. I can see Elizabeth feels the same. Tell us your reaction at the precise moment you socked it to Bruno the Brute. Smacking that paperweight into his thick skull must have been the ultimate thrill after what he subjected you to. Do you agree Georgia?'

Georgia wasn't as sure as the others that murder, whatever the circumstances, was a life-enhancing experience. She'd seen so much violence, taken too many thrashings to see damage in any guise as rewarding. In the shocking aftermath of Bruno's downfall, bewilderment and depression set in. Her post-killing mood was a monumental all-time low. Probably like that of the first moon walker – a grey void after the big build up, flatlands, a February walk in the fen country. Nobody gave her a prize for her effort. At least Neil Armstrong had taken one giant step for mankind before the 'Now what?' set in. All she'd taken was a step towards her adversary instead of the usual two steps back. The element of surprise and that small advancement had been the conduit for her enormous reserve of pent-up strength. She knew she'd only get one shot, one crack at the target. The paperweight, her lucky charm, did her proud.

She had stood examining it through a veil of tears, its power of reflection dulled by a thin tracery of Bruno's blood. She was disturbed to recall that his blood softened the beauty of the object, muting the glitter into a rosy glow so that it resembled a priceless piece of cranberry glass and looked nothing at all like a deadly weapon.

Bruno had keeled over like a felled tree, fixing on her an ice-blue gaze until droplets of blood appeared and paused on his lashes before rolling down his drink-veined cheeks – a cocktail of blood, sweat and tears. The familiar leer frozen in a rictus smile, his lips were drawn back over the gap in his gums. He used to plug a wine bottle into this gap and lifting his stubbled chin throw back his head and drink it in one go – sometimes a whole litre. This was his party piece although he didn't need to perform. There was always an audience for Bruno.

Not this time – she was alone with a dead lead player. Georgia was no longer the understudy.

She knew them by heart but had never been allowed to examine his features very closely. In life he didn't stay still and should she have tried to steal a glance at him he would have cuffed her for giving him one of her 'funny looks'. Even in sleep he would growl and writhe under the duvet claiming the lion's share – as with everything – for himself. His tangled dreams and nightmare mutterings punctuated her nights. She found his new stillness awesome, expecting him to spring up any moment and chuckle 'Fooledya bitch!' while breaking her wrist or spitting in her face. There was no movement. The sovereigns lay in his calloused palm. Georgia reclaimed them, recoiling at the touch of his hand. He'd never held her hand or kissed her in life. He stank of lager, blood and piss. Rotten bastard. You're dead meat, she'd thought at the time.

'He looked like dead meat,' Georgia said in answer to Penny's question. 'And I loved him, really adored him now that I had delivered myself from his evil. Weird isn't it? Every time I see a boiled egg I throw a tantrum. I hoped against hope that Letti wasn't going to give us stuffed eggs for starters.'

6

No Regrets

Letti emptied Georgia's ashtray and selected a
Walker Brothers CD which she studied and slotted
into the player. The powerful cathedral-like quality
of Scott Walker's voice never failed to entrance her.
She felt her choice of ballad with its echoing
tortured quality was very apt to accompany this
point in the proceedings.

'No regrets,' sang Scott, a golden-haired
boulevardier refusing to dwell on lost love –
forging onward, leaving loss behind.

'I've heard three amazing accounts tonight,
diverse but interwoven with the same irrefutable
fact. You have each begged to differ, turned your
lives around from victimisation to survival –
superiority even. Equally you've been punished,
served your sentences. Hear me out now and

absorb this man's voice. He's singing from the heart, soaring from his cell over the rooftops, bursting with optimism. You can hear the pain in his voice, it adds to the maturity, the wisdom. This man has seen life and not been afraid to dabble, wandered on the wild side and come out of it strengthened. He's of the genre of Jacques Brel, Bertolt Brecht – Gothic-minded souls with equal capacity for doom and revelry and nothing done by halves, living to the hilt. No regrets.'

Elizabeth, Penny and Georgia, like dedicated sixth formers, bent their heads towards the woman who used to be their counsellor. The woman who used to be their counsellor persisted with her personal views. This was not by the book but the book was officially closed on these three. Letti was determined to make her addendum. Off the record she continued, 'The slate is clean, girls.'

She did indeed resemble a favourite school mistress which made it easier for her three guests to believe what she said. They felt comforted, transported back to the classrooms of their teens when what Miss said was always wise, correct, factual.

'Whatever you chose not to reveal to me during the time I was your counsellor has surfaced naturally tonight. This is because you've been introduced to each other for the first time, resulting in tremendous support for each other. I personally have no first-hand knowledge of what it feels like to take a life. I've met many killers but my grasp of the concept of disposal or culling or whatever disguise deliberate death is cloaked in, is based on second-hand information. I can only use my ears and my powers of analysis, my training and my gut feeling. I never assume.

'May I say I am humbled? You three all accept full blame and have truthfully admitted you were sane and wholly responsible for your actions. Yes, Georgia admits to being aware that she was 'coming unravelled'. Battered women have every right to become unravelled. It's the continued boxing of ears that has most likely altered the brain function, opened up a few channels into dangerous areas. A crack around the head can cause incredibly altered behaviour – look at boxers, look at road accident victims.

Georgia is more than justified in being a little eccentric and it's extremely interesting to learn that when she finally fought back she chose to batter Bruno's head. She was aping what she had learnt from him, copying what he regularly did to her. She used to recover from his assaults, she probably expected him to do the same.

'Surely Georgia, who we can all see is an intelligent, perceptive woman, knew Bruno was flawed. Yet she waited on the sidelines, patiently and in vain, for a crumb of affection, a spark of hope that his good side would triumph. Her one violent retaliation wasn't premeditated. Half of her still adored him. She's just told us that when the threat of abuse was removed, when he lay dead, she felt love.

'Georgia was fighting a loser's battle, a hopeless cause. It was the realisation of this that guided her to kill Bruno. Not even self-defence: he wasn't prepared for battle, merely marking what he believed to be his territory. Georgia's best ally was the unexpected. Off guard, a mistake almost, the element of surprise killed Bruno, definitely not a structured and preconceived plan. I propose we pronounce a verdict of 'not guilty' despite the previous verdict a decade ago in a court of law.'

Everyone clapped, there was a buoyant mood of bonhomie around the table. Without exception the women were wreathed in smiles, Georgia in particular. She expelled a long sigh, pain, fatigue, regret, guilt escaping through her purple-stained lips. Letti, enjoying her platform, her articulateness heightened by a third schnapps, continued her pronouncement.

'I suspect the other two of you would go so far as to say the final gesture was extremely satisfying. I find that admirable. Not excusable, but nevertheless, when fate thrust an intolerable situation at you, rubbed your noses in misery, dared you to respond – you fought back. Penny killed through disappointment. One excuse, one let-down too many and an unfortunate collection of circumstances led to Perry's downfall. Had he not been so arrogant as to barge back into her life on a dull Sunday he might still be strutting his stuff to this day. He lacked the brains to coax and court Penny first, lacked the judgement to wheedle and plead. Surprising because these were just the qualities – if they can be called qualities – in which he excelled. Had he not been so lazy, so cocksure, Perry might have sweet-talked himself out of the woods, and the sorry charade of this apology for a love affair would more than likely still be playing out to some other tragic finale.

'Penny, so ladylike and compliant had swallowed the bait, been duped into believing Perry was separated, in the throes of divorce. She saw her promised land gazumped. That territory so elusive to single women of a certain age had been reclaimed, marked by the wife. Respectability, the opportunity to be the other half of a rosy apple, had vanished. The apple revealed a maggot. Penny saw the magic status slip from her grasp, callously removed.

'Perry was a womaniser, a cad, a Walter Mitty. These aspects can be devastatingly attractive if two people conducting a relationship agree upon the ground rules. If they admit it's marvellous fun, terribly sexy but merely a fantasy. The cracks emerge and the rot sets in when one partner begins to plan a future, dares to introduce the element of reality, domesticity into the game. Mortgages, matrimony, menopause are garlic to the vampire, the stuff of horror to an accomplished Lothario, an ageing playboy, a roué.

'There is rarely a balance. Always there is one who loves, one who is loved. Penny's priorities changed, she was initially satisfied with their arrangement but Perry demanded her entire attention, got to her heart with a studied campaign of one hundred and three love letters, hard facts, lies that he really meant business, wedding business.

'Penny planned for this future together only to have the magic carpet swept from beneath her. Champagne Perry dangled his carrot once too often. It was he who became the ass. When Penny drowned him she was drowning her sorrows, pushing beneath the bubbly bath water her embarrassment, a huge deceit unbearable and undeserved. It wasn't Perry she effectively buried, it was her own disappointment.

'A judge wouldn't have had the remotest idea of Penny's mood that Sunday. His Sunday would have consisted of a leisurely, late breakfast *à deux* with a submissive but elegant spouse. The type who tactfully finished his sentences and hung on to every ponderous word. After the kedgeree and Newmarket sausages, they would have pottered in the manicured garden around their mock-Tudor manse before a dry sherry and the Sunday newspapers. In the afternoon there would have been company – perhaps two or three successful offspring plus grandchildren – for scones, honey and an unchallenging chat before dinner. All in all, a lovely cosy bland day before chambers on the morrow.

'By contrast, Penny, who has categorically stated how she loathed solitary Sundays, would have risen, downed a couple of black coffees to stave off the previous evening's hangover and started her vigil beside the silent telephone. She'd have painted her toenails, waxed her legs perhaps, read and re-read Perry's bundle of beribboned bullshit – living on dreams. She might have scrambled eggs and toasted a croissant to create a facsimile aroma of a family home.

'As the day wore on her optimism would have been as congealed as her untouched breakfast. The wine bars would have been filled with couples brunching and bantering, billing and cooing, always in a brace on a Sunday. On that grey day, unremitting rain would have weighed down the blossoms on her lilac tree, tears streaming down the elegant bay window of her town house.

'She would have reminisced, wallowed in Bette Midler, wondering where he was with the wind beneath his wings. She'd have sobbed silently to 'their song' while the object of her desire, the real bag of wind would have been spouting hot air to the great Dane, the official wife, the vitriolic Valkyrie. Towards mid-afternoon Penny would have hit the bottle big-time, composing countless little scenarios where she'd hear his footsteps squelching ardently across her crazy paving – up the garden path.

'Then girls, imagine the swoop, the swing, the big dipper sweep into ecstasy when against all odds her telephone heralded His Lordship's imminent arrival! How she would have glowed, sung, thanked God, heavens, her lucky stars while sweeping the cold eggs into the pedal bin with one hand and with the other ironing his favourite piece of easy-come fetish lingerie. In moments she would have blown a fiver's worth of fragrance, permeating the bedroom with musky promise, hauled out the best fizz, the antique crystal and in a frenetic opera of activity, set the stage. All Perry's past misdemeanours would have been filed away, his attributes fished out of her memory banks, past failings deleted as she convinced herself, perjuring his case, easing his path. She'd have waited like an orphan for a mother, a sheltered animal for a happy home, a sparrow for a crumb.

'Just imagine the euphoria ladies. Penny's self-esteem would be patched up, there would be plenty of memories from this afternoon's delight to keep her going through the next batch of broken dates, enough to convince herself it was all fine really. Suddenly, there he was, corpulent and cocky, desperate for his bit on the side, his lovely willing forgiving plaything. Good old Penny, his walking talking living sex-doll.

'Unfortunately for him, Perry had made a big mistake, been too presumptuous, too greedy. His Saturday night pacification of 'her indoors' involving matching baskets of scampi and French fries and the mildly titillating French film to follow had resulted in a rare leg-over. She-who-held-the-purse-strings, after two campari and sodas had demanded her conjugal rights. Over-generous on a bottle of claret and three crème de menthe frappés Perry had let his wife fasten her expensive little rodent dentures on his fat neck.

'Penny drowned Perry because of a love bite. She was jealous. As sure as shit, Perry's murderer had been stalking him for weeks. Patiently, jealousy held him in its glittering emerald gaze, biding its time. His mistress killed Champagne Perry but jealousy was the motivator.'

'Thank you Letti,' murmured Penny.

Georgia raised her whisky tumbler in an admiring salute and Elizabeth – not given to tactile gestures – squeezed Penny's hand.

Letti warmed to the theme.

'And now for Elizabeth,' she continued. 'Elizabeth killed out of loyalty to a childhood friend who she had failed to save. She also killed to save a cherished brother from himself. She did it to give him an option from madness, to take away his life before he came to terms with what he'd done and to rescue him from a lifetime in an institution. This selfless and misguided loyalty backfired on

Elizabeth whereby she herself was incarcerated for socially unacceptable behaviour and effectively removed from society for many years. She became the scapegoat, took the rap, carried the can – of worms.

'Elizabeth's desperate gesture evened the score for her little playmate Marjorie and saved her brother both from himself and a jury. A jury would have coolly looked beyond Philip's beauty and eccentricity and urged the judge to deliver sentence accordingly. Elizabeth was a crusader, a fighter for the cause, the family bond and yet she landed herself in as deep a hole as Philip. This monstrous incident shattered her relationship with her mother and blighted her comfortable future.

'Now in exile from her beloved village and the yearned-for teagardens she must find resources of willpower to enable her to return. To carry on the family business with James, her new partner, she'll have to somehow make peace with her mother – impossible probably. Philip was the favourite, the golden delicious son, apple of Mummy's eye. James may persuade Elizabeth to recreate a tearoom in another location but news travels and controversial news sticks in the collective craw of tight communities.

'The grapevine will resonate with whispers. There will be hastily curtailed conversations and twitching net curtains whenever and wherever she passes. The village wives are now possibly too hi-tech to gossip amid billowing sheets over the privet. Whatever the methodology, whether they e-mail the 'Guess whats!' and 'Did you evers!' or fax their facts, warped and multiplied by six, the practice of rank-closing remains a thriving art. Elizabeth will need the shoulder of her new, strong man and she'll need a core of steel.

'This wasn't murder, it was survival of the fittest. If she hadn't got Philip first he would have damned well got her for rumbling him – extracting his confession – engineering his return to the scene of the crime and finding him out.

'Subconsciously Elizabeth might have harboured grave suspicions prior to Philip coming clean. She has revealed his oddball traits to me in many of her therapy sessions, unburdened her doubts. I shall not betray her confidences by quoting her revelations but I will say Philip was a spiteful, destructive child who carried that capacity into adulthood. He wouldn't have thought twice about killing his sister to shut her up once she had the knowledge. It would have been Elizabeth who joined Marjorie down the well instead of him. It's a miracle he didn't make a job lot of it on that spring day when he killed Marjorie – two little trembling birds with one stone. Even at that stage Elizabeth knew too much.'

Letti paused, silently recalling the earlier sessions with Elizabeth who had described in graphic detail Philip's penchant for trapping, maiming and aggravating small wild animals. He progressed, or more aptly deteriorated, to the drowning and torturing of his domestic pets if they snapped or proved disobedient but usually for no particular reason at all. Impatient for small corpses he was known to hurry nature. Ginger, Brighteyes and Fluff had all died prematurely and in dubious circumstances. None of the family cats approached anything near their span of nine lives.

Mother's chapel rota and Dad's obsession with his Maris Pipers gave Elizabeth and Philip free rein to amuse themselves unsupervised. It was just that Philip, such a beautiful and cherubic country lad, preferred bloodthirsty games. Elizabeth trained herself to turn a blind eye, in fact, mused Letti. She didn't lift a finger against this favoured child's activities until he committed the ultimate atrocity. She then felt justified in suddenly drawing him into line, avenging not only the blood of Marjorie but that spilt by a whole menagerie of unfortunate rabbits, hamsters, kittens and puppies, not forgetting Joey the budgie and the white mouse to whom he'd administered bleach.

Coincidentally, while Letti was reconstructing these silent facts in her mind, Elizabeth's thoughts had registered the irony that it was small creatures that eventually enjoyed the unexpected pleasure of feasting on Philip's broken carcass.

'So!' said Letti, 'Elizabeth acted quickly to save herself. The farm hand who witnessed Philip's demise at first hand made a statement to the effect that "The lady didn't seem to know the location of the well and she only turned into a raving lunatic after her companion's confession."

'Hardly plotted and planned was it? And she'd covered up a multitude of childish cruelties for him. It's painfully obvious she loved and admired her brother dearly, was always in his shadow and considered second best by her parents. She knew his capabilities but couldn't believe he would ever exercise his dark compulsion on a human being. The shock of realising she had conned herself, the hard truth that she had misjudged her brother's endless capacity for evil, this lethal cocktail of disappointment along with the universal desire for self-preservation, caused Elizabeth to commit fratricide. What's the verdict ladies?'

'Not guilty!' roared Georgia and Penny. In the background Scott Walker, in credible grim reaper guise, applied his achingly perfect voice to a mournful melody. The song: the deadly, cynical and more than appropriate 'Funeral Tango'. How come he died so young, or was he very old? Is the body still warm, is it already cold?

The doorbell buzzed.

'That'll be Angela – great timing. Now we can all have dessert. Something frothy or a piece of sharp tart fruit I wonder? Lightweight or acerbic –

Angela has many moods – I hope she's on form tonight. She's a bit of a comedienne, a raconteuse. Despite being sectioned after exterminating her own particular Emperor Rat she's retained her unique brand of humour. You'll like her,' said Letti as she went to the door to invite Angela to join the motley crew on this fascinating evening.

7

Just Desserts

Angela burst in on the gathered company like a court jester, her tiny figure a miniature whirlwind of flame hair and black and orange clothes, tangerine jacket, sooty eyes, black boots and bronzed lips. Effervescing with energy and full of apologies, the firebird flew over to the table and sank into the vacant chair.

'God! Sorry I'm late, Letti, I nearly didn't make it at all. I bumped into my friend Elouise en route from work and she frog-marched me into a wine bar, not that I needed much persuasion after the bitch-day I've had printing posters for shop-soiled saucepan sets!'

'No problem, Angela. We've been amusing ourselves with tales of life and love and as a penance you can tell us yours – that's if you feel so inclined. It's fortunate you stopped on the way for a drink or else you'd have had rather a lot of catching up to do. I believe pleasantly plastered is an accurate assessment of our group condition!'

'What exactly are we celebrating?' asked Angela.

'Girl talk, new beginnings, new jobs and nice harmless new men,' explained Letti with a smile.

'Well here's to it then. After basking in Elouise's reflected glory for an hour I feel like taking a lead role,' said Angela as she handed over her welcome offering of two litres of dry sparkling wine, warmish from being clutched during its transportation from the wine bar – but who was arguing!

Introductions were made, outfits admired and the fizz whisked away to be chilled. Letti returned with a huge platter of death by chocolate and double cream which she positioned in the centre of the dining table. Penny passed round the crystal bowl of peaches and apricots which was arranged next to the stilton. The cheese shone like a piece of pink marble as it sweated in its moat of port. It brought to Elizabeth's mind the pinkish marble gravestone which marked Marjorie's small child-sized grave behind the village church. Throwing back her head in defiance she gulped her Cointreau, determined to forget The Incident at least for the rest of this evening now that she had retold the whole sad sorry story.

The reflection from the newly replaced candles flickered on the silver fruit knives and the long-stemmed wine goblets. Pure white bone china dessert plates completed a banqueting scene comparable with the most obsessive food stylist's display. Letti the perfectionist needed to make this harmonious domestic statement. There was so much chaos in life she insisted on maintaining high standards of order, comfort and visual pleasure in her home environment.

Angela was allowed to choose the music. Little wonder that with her shock of vermilion hair and exotic self-styling her ankle-booted foot was soon tapping along to chameleon Bowie: Bowie in the most vibrant of his multi-personalities, Ziggy Stardust.

'I love blokes in make-up,' contributed Georgia.

'Would you like to enlighten us?' Letti asked.

'Tell you later,' came the reply.

Letti was intrigued and made a mental note to extricate more details of this snippet of hitherto unknown information from Georgia. She sensed that self-confessed celibate scarred and scared Georgia had a secret tucked up her velvet sleeve. Letti knew Georgia had a 'new best friend' – tall, beautifully made-up and extremely narrow-hipped for a woman, by the look of the few photographs Georgia had shyly produced. Perhaps this beauty, who was the one friend who'd penetrated Georgia's armour since Bruno encountered the paperweight, was not quite what she seemed. Letti didn't push it.

Penny was allocated the job of cork-popping and fizz-pouring using her skills from the Champagne Perry period.

'Dive in, girls,' said Letti. 'Help yourselves to the food, the fizz and the free speech. You need pampering – and so do I, actually.'

Ziggy still played guitar but Angela, Georgia, Penny and Elizabeth were stunned into silence, glasses poised in midair, collectively surprised. Letti, their Letti – teacher, mentor, counsellor, nanny – feeling vulnerable? She who knew all the answers surely didn't suffer from insecurity or depression. It was unthinkable. She was tough, reliable, constant.

'What on earth do you mean, Letti?' asked a concerned Penny. 'You haven't said much at all about yourself – you never do.'

Letti voiced her doubts. 'It's just that Jon's away and when he is I dwell on the fact that I hardly know anything at all about him. I'm accomplished at extracting the deepest secrets and great chunks of information from the world and his wife in my working capacity but as a girlfriend and supposed soulmate I've found it impossible to probe and extricate anything about his past history or even his current lifestyle. He simply isn't forthcoming.

'He tends to disappear to seminars and

symposiums after showering me with lilies, kisses and promises and reappear with comforting regularity – yet I have this vague nagging feeling that he isn't quite real. We have little past, a hazy indistinct future and only the present. The times when we do get together everything's so intense. Jon is the man of the moment in every respect. I feel that if I do try to know him better the magic will evaporate.

'The aura of mystery I've always insisted on maintaining and have preached about to you tonight is too much in evidence in the case of Jon and I. My ground rules for harmony are slightly unsure. I've been caught at my own game. I long to visit his family as mine is so depleted by the unrest in my homeland. I yearn to browse old photograph albums bearing evidence of his earlier life.

'Lord knows why I'm sharing this, it's probably a legacy of my own past history of disastrous romances combined with the effect of the schnapps. It's a well-known tongue loosener, isn't it? I love him too much too soon. I'm becoming obsessive. He says he loves me. Don't laugh, please don't laugh, he has a pet name for me – no, I can't reveal it, it's too silly, too frivolous. I chant this ridiculous endearment every minute of every night we're apart. It's my mantra.

'My role as your prop and your strength must be so familiar to you all that this little outburst, this regression, must seem completely alien. Are you disappointed? Please try and see me as less of a textbook, less of an oracle and more as a real woman with human frailties – a sister, a friend.

'Hearing your confessions over the long and difficult counselling sessions has underscored the fact that there has been nobody to share my own insecurities. Suddenly it's dawned on me that who better to lean on than yourselves? What a broad shouldered lot you are! You've each survived trauma and found happiness. I too want happiness but I'm petrified to commit and it seems that Jon is too. I hardly dare reflect on the catalogue of his inexplicable absences or his reluctance to share a past or plan a future.'

Her guests with murmurs of encouragement urged Letti to continue. She looked drained and resigned. To regain composure she was furiously repeating inside her head the secret name by which Mr Right called her in their closest moments – Honeybunny, Honeybunny, Honeybunny . . .

'As much as I deceive myself and bury my heart in my career, my home, my books and my writing, things still don't seem normal. Perhaps because comparing dysfunctional behaviour with accepted norms is my business I'm over-emphasising petty doubts. Maybe my own paranoia and troubled psyche is rotting this potentially great love affair. How ironic that you might all tell the learned counsellor that "It's all in her mind!" I'm supposed to have all the answers but this time I'm up against a brick wall.'

Letti ran out of steam, put her elbows on the table, cupped her chin in her hands and awaited reaction. Penny was the first to speak.

'Letti, thank you for tonight. We, in our pain and self-absorption have been totally oblivious to your needs and emotions. Without consultation I'll stick my neck out and be the first to say I'm in the same boat as you. Please don't feel alone. I too am bound up in dreams of the future and plans for the perfect partnership each time Jeremy and I meet.

'My particular boat is heading for the rocks because if you think Jon's secretive and difficult to read, my gorgeous arty Jeremy takes the biscuit for avoidance and evasiveness when it comes to hard facts and family history. Christ! I don't even know where he lives. I don't want to know because although I say he's my saviour, my new hope and a pussycat after the long list of rats, I'd put a year's salary on a sure bet that there's a wife or a live-in partner tucked away somewhere in a fashionable part of town.

'Most of my suspicions I've put down to the damage done to my trust and self-esteem by Champagne Perry but sitting here hearing the very brave and naked truth from Letti I'm going to admit to you all that I'm scared. I too haven't dared push the business of marriage or permanency. I sit and wait. I kid myself that we have the perfect arrangement but all I have in reality is a devastatingly dashing new lover who is convincingly devoted while he's there, but once a week for ever isn't enough. This mystery wife or his art gallery directorship must have a pretty powerful attraction to prevent him giving more of himself and yes, when push comes to shove, as much as I've advocated the bachelor girl state I in my heart, like you Letti, damned well want more!'

Elizabeth who had been taking it all in with a shocked and superior expression on her face was intent on having her say.

'My James only sees me on a Wednesday at the moment and I trust him implicitly. Being a sales representative for a tea and coffee merchant with a huge area to cover takes up a great deal of his time. He spends weekends with his elderly parents in Suffolk and knowing the cantankerous traits of my own mother, even if invited, I'd never join him there. I've no desire to poach him away from them prematurely. They'll be dead soon anyway and I want to take things very slowly.

'James is my first real boyfriend. I was always too bound up in my brother Philip's arrangements during my teens, especially after Marjorie's death. I followed him around everywhere. It was as if before I knew the truth I was aware on a subconscious level that he had to be observed constantly in case a confession was forthcoming. Then my best courting time, my hunting season to be quite honest, was stolen from me by the prison sentence. I wasn't released until I was well into my thirties and I was so inexperienced when it came to dealing with men that I hadn't a clue what to say when James walked into the coffee bar where the rehabilitation people had placed me.'

Letti passed the Cava along the table and Elizabeth absent-mindedly filled her glass and swallowed the sparkling contents as if it were the cola she'd so often shared on picnics with Marjorie. Flushed and still indignant she continued.

'It takes all my emotional resources to make myself interesting every Wednesday. To keep bright and witty for just that one day we spend together requires a major effort at the moment. I concentrate all my lapsed femininity into making my 'James Wednesday' as I call it extra special for him. By the time he's ready to go into business with me using his parents' legacy and we make our tearoom dream come true he'll not have the punishing schedule and I'll have recovered my confidence and sense of humour enough to command his full attention and be able to fill every day with being a true partner in business and in marriage if I'm lucky enough.

'If I may say, you Letti and you Penny don't seem very trusting. Dare I suggest you should be more like me, bide your time and wait. We'll get our men in the end. It's the earlier wounds that cause us to mistrust. I'm surprised, Letti, that you haven't realised this but when one's doing something daily for a living it must be hard to practice what you preach. Isn't it often said that the taps never work in a plumber's house or the paintwork's usually shabby in a decorator's home?

'Please don't be so suspicious, especially you, Letti. Surely you don't really suspect Jon of double-crossing you just because his job takes him away at short notice? Just look at those beautiful lilies – a symbol of honesty and purity. Surely he wouldn't be so generous and loving had he anything to hide?'

Lilies, pondered Georgia. Sharp green bittersweet-scented crypt decorations, symbolic of death and funerals. She felt uncomfortable with the silence that followed Elizabeth's protective little speech in praise of James, purveyor of fine teas and coffees – what a grind! Georgia smiled to herself. She was now prepared to share the pleasing secret of her 'new best friend'.

'I'm going to tell you all about my beautiful new friend. I call him Jean/Jeanne,' announced Georgia confidently.

The background music switched to the thud, thud, thud, repetitive beat of the introduction to Bowie's clipped and cynical rendition of 'Jean Genie' and struck yet another chord of coincidence with Letti.

Angela, the latest arrival, didn't mind taking a back seat. She didn't feel quite as integrated as the others because she'd heard none of the 'disposals' and only the details of the new loves. She played for time, enjoying the rich dessert, the wanton consumption of alcohol and the generous exchange of fascinating information.

'I can't bear blokes near me since Bruno.'

She turned to Angela.

'Angela, you didn't hear what I had to say earlier but it's enough to say that I killed a lousy lover, a cunning man with a capacity for immense cruelty, who underestimated my desire to escape and be free at any cost. After he cornered me for the final time and I shut him up permanently with a paperweight, he left me with a legacy of distaste, a pathological hatred of blokes, beards and boiled eggs. It will drain me and bore everyone else if I have to go through it all again. Suffice to say, if a man comes anywhere near me I go into a phobic panic but I've found an amazing compromise.

'This is going to be the weirdest thing you've heard tonight. I've fallen in love with a cross-dresser. Not a gay boy nor a freak. Not a screwed-up closet queen nor a knicker coveter. He has no sex drive or leanings of any persuasion. He's got all his bits and will 'do it' if I ask but he feels or wants nothing. The act with him is automatic, robotic. He's quite happy to give but able to take it or leave it.

'Jean/Jeanne I call him. He's like a great golden doll, an animated mannequin. Someone to dress up and play with. We share make-up, gossip, secrets, jokes. Jean/Jeanne works on Sunday afternoons and on a weekday to suit the club owner. He performs in a gay bar but I can't describe it as a drag act because he doesn't look bizarre or out of place in women's clothes.

'Jean/Jeanne crops up at my place after work in satin, feathers and fishnets. Sometimes he turns up as the pretty boy he is, in leather trousers and silk shirt, all floppy blond fringe and shades like a nervous rock star. He kisses me like a man and will adore me forever because I accept – I don't question his actions, his motives or his whereabouts when he's not performing in the bar or spending time with me. I let him be free. He's like an exotic, wild creature who continues to return because there's no threat of entrapment.

'We paint each other's toenails, wax our legs, squabble over Brad Pitt videos, eat popcorn and read glossy magazines. Jean/Jeanne wants to be me, to learn all about women from the inside out rather than the outside in. I let him get inside my head and in my bed.

'I want all the love of a man without the sweaty sordid soul-trapping sexual slavery and certainly without the abuse. Whether this makes me a fruit fly or a fag hag, a bluestocking or a sad facsimile of a lesbian I don't give a toss. Whatever Jean/Jeanne's got I want and it's all I'm ever capable of accommodating ever since I touched

Bruno for the last time as he lay on my floor with his skull cracked open.

'The one good thing that came out of Bruno's death is that I was left with no prejudice. Jean/Jeanne was stunned to find a friend who was completely non-judgemental. Anything goes. We are comfortable with each other. I've even told him what I did to Bruno. I don't think he believes me but if he does he's attached no importance to it. We live for the present.'

'How did you meet him?' asked Elizabeth who envied Georgia this brotherly/sisterly bond she had managed to develop.

Of all of the women seated around the table Elizabeth understood best the deep affection Georgia had described. She wouldn't have championed her brother Philip's wrongdoings for so long had she not experienced exactly the same brand of affection herself. How marvellous, thought Elizabeth wishing her James was gentler, less typically male. Someone like Jean/Jeanne would give her time to adjust in a growing relationship. Lucky Georgia. Elizabeth wasn't the least bit shocked by the eccentric behaviour of Georgia's new best friend.

'I met Jean/Jeanne at the salon where I have my purple streaks put in. He was in the seat opposite and we kept grinning at each other in the mirrors. He was having highlights but then asked to try on the wigs. The two customers flanking him kept sniggering but when he was wearing the wigs his face was transformed so strikingly into a woman's that they actually shut up and complimented 'her' as she then deserved to be referred to. I invited Jean/Jeanne for a ladies' lunch to compare hairdos afterwards and we chummed up from there. Jean/Jeanne changes, he isn't any particular gender, he's just Jean/Jeanne.

'I have no idea what he does with his 'non-me' time. I don't give a damn. Like Elizabeth my scars go too deep to devote everything to a new relationship, or not for a very long time. So I have a workable solution to post-Bruno loneliness. Best of all I love Jean/Jeanne and I wish you could all meet him. I'm positive you'd feel the same. We're all social outcasts now but none of us more than he is. He'd fit beautifully tonight into our newly founded girls' club, our coterie.'

Letti was thinking. She was fascinated. So this was the 'new best friend' in those photographs she'd seen. She toyed with the idea of inviting Georgia to bring her 'big golden doll', this Jean/Jeanne into their midst. It wouldn't be breaking the strictly female house rules because Jean/Jeanne would be in female guise and in empathy. Letti pushed the idea to the back of her mind. She was jealous. Why, after all, should Georgia be allowed the luxury of flaunting her prize, her happiness when doubts were beginning to emerge amongst some of them concerning the dedication of their respective suitors? No, Letti decided to curb her curiosity. However it would be a great idea to meet Jean/Jeanne at some stage. He sounded like a prime case for counselling.

Penny was a man's woman and was finding the concept of a physical relationship with a feminine man in full drag hard to take on board. She said little but was generous enough of spirit to acknowledge the importance of Jean/Jeanne in Georgia's life. After all, what did she herself know about assault and battery? Laughable in the circumstances she was averse to violence and saw the drowning of Perry in the bath as a civilised and necessary evil. Well there had been no bloodshed had there? Apart from a few inches of fragrant bathwater there had been little mess in the aftermath – except the irritating matter of her conviction and the subsequent sentence.

Penny sat on the fence wisely telling herself that the subject of cross-dressers and their proclivities was out of her field. Nevertheless she was itching to take a look at this Jean/Jeanne, this paragon and life-enhancer. For all her faults she was open to change and Jean/Jeanne did sound a little more amenable than her Jeremy although just as secretive and elusive. Perhaps the slight flaw in their liaison lay in Penny's inability to trust anyone since Perry's lies. She decided to learn from

Georgia's story, take Elizabeth's advice and stop worrying about Jeremy's wanderings and art gallery comings and goings. She poured another Cava and visibly relaxed.

The visitors knew this would probably be a one-off meeting, the last time they would see each other before going their separate ways. The camaraderie around the dining table was a wonderful illusion but each knew it ought to be temporary. Letti was right. Now was the time to purge the nastiness and then repair the individual threads of their lives and face the future without the support of either Letti or each other. To cling together would create a bigger mass of weakness similar to a leper colony, a hospice. None of the murderesses wanted to be like lemmings.

New skin would cover the scars much more effectively if each struck out for shore alone, well not quite alone – with their present partners of course. After Letti and Penny shared doubts about their relationships with their new men the women were collectively coming to realise that even a new man couldn't or wouldn't supply complete protection and support. Jon, Jeremy and even James and Jean/Jeanne were beginning to lose their power as props and heroes as the evening progressed and previously unaddressed doubts and insecurities became more apparent. The golden boys were ever so slightly tarnished.

'This is rather like the Last Supper,' observed Penny. 'Let's savour every moment. It's Friday night, none of us are working until Monday so I think we can afford to have hangovers.'

Their cosy environment resembled a time warp. Letti's apartment was neutral territory. All their boyfriends had been put on – or had put themselves on – the back burner and now that Angela had finished her late shift there were no commitments for the weekend. Those who had families were either ostracised or partially alienated except for duty and festive occasions, the strain of which made a mockery of the true meaning of festive. The prison gates were closed behind them, the psychiatric units had meted out the required span of temporary hospitality and thanks to this generous and glorious orgy of normality courtesy of Letti, it was beginning to dawn on all concerned that they were free. A sobering thought but nobody was staying sober.

More peaches were sliced, apricots dipped into Cointreau and second helpings of death by chocolate smothered with cream, reinforcing the belief that if you couldn't count on your man then why the hell count calories? Women who have been shut away behind bars need building up.

General opinion decreed it too early for coffee and Angela, the joker in the pack, was now eager to perform. Elizabeth chose the music showing a rare glimpse of humour as Helen Reddy's strong antipodean twang related the warped ballad of 'Angie Baby', a very special lady indeed and a classic victim of the promise that would never materialise. Everyone identified with her, more corks were popped and ears pricked. The ladies were in waiting.

8

Homicide's Funny Side

'Oh to be Elouise! You should have seen her in action in the wine bar earlier on!' said Angela well aware that a warm-up was expected of her before she joined the others by relating the heavy stuff, her personal account of what she did and to whom.

Angela had convinced herself that this particular nasty little episode was not worth dredging up. She'd planned to stick to her repertoire of funny material. She thought Letti had invited her as the light entertainment, the cabaret. Letti was such a serious and learned woman. There was more than an element of surprise for Angela on arriving, settling around the table and learning from the fragmented conversations just what had gone down with the other women. Gritty stuff, real problems exactly like her own.

As the wine flowed the tongues loosened and hitherto padlocked doors to scary memory corridors had been flung wide. Angela soon cottoned on to what this evening was about. This was confession time and these women were right up her street. Angela wished she'd met them during her long-term stay in the secure hospital. Her fellow dinner guests didn't seem like standard jailbirds – the drug baronesses, hairy old dykes and child killers – whom she expected peopled women's prisons nowadays. Her hospital inmates had been weeping wrecks of womanhood, automatons striding the disinfected corridors, the deeply disturbed and those wracked with loss, guilt and regret. The latter were very like herself but she had been unable to form friendships or bond with them. There'd been no cameraderie, no sisterhood.

Angela deduced that a selection of tonight's audience hadn't exactly been jailed but incarceration in a nut house was probably even worse.

She was right. Doe-eyed and countrified Elizabeth looked remarkably together considering the wattage that had been forcibly sizzled through her brain. Georgia of Gothic leanings with those achingly delicate blue shadows beneath her eyes and the bruised bee-stung lips seemed almost tamed after the array of chemical cocktails administered to eradicate her demons. Georgia would have looked more at home wandering a graveyard sobbing for whoever had got her into this blanched state, but she was bearing up. Bearing up very well – considering.

Penny wasn't really Angela's *tasse de thé*; she was a bit posh. Nevertheless it was nice to know this elegant chic woman had an equal amount of guts as the peasantry when it came to slaying dragons and doing time.

In reality a wardrobe full of up-market fashion in lieu of payment for her services in Cassandra's boutique were Penny's only material assets since the divorce courts had robbed her of her so visually challenged but so financially sound husband. 'More flash than cash' aptly described Penny's present circumstances. Penny herself was reasonably pacified by the fact that in general, because she was so well turned out, people perceived her to be a woman of means. This could only bode well in her quest for her next husband.

'What dirty deed did you perform to secure a place around Letti's dinner table tonight, Penny?' asked Angela outright. 'I hope you don't mind me asking but I need a thumbnail sketch in order to catch up!' she added.

'Not at all. I gave a fat liar his comeuppance, his final blow-job with a champagne bottle. Choked him to death while I sat on his dick and drowned him for good measure,' answered Penny obligingly.

Angela resolved to make allowance for the enviable Chanel earrings and aristocratic demeanour. 'I'm going to like you!' she smiled.

Elizabeth chipped in, more to herself than to the others, 'I pushed my brother down a well shaft twenty years after he did the same to my best friend, Marjorie. I suppose that too was an intended drowning although the well was dry.' She reflected for a moment and whispered, 'At the precise moment when he hit the bottom he probably wished he'd drowned.'

Elizabeth wasn't to know that Philip had lived for almost an hour at the bottom of the well. Little Marjorie's shattered thigh bone had lain there waiting for him all those years, sharp and yellowing and picked clean as a knife blade by two decades of blind mud-dwelling creatures. Philip had spiralled downwards, ricocheting against the slimy walls, losing on the way an eye, an ear and most of his fingers. As he met the well floor he saw with his remaining eye, Marjorie's femur slice into his chest like a serrated knife into a cabbage.

Philip lay impaled, his past life flickering across his memory, especially his childhood. The pets were all there, replayed in his mind's eye, reproaching him: Patch holding up a maimed paw in supplication; Bright Eyes staring blind and bewildered after Philip had cruelly administered disinfectant; the kitten he'd turned into a Manx without an anaesthetic.

In that endless hour Philip wished he hadn't been such a wicked boy. He came to believe that pain wasn't such an enjoyable experience after all, especially when the boot was on the other foot – or what was left of his foot. Marjorie had her last laugh, not the high tinkling peal of childhood laughter in sunshine, but the hollow vengeful chuckle of a long-dead child echoing in the dark cavity from the depths of the well. It was she who planted a bony stake through her murderer's heart. All Elizabeth did was push him down to meet her. She and Marjorie had always done things together.

Angela by now had a pretty good idea of the picture. She was pleased she'd extricated herself from Elouise's rapidly multiplying legions of male admirers in the wine bar. Willowy Elouise of the Titian hair and endless legs who had wafted past Angela's place of work earlier and delightedly lured her off for a 'quick drinkie'. Elouise was quite capable of hunting alone but one auburn and one carrot-top added up to two head-turners, doubling the stakes in Elouise's book. Angela mulled over their earlier encounter and related its highlights to the others.

'Elouise was wearing a three-quarter-length fake leopardskin jacket. "Try it on," she purred throatily. I looked like Bud Flanagan. It drowned me, I'm only five foot two! Then she plonked her hat on my head, knowing I'd been covetously eyeing it. It was an extravagant chocolate velvet affair and what did I look like? Secret Squirrel. I don't know why I hang about with her. She's always giving me her Louis Vuitton lizard-skin briefcase to carry; my supermarket carrier bag makes her cringe. She sometimes gives me her cast-off clothes. Very generous but I look like Swee'pea as she's so curvy and tall. Second-hand Rose, that's me.

'Anyway, we arrived at Hades – funny name for a wine bar but I think it used to be called Shades and the gold leafed 'S' rubbed off. It's a steamy pit of sin in any case so perhaps the name is quite apt. After a day's work Elouise looked immaculate. I was sweaty, she was sweet. She'd been power-brunching all day for her radio station and I'd been slaving over a printing machine churning out posters for an event at the store. The opposite sex materialised from between the fake beams and Elouise gave them a fake beam. She has wonderful teeth. I secretly call her 'Tits and Pout'. It could be said that I envy her.

'You should have seen the talent! They were like bees to a honeypot, moths to a flame. "Elouise darling, what'll it be – a white wine and cassis, a papaya juice spritzer with an acacia blossom and a plastic mammoth?" – that sort of sycophantic drivel. Then as an afterthought they became vaguely aware that she wasn't on her own. Gamely waiting for attention, the bright little corgi to her bored Afghan, I heard from Harry or Hugo or whatever that city dealer type are christened – "What'll your friend have – lager and lime, pineapple juice, does she want a cherry?"

'I'd be lucky if I got a glance. The conversation buzzed to and fro above my cross little head. For Christ's sake my hair's dyed vermilion, you'd think that'd get me noticed! The beautiful people continued their banter, privileged to breathe the rarefied air we stunted examples of midgetry can never get at. I felt like a spectre at the feast ready to explode at the injustice of it all. Just for the hell of it I blew down my straw and spattered Elouise's beige chamois coat-dress with blue curaçao.

'I've done impulsive things like this before. Sometimes I get out of control. My fling with Bill started as a wacky fun thing. Penny, I think, knows exactly what I mean – it all starts innocently from some chance encounter, goes swimmingly until you begin to get keen and ask questions and then you find out they're married with two kids and another on the way, they're halfway through building a granny-flat for the mother-in-law, they're screwing the wife every Friday night after five pints and a vindaloo, whether she likes it or not, and you get angry, furious – well, murderous actually in my case.'

Letti, having gone to make coffee, returned and served her guests who were heartily amused by

Angela's way with words. They'd been told she could be a comedienne if the circumstances were right. Tonight the circumstances were ideal. Elizabeth, enjoying her turn as the disc jockey, was congratulated as she browsed Letti's nostalgic collection of 'oldies', sourcing and selecting just what she was looking for. Mick Jagger whined his beggar's ballad to 'Angie, Oh Angie' as cream swirled in coffee cups, florentines and bitter chocolate were passed around and the levels in the liqueur bottles, glowing varying shades of amber by candlelight, dipped considerably.

'Elouise didn't give a damn about the booze I'd splattered onto her dress,' continued Angela. 'She'll probably give it to me like all the other stuff rather than bother to have it dry cleaned. She knows me and my moods very well. The Hoorah Henrys were not impressed though. They closed ranks around her like drones protecting their queen bee, horrified by my avant-garde behaviour, so I left.

'I do exactly as I please nowadays. The discipline I bowed to while receiving treatment has left me very selfish. I used to be much more popular with fellas than I am now. I might as well have 'ex-nutter' tattooed across my forehead. The stigma of mental illness stinks and sticks as does the stigma of a prison sentence. A defensive, wary expression lingers in your eyes and around your mouth. Georgia knows all about it I'm sure, just look at her. She won't mind me commenting that she's a prime example of secret sorrow. Involuntary confinement leaves an indelible scar, it doesn't rub off easily. I'm positive people can tell.'

They all agreed.

Letti had created a unique 'couch-potato' area beyond the archway leading off from her dining room. In contrast to the stark linear taste reflected in the rest of her apartment this was a real den. Two long low settees covered in navy velvet faced each other. They were heaped with the cushions Letti liked to collect on her travels. Each was original: embroidered or appliquéd, of suede or in animal prints, some sequined others splashed with bold jewel colours – emerald, turquoise, ruby red.

The coffee table separating the seating had a papier-mâché base resembling a full-sized Egyptian mummy case. A huge sheet of plate glass formed the table top. It rested on the gilded upturned feet, the chest and the forehead of the regal effigy moulded into the lid. Through the glass could be seen the impassive kohl-ringed stare of what represented a long-dead pharaoh. It was a striking piece of workmanship in ochres, turquoise and black, indistinct in the darkened room except for the generous application of gold paint which gleamed by the light of two scented candles held aloft in the scaly claws of a brace of squatting gargoyles, evil little devils, arranged on the glass table top like tomb guardians.

The walls and ceiling in the den were painted midnight blue. The centrepiece of the ceiling was a Middle Eastern brass hanging lamp which as it slowly rotated threw a moving pattern of fretwork minarets around the walls and across the two enormous prints – light, shadow, light, shadow. The two prints were terrifying – huge grey photographic blow-ups of ancient griffins and dragons with crumbling gills and broken frills. Scary monsters frozen forever in stone.

Penny had found herself in a Tunisian discotheque once. Letti's den brought back memories of Jamal and MoMo and Rachid . . . Reminiscing, Penny smiled to herself and settled against a sequined cushion.

'Where did you find this table, it's fantastic!' exclaimed Penny.

'Oh it's a theatre prop, it's only papier-mâché. I put in a bid when the Tiffany theatre closed. I got these handsome fellows too, as a job lot.' Letti caressed the nearest gargoyle and continued, 'I couldn't buy a table to match the length of the settees so I used a bit of imagination. The glass top is a second-hand supermarket door, it weighs a ton but the sarcophagus is quite light. I enjoy making something out of nothing, gathering together lots of broken bits and reassembling them to create something beautiful and strong.'

Letti did indeed get a buzz from making a perfect whole from flawed components. She was delighted that a tightly bonded group of women were evolving from the crushed individuals that had been the sad and sorry material she'd first worked with. Letti was feeling satisfied, smug almost. Her achievement tonight was beginning to cancel out the niggling fears she'd voiced with regard to her own doubts concerning Jon. She would have liked to have introduced him to her guests but true to her business ethics she'd barely mentioned them save for now and again obliquely during her time as their counsellor. Perhaps now her services were no longer officially required the occasion might arise.

Letti considered and knew in her heart that she'd probably never see any of them again. They'd need to go their separate ways by morning. Morning . . . Saturday morning. Letti had no commitments, business or romantic. Neither did Penny as Cassandra was overseeing the boutique herself this Saturday. Elizabeth, Letti knew, didn't work on Saturdays. Possibly the coffee bar proprietors knew her history and thought her state of mind too introverted and delicate to inflict on their customers on their busiest day.

Elizabeth was a hard worker but she was like a zombie in her working environment – the living dead. She only spoke when spoken to, not conducive to good customer relations especially on sociable Saturdays. It was a miracle James had managed to strike up and elicit conversation from her let alone conduct a relationship. Their relationship had probably thrived because Elizabeth was so undemanding and not in the least inquisitive about how James spent his time when they were apart.

Her compliance gave her the edge on the other women who craved more attention than their partners were willing to allocate – except perhaps for Georgia who was quite interested in Jean/Jeanne's other activities but settled for his feminine persona, the piece of him she considered exclusively hers.

Georgia's friendship was quite a comfortable compromise. Georgia's office job didn't require her to work on Saturdays and she wouldn't be expecting to see Jean/Jeanne until after his drag act late on Sunday evening. Angela had earned her free Saturday by doing overtime tonight at the store.

This fortuitous collection of circumstances enabled Letti to turn over an embryo of an idea in her mind until it matured into feasibility. She was a person given to practical analysis followed by swift decision. Letti put her cards on the table.

'We haven't heard Angela's account of how she dealt with Bill yet, nor with whom, if anybody, she is dallying since losing Bill and a large part of her life while taking her 'rest cure'. Shall we admit to being drunk as skunks and decide upon some strategy because I have a proposal?'

Letti didn't want the evening to end. They were on their second cafetiere and to a woman, were 'three sheets to the wind' as Elizabeth would have said, 'pissed as a parrot' as Penny would have admitted, 'legless' as Georgia would have termed their condition and 'drunk' as Letti, who called a spade a spade, realistically stated. Angela was tipsy but catching up fast.

'Stay the night and we'll reconvene in the morning. None of us has anywhere pressing to go, our men are otherwise engaged and there's a bakery over the road that does an irresistible hot Danish take-out for breakfast. No Angela, a pastry, not an accomplished Scandinavian hunk called Sven!' Letti predicted and countered the smart remark that she knew Angela was about to make.

Angela laughed and shut her mouth. Letti knew her well – Letti knew them all well.

'I propose,' she continued, 'that we draw up the drawbridge, have one more nightcap and extend this party to Saturday or even Sunday for those who so desire. There's the other bedroom, and these settees will sleep two. What do you say girls?'

'I'm game,' said Angela immediately. She felt cheated in any case, having missed most of the meal and the meatiest bit of the conversation. Above all she was anxious to tell her tale and welcomed a few hours during which to order it in her mind.

'How lovely, Letti!' purred Penny already in repose like a languid cat amongst the cushions.

Elizabeth readily accepted Letti's offer, as she was seeking a way of amusing herself while James was spending the obligatory weekend with his parents. She'd have plenty to tell him on her 'James Wednesday' if she spent a couple of days in this fascinating little enclave! She would divide it all by six, leaving out the 'the nasty bits' rather like she'd done a while ago when she'd attempted to tell James about 'Before'. James hadn't believed her. It suited him to believe Elizabeth had had a nervous breakdown, a delayed reaction to little Marjorie's death, and so Elizabeth had made a decision to 'let sleeping big bad wolves lie'. Having always played second fiddle to her brother she was content not to reveal too much about herself. This was why she respected James' need for personal space and didn't delve as deeply as Penny or Letti did into their Jeremy and Jon's unexplained comings and goings.

Georgia, used to solitude, had doubts about prolonging the get-together. She became anxious if she didn't get back to base at night, preferring her own things around her and to sleep in her own bed. She'd only been allowed the farthest edge of the bed she'd shared with Bruno after he'd used her for his drunken gratification. She was then cast aside like an empty pint glass, of no further use. Prison had taught her that privacy was to be treasured, as had the constant monitoring during her subsequent stay in the psychiatric unit.

Although flattered to be considered worthy of taking part in the dinner party, Georgia was feeling crowded. Jean/Jeanne wasn't likely to crop up until Sunday evening after performing his drag act so there was nothing awaiting her at home. But 'nothing' was what she craved. Letti, perceptions honed despite the schnapps, sensed all this and offered an option.

'You could go home and sober up, gather your strength and return tomorrow if you prefer.'

While the others were deciding on sleeping attire, squabbling light-heartedly over Letti's collection of outsized T-shirts and sharing out bedding, toothpaste and the like, Georgia bade her goodbyes and followed Letti into the kitchen where together they stacked the dishwasher. Then between them they hauled a brimming bin bag of post-dinner debris outside the apartment to the doors of the rubbish chute. As they hefted and tipped down their burden their eyes met in the dim outer hallway, revealing identical thoughts. Both at that moment thought of Elizabeth who had pushed her brother down a deeper, darker hole. Georgia knew exactly what had driven quiet, reserved Elizabeth to show her claws, she herself had demonstrated all the same skills. Letti didn't know exactly but she could imagine.

Georgia thanked her hostess.

'I'll be back tomorrow, Letti. I've had a brilliant time but I'm drained. I've said too much and drunk too much.'

'You've just lived too much,' answered Letti quietly more to herself than to Georgia as she turned back to her doorway, self-contained and neat in her black dress and as bright and observant as ever despite the indulgences of the evening.

Georgia lingered in the stairwell for a minute gazing at the now-closed door. She envied Letti her interesting career, her man – this Jon who sent lilies and was something in computers – this perfect man who came and went but always came back again and wasn't any trouble. Georgia bet herself Jon had never raised a clenched fist in anger at any living creature, especially a woman.

She envied the designer lifestyle, the mock-Egyptian coffee table, the octagonal plates, the crystal. She bet Jon wasn't a plate-smasher, a destructive type. She envied Letti's ability to extricate pain and exorcise demons. Above all Georgia envied the fact that Letti hadn't committed murder. Letti had a clean slate. Georgia's was scribbled on. She descended the remaining flight of stairs, turned up her collar and left the building.

It was raining. Georgia wasn't afraid to walk the city streets at night. What was there to fear? She knew how to kill and she was well schooled in self-defence; fending off Bruno had taught her a lot. Identical to a thousand other lost souls going nowhere at 2 a.m. on a Saturday morning, her painfully thin frame and pinched features came as standard amongst the night people.

She took advantage of her anonymity and rain-streaked appearance, and surrendered to tears. Georgia didn't know precisely why she was crying. Perhaps for Bruno and the sham love affair she'd tried so hard to shore up and which he'd neglected and destroyed with little effort. Maybe she cried for Luke the pitiful scrap of life that didn't make full term.

More likely the tears were for herself. She'd sat at a laden table in like-minded company after surviving Bruno, Luke, prison and a psychiatric unit. She'd said her piece with minimal emotion, expecting to exorcise her ghosts. She had the support of Letti and was placed in reasonable employment. Her life looked potentially 'not bad', but Georgia didn't want 'not bad'. She wanted the feel-good factor, not this permanent feeling of despair. As she splashed through the puddles beneath her umbrella Georgia knew it was all pointless, her scars went too deep. Her soul had been destroyed.

Digging for her hip flask she took a long draught of Scotch. Revellers were emerging from a club. She stepped off the pavement to avoid contact. A man hurried past. She thought it was

Jean/Jeanne and made a half step towards him but it was another guy of identical build but conservatively dressed. His hair slicked back with more than his share of gel – not a habit of Jean/Jeanne's – and his eyes instead of baby blue were dark behind glasses. Georgia had held his gaze for only a moment. Most of his face was obscured by the collar of his jacket turned up against the weather. Then he was gone, shouldering his way through the traffic. As she tried to recall his face through a haze of whisky and wine Georgia registered that he'd seemed shocked.

If she could have seen herself in her wringing velvet clothes, black hair plastered down like a crow's wing, mascara coursing down pale cheeks. In one hand the hip flask, a bat-like umbrella in the other, she wouldn't have wondered why a stranger would be startled by her appearance. Georgia looked like a shipwreck. All washed up.

'It's the Scotch,' she muttered to herself as by remote control she located her home and in a disjointed, modern ballet divested herself of her clothing and lurched into the shower. Scrubbing furiously, Georgia eradicated her war paint. Her skinny body still bore areas of raised, spoiled tissue – the legacy of Bruno's abuse. The water was scalding, the soap fragrant but both failed to put roses in Georgia's cheeks. 'I'll be all right in the morning, it's the Scotch,' she repeated as she fell into her bed.

Not a million miles away, also in solitude but a thousand times more self-assured, the man who looked like Jean/Jeanne shrugged off his expensive jacket, wiped the steam from his glasses, smiled at his devastatingly handsome reflection and also turned in for the night. While Georgia dreamed of a blood-spattered paperweight and a porcelain doll with a shattered face the nameless stranger stretched, put his hands behind his head and lay contented – long and lean like a great satisfied he-cat – considering a nameless woman, his next choice, the lucky recipient of his attentions in the very near future.

9

Non-Gay Paris

Paris was a delicate and premature baby born to a bitter mother of independent means and fading beauty. Mummy had been dumped by Daddy as soon as her pregnancy became apparent and she was deeply disappointed. It was the last straw. She had hoped her wealth would have been enough to sustain his interest but it was not to be. Mummy, teetering on the cusp, turned into a vehement man-hater. Paris had the misfortune of emerging from the womb in possession of a penis which seriously hampered his mother's plan for an all-woman household. From the age of two Paris was habitually required to wear girl's clothing: peach cardigans and smocked dresses of ivory silk and often vivid blue to match his eyes and complement his halo of golden curls. Paris at two knew no better.

At four and a half years old Paris attended nursery school. He began to realise he was different. The other little boys had names like Kevin and Paul. When they went home they were allowed, unlike Paris, to keep their grey flannel shorts or denim dungarees on. Their mummys didn't make them wear dresses. Toddler talk at milk and biscuit break with his peer group had enabled Paris to elicit this important information. Kevin and Paul didn't know what Paris was getting at. Paris kept quiet, it was just his and Mummy's secret. He was a bright boy but he couldn't work out why Mummy wouldn't let him have his hair cut either. He began to demonstrate unacceptable behaviour, tantrums alternating with long periods of sulking in his pink gingham bedroom.

By the time he got to junior school his feelings for Mum see-sawed precariously between love and hatred. He blamed her because he didn't have a dad like Kevin and Paul. He wanted brothers and sisters too. Mum told him he was a blessing, a miracle because she'd nearly lost him at birth. She didn't clarify the matter by mentioning the litres of Chablis she'd poured down her love-starved unkissed throat while others in the antenatal classes dutifully popped their folic acid.

At thirteen Paris hated his name. By now he'd been subjected to systematic bullying and mocking sniggers every time the register was called. He started hanging around with the girls. He was tall for his age and slender. Mum fed him the same diet she religiously followed: cottage cheese, tuna, broccoli, greenery of all descriptions except processed peas. Mum said they were common. Dad had liked processed peas. Paris wasn't allowed to have anything in common with Dad.

Not that Paris could remember. His earliest memory was of lying in his pram under the lilac tree screaming and scarlet of face because an earwig had dropped into his open mouth. Mummy had soon made it all better but even then he didn't trust her. Together with the strange diet – Paul got chips a lot and Kevin always had pockets full of sweets – Mum gave him wine. She used to dilute it in his bottle to make him sleep. At thirteen Paris could put away two or three glasses a night. Always before bathtime.

Bathtime was bizarre. Mum still bathed him. Sometimes she got in too. Paris secretly thought he was too old to still be on the breast at thirteen. Mum thought otherwise. She would kneel beside the bath, shampooing his hair. She loved his long hair. Somehow her robe would fall open. She would fix Paris with a determined no-nonsense look and like a moth captured in a flame he would remain unable to escape, blushing but willing.

She would climb in with him, a voluptuous study in rose and cream. Her generous white body pressed insistently against him in the vast luxurious bathtub. Paris would close his eyes as she murmured endearments and inhale her familiar scent: a combination of dark velvety autumn flowers and expensive French wine. Paris would sink into her depths eager and ready, helplessly hating himself, kneading her cushioning breasts and biting her hardening nipples like a suckling kitten. She would haul him wide-eyed and pink from the fragrant water and lie with him on the tangle of warm white towelling caressing her beautiful boy, rubbing him dry, rubbing him slowly and then faster and faster. The things she did to him and guided him to do to her often made him cry himself to sleep with a contrasting mixture of emotions. Guilt and panic, embarrassment, excitement, ecstasy.

Mum clung. She told Paris she was all he needed and not to court the girls at school, they were all tarts – like the strumpet who took Dad away. He wasn't sure what a strumpet was although he hated the strumpet who'd lured away his father. He decided it might be someone who was loud and brassy like a trumpet. He was dead right.

Paris ignored Mum's warnings. He didn't need to keep his distance from the girls, they came to him – in droves. At fifteen Paris was so beautiful the girls at school, even the older ones, followed him around as they would a rock star. The boys shunned him and called him a pansy. Paris wasn't gay. He desired neither boys nor girls. Paris had Mum. He showed no teenage emotions and didn't have any crushes but because his carnal knowledge was extensive, thanks to a long succession of highly instructive bathtimes, there was nothing he didn't know and word soon got around amongst the nubile sixth form girls, all quick learners.

At seventeen Paris was a big boy, tall for his build and the possessor of a leonine mane of tousled golden curls. Paris took what he wanted, loved them and left them. After all it was the sixties – free love and one-night stands epitomised the era. His conquests were willing to be flavour of the night and castoffs of the dawn.

Paris of course always played away matches. Mum turned a blind eye, she was secure in her total possession of him. She had created him, he always came home. Mother knew best. He shuddered at the consequences should he have suggested bringing any of his strumpets home.

Paris despised his prey. Because he was so fair of face he didn't have to try. He was bored and longed for a challenge. Even the forbidden heart-thumping very naughty acts with Mum, especially now that he often instigated proceedings, were becoming predictable.

Because of Mother's wealth Paris didn't have to work. He spent his time acquiring a range of diverse skills from applied mathematics to appreciation of the arts. Perhaps because of his early childhood experiences in the guise of a girl, he saw dressing up and acting as a diversion from his other pursuits as a sex symbol. He became quite good at the application of cosmetics and Mother encouraged him. They'd spend hours on end in her suite impersonating royalty and drama queens. It was a seductive game. Paris realised he could be anybody he liked. Taking into account his off-beat upbringing this was fortunate. Paris could hide his disturbed and flawed self behind a myriad of personalities and many mantles of disguise, egged on by Mother who was running out of ideas to keep his full allegiance.

In his mid-twenties Paris met a girl who looked just like Mother – in her youth. The girl was buxom wealthy and self-assured. She didn't care whether she saw Paris or not. Her indifference was a revelation. Paris was intrigued. His days as a serial lover were numbered. One by one he dropped Flora and Lucy, Beth, Nicole and Helen, the nameless ones too – the bank cashier, the blonde he'd met on a train, the one who gave great head, the one who didn't, the one who dressed up for him. Gradually Paris became entranced by the girl who looked like Mother.

He was becoming increasingly irritated by Mother whose body by now left a lot to be desired. She'd developed a dowager's hump and an extra chin and quite frankly what had once been a luscious banquet of forbidden fruit had become wind-blown, over-ripe and spoiled. Rubenesque was now an exaggeration of her charms. Mother was fat. Her face remained unlined, her hair, artfully coloured, was still luxuriant but from the neck downwards the once-alluring and magnificent body had succumbed to gravity. Paris, even with his customary indifference, found it impossible to become aroused. He felt no loss, his mother's substitute was more than enough to secure his attentions.

Mother, however, felt a vast loss. She was livid, furious with Paris for being less than attentive. She was annoyed by his new habit of bathing alone, barricading himself within the opulent bathroom, soaping, oiling, powdering, massaging and Lord knows what else, excluding her, not needful of her ministerings, unmindful of her hunger.

Paris, bewildered by the alien emotion he was experiencing since falling under the spell of the 'younger model of Mother', fretted that he was no longer in control and concluded to go with the flow and surrender to love. When his new love desired his company her wish was his command. Often he wouldn't return home to Mother for three or four days at a time.

Mother tried very hard to keep Paris amused and interested, producing ridiculously expensive gifts and stacking the house with tempting delicacies, obscure and rare European chocolates, truffles, guineafowl, pheasant, aged claret, Cognac. Paris, in the throes of his first major love-affair, was off his food. Mother, finding herself alone in the house, now appeared a figure to be pitied – over-painted, over-dressed and over-eating.

For a woman who had spent her life grazing on steamed vegetables, tuna fish and assorted designer leaves, the indulgences of her self-pity had a noticeable effect. Becoming bloated, she took to wearing unstructured flowing clothing, let her hair hang loose, neglected her manicure, ceased to attend to her underarm and facial hair. No longer the well-preserved and immaculate example of mature womanhood, this parody would pounce on Paris on his increasingly infrequent forages home, her kaftan agape, the shrivelled, brown nipples of her flabby breasts aching with desire. She would grasp handfuls of his golden curls and force him to look at her while murmuring all the endearments he knew by heart.

Breaking point had been reached. Paris, on one such occasion – not bothering to disguise his revulsion – threw up over her disproportionately tiny brocade-slippered feet. His home-life deteriorating, Paris stayed away as much as he could. This irritated his independent girlfriend somewhat but Paris was blissfully unaware that here was a woman who was quite keen but didn't like to be crowded. Neither did she encourage impromptu visits.

Paris considered Mother still capable of looking after herself and more than capable of feeding her face if not her sexual cravings. Mother transferred the goodies Paris had rejected to her suite and idled away the hours anticipating his infrequent returns by gorging on chocolates and devouring whole jars of asparagus and antipasto, the olive oil glistening on her chins.

She would mix cocktails of Krug and cognac and slump on her king-sized bed, watching the clock while playing and replaying a crackling LP track, their song, her anthem to a son who'd once adored his mummy. The plaintive ballad would drive the neighbours to post polite notes to her, requesting that she at least change the tune if not lower the volume. Mother refused to put a sock in it, humming along to the lyrics describing a black sheep boy with 'golden curls and envied hair' who shone beside his swarthy peers, a dove amongst crows.

She painted her eyelids silver and applied baby-pink lipstick in a great sticky bow overspilling her natural lip-line. She looked like a terrifying inflated rubber doll. Her fevered efforts at cosmetic improvement were interspersed with periods of inertia and depression but always she ate and drank, swilling down bejewelled handfuls of tablets to hasten sleep and oblivion.

Paris inevitably found her decaying gently in a bed full of putrefying smoked salmon leavings, half-eaten chocolates, empty pill bottles and bodily eliminations. In her hand – rigor mortis causing her to clutch possessively – she held a photograph of a boy in puberty with bee-stung lips and an angelic, adoring expression. His eyes seemed to be saying 'You shouldn't but you can.' This was her prized portrait of Paris when he had been exclusively hers and when she had been all his. She was an eternal noose around his neck in life. In death she would never desert her blue-eyed boy.

The grown-up Paris, with customary coldness, arranged a swift cremation and the uncomplicated transfer of Mother's wealth to his own accounts. The practicalities dealt with, he couldn't wait to present himself at the door of the woman who looked like Mother and declare himself free of encumbrance at last.

The woman was mortified at the sight of Paris on her doorstep flanked by a pair of expensive crocodile-skin suitcases, a sheaf of lilies in his arms. Paris considered it a natural progression to move in with his sweetheart now that Mother was gone. He'd never known rejection. The possibility that he might not be wanted on a full-time basis was unthinkable.

He stood out in the street as the object of his desires coolly refused to accept Mother's emerald-and-diamond knuckle-duster – Paris' idea of an engagement token – but graciously accepted the flowers. Impressing on him that she preferred to make her own decisions with regard to shacking up and commitment, she politely but firmly shut her elegant mews front door in his beautiful petulant face. None of this was in Paris' script. He stood for a few minutes staring at the snarling brass-lion door-knocker. Inside he too was roaring.

He made his way back home in silent fury. Having intensely disliked Mother for some time he now felt hatred. He blamed her for dying and creating this intolerable situation. He'd been almost all right before, juggling both domestic situations. Both versions of Mother had betrayed him, one by letting herself deteriorate into such a joke and the other, the younger model, his replacement icon, by casting him away like a trinket she'd become bored with.

The female of the species was not to be trusted. They all betrayed you, concluded Paris as he stormed into his elegant if cluttered residence – all his now that Mother was out of his hair. By some miracle the old cow had overlooked a bottle of brandy during her foraging. Paris helped himself to a generous measure and wandered the rooms, pitying himself, giving vent to his hatred.

This wasn't the vague abstract disdain he felt for his father or his strumpet, the familiar resentment of a bewildered, rejected boy. This was a hot insidious creeping hatred which, as he surveyed the clutter and chaos in Mother's bedroom, manifested itself in a red flash of anger. He gathered together the collection of photographs of himself that she'd grouped on every available surface and trod them into the carpet, grinding the glass and bending the silver frames beneath his heels until the charismatic faces recording the various stages of his flowering youth were ruined and unrecognisable. Paris laughed at the destruction, tossed back the brandy then held the balloon high and hurled it into the ornate fireplace like a celebratory ritual in a Greek taverna.

Destroying all the simpering posturing photographs of the Paris of old helped focus his mind. Paris promised he would reinvent himself from this moment. Absolutely free now of cloying maternal demands and no longer a victim of the indifferent whims of his first and last love, Paris made a pleasant discovery. He belonged to nobody, he could be anyone he damned well chose to be.

10

Dream Lovers

The rain continued throughout the early hours of Saturday morning. Georgia slept in the tangle of her duvet, clutching a mascara-streaked pillow to her thin body. Images of Luke the lost child and Bruno the late lover visited her dreams. Bruno danced a grotesque, slow-motion, drunken reel across her mind's eye. She too featured in the dream, behind an impenetrable sheet of rose-tinted glass which formed a barrier between them. The glass was the same colour as the blood-spattered paperweight with which she'd slain Bruno.

She pushed at the surface which divided them in an attempt to reach Luke, her imagined six-year-old. Taking Luke's hand in his larger-than-life-sized paw, Bruno turned and fixed Georgia with a puzzled wounded gaze. She couldn't hear through the glass but she could see a bitter smile form on his ruined face, the gap in his gums, and his broad shoulders convulsing with what she knew to be that husky nicotine-damaged laugh. Blood coursed down his neck but he seemed unaware.

As she watched, Luke snatched his hand free from the hulk who would have been his father and charged towards the glass. He gazed up at Georgia through the glass, a mended miscarriage, the son who nearly was. His eyes sparkled like the innermost facets of her treasured paperweight. Luke closed his eyelids and blinked at her. He didn't know her. The skin beneath his eyes was a delicate, bruised blue just like her own. Dreaming on, Georgia waved goodbye to Luke, and to Bruno whose skull gaped open exactly as on the last time she'd set eyes on him. He didn't seem to be in pain and his laughter continued.

Suddenly she was back again in her prison cell where the heavy door swung open silently allowing a cacophony of sound to assault her ears – the clattering of spoons on mugs, the foul language of fellow inmates. There stood Jean/Jeanne, silhouetted against the harsh outer light. He beckoned her with a perfectly manicured hand, a complete contrast to Bruno's nail-bitten rough-skinned hand. He beckoned her to freedom.

Georgia smiled in her sleep and hugged her pillow closer. She descended to a deeper level of subconsciousness where, if she experienced further dreams, they were forgotten by morning. In reality the rain persisted, thrumming against the windows. In oblivion and peaceful at last, her memories at bay for a few hours, Georgia slept on. The thought that she would probably have the courage to return to Letti's apartment, maybe not for breakfast but at some point during the weekend, was an oblique idea slowly formulating in her mind.

Across town, in Letti's apartment four more-than-slightly inebriated women had settled down for the remainder of the night.

Penny had stretched like a pampered Czarina and collapsed where she'd been sitting drinking coffee and brandy amongst the embroidered cushions in Letti's den. Fully made up, she'd succumbed to Morpheus' kiss. On the opposite sofa, Elizabeth had made a bed with one of Letti's duvets and her own quilted jacket. Face scrubbed of her minimal lipstick, cheeks rosy with the effects of the Cointreau, she looked like the country girl she was, a Gretel under a flower-sprigged, patchwork quilt. It was hard to imagine her as a killer.

Between them, the sarcophagus was fully visible beneath the now-cleared glass top. The casing bearing the image of the dead Egyptian king looked remarkably authentic. His gold-painted amulet glowed in the narrow shaft of street light which had crept through a chink in the window-blind. His turquoise-and-kohl decorated eyelids glittered under the heavy plate-glass table top in the otherwise darkened room.

Letti had allocated the spare bedroom to Angela, feeling she deserved extra privilege having missed most of the conversation and three parts of the meal due to her late arrival. Angela graciously accepted. She wanted a few hours of solitude to order her story in her mind. Her turn to tell why and how she killed Bill would come over breakfast.

Initially en route to the gathering she'd convinced herself she wouldn't tell her tale, but on meeting the others something about them touched a spark which ignited a small flame of kinship in her heart. Angela loved to perform. The history of her love life had been a technicolour collage of promiscuity, full of ardent adventures with all sorts of Toms, Dicks and Harrys. Being such a 'shortie' she loved long-limbed men. It didn't matter if they were academics or boilermakers' apprentices, or if they were sixteen or sixty as long as they were over six feet tall and interesting. Great in the sack was a bonus and not always the case. Angela thought about her past and found it difficult to sleep.

Georgia had vanished into the rainy night, and Letti, after bidding goodbye and urging her to return for breakfast in the morning, had taken her turn in the shower and retired to her white bedroom. Despite the effect of the schnapps, she had folded and hung her clothing, having restored the kitchen to its customary neatness. The swishing of the dishwasher combined with the low hum of the water-heating system and the patter of rain on the windows had lulled her guests to sleep.

Letti slipped under her cool quilt and wondered why Jon hadn't phoned. His endless round of hi-tech seminars had probably exhausted him. She felt a little guilty at sharing with the other women her doubts about his remoteness, because it was so typically considerate of him to send the lilies. She tried to picture his features, recreate the familiar contours of his face in her mind's eye but all she could visualise were his tortoiseshell glasses and the brown eyes behind them, always smiling. The greenish glow of her bedside alarm clock illuminated the gift tag that had arrived attached to her flowers. She re-read his message, 'See you very soon Honeybunny. Yours, J.'

Reassured, Letti smiled to herself.

'Mine,' she murmured, 'all mine,' as sleep claimed her.

Letti had a dream. She was a child again, in a classroom struggling with her arithmetic. Her teacher came towards her, brown eyes sympathetic behind tortoiseshell glasses. He held out his hands and asked the Letti-child to tap one of them. She chose the left hand. Jon-teacher opened his left hand. It concealed nothing. He opened his right hand to reveal a calculator.

'Thankyou!' said Letti-child.

'No!' said Jon-teacher, 'you made the wrong choice, you misjudged – you'll always get your sums wrong!'

He laughed at Letti, who picked up an inkpot and smashed it into his glasses. Jon-teacher couldn't see Letti clearly through the shattered lenses. She scrambled down beneath the school desks, tunnelling her way towards a doorway. She could hear him blundering towards her. She opened the dream-door and crawling through found herself not in the expected corridor but in an anteroom filled with decaying lilies. Each bouquet bore a gift tag inscribed 'Honeybunny'.

Penny, anaesthetised by the cognac, dreamed deep and sluggish dreams. The images paraded across her mind's eye in slow-motion torpor. She observed a series of rooms and somehow she could see into all of them. Jeremy's art gallery interlinked with the Victorian bathroom in her old town house. A luxurious hotel bedroom, where years before she'd enjoyed a one-night stand (or flop in his case) with a gentleman of Middle Eastern persuasion, was also bizarrely connected to this dream suite. The imagined occupants of each of the rooms were clearly visible to her but she remained unseen yet present in every situation.

She could see Champagne Perry, his thick lips twisted in an accusatory grimace, his eyes bulging with surprise. His drowned bulk bobbed lazily just beneath the surface of the cold water in her ornate bath. Penny didn't know how she knew the water was cold. Perhaps because Perry's face was blue-grey in the early stages of decomposition. Ingres blue, thought Penny in her dream.

She suddenly recalled a watercolour Jeremy had had restored and had re-framed by his gallery as a birthday gift for her. The mount was ingres blue, the exact shade of Perry's drowned face. Peculiar how dreams can link the most diverse happenings and objects, pick them up at random and reassemble them into a complicated jigsaw which makes perfect sense to the dreamer but on awakening appears a rambling, nonsensical memory.

Penny made this observation while she dreamed and urged her sleeping self to wake up. She didn't like the look of Champagne Perry at all and feared he might rise from the bathwater like a zombie in a second-rate movie but she was spared. The dream relocated to Jeremy's gallery – oddly next to her bathroom – where Jeremy was dressed as a bridegroom. He wore a wedding ring on each of the fingers of his left hand and one on his immaculately manicured thumb. Five gold rings, sang Penny in her dream. None of it made sense.

Jeremy couldn't see her. In the adjacent room –

the luxurious hotel bedroom – sat an Arab, black-bearded and naked among the crumpled sheets of a king-sized bed. 'You drink too much,' he reprimanded a woman who was plundering the mini-bar and methodically downing the contents. Penny was shocked to see that she was observing her younger self.

'I drink too much,' muttered Penny as she jolted awake in Letti's den and bolted clumsily in the dark to the bathroom, where she threw up her dinner in as quiet and ladylike manner as she could manage.

'The fare was too rich for the palate of a poor ex-prisoner!' she commented to the relaxed shape of Elizabeth who stirred slightly as she continued to sleep underneath the patchwork quilt.

Penny sat shivering despite the warmth in Letti's apartment. It was 4.30 a.m. She sipped a tooth mug of water and reflected on her dream. She often dreamt of Perry, who usually appeared in various stages of decay. Jeremy too graced her dreams – especially of late – with his elegant presence. Usually her Jeremy dreams were erotic. Penny, half awake, wondered what the excess of wedding rings symbolised. Probably it was her subconscious warning her not to pursue hopes of matrimony! Penny resolved to pose the question to Letti in the morning. It would make an interesting subject for analysis.

The Arab she recalled from her early twenties,

her carefree promiscuous years prior to her marriage. She was more frivolous and blonder then. The very idea that she would ever see the inside of a prison cell would have generated gales of her trademark throaty laughter.

The diminutive dusky gentleman had once offered her a drink or two which had progressed to seven or eight in a country pub. Easily impressed in those days, Penny had subsequently found herself being groped in a Panther de Ville. He'd taken her to a ridiculously over-priced riverside hotel where, after ruining her complexion with the cheese grater-like action of his black beard ground into the general direction of her face, he had prematurely ejaculated and fallen into a noisy sleep.

Penny had spent the remainder of the night rifling his silken pockets and feeding coinage into the room's mini-bar. The resultant cocktails became stronger as the night went on. By dawn Zid or Zod or whatever his name was appeared attractive enough through the vodka/martini/gin-induced haze to have his suggestion of a little sojourn on his love-boat taken seriously. Penny couldn't remember the details but the galley of his yacht with its compact units and crisp navy and white decor was very similar to Letti's kitchen.

Eventually he had tired of her – as they do – and sailed away into the sunset leaving her with a face rubbed raw and a pair of obscenely chunky mock-Baroque earrings worth their weight in Arab gold. These she converted into hard cash at a dockside pawnbroker's the minute she regained landlubber status.

Penny grinned to herself while thinking back to the days of this swarthy little billionaire and thought it a reasonable example of how she'd conducted the swingin' sixties and her freedom years. She thanked her lucky stars for the man who, since her temporary descent into the madness during the Champagne Perry episode, had restored her faith and equilibrium. Jeremy, tall cultured Jeremy.

In the early hours of Saturday morning she sat propped against Letti's exotic cushions listening to Elizabeth's rhythmic breathing on the opposite sofa and wondered what he was up to. She felt sure he'd crop up during the early part of the following week, wearing one of his exquisite hand-painted silk waistcoats and a generous splash of expensive Italian cologne – Oh! how she loved him, even if only for his elusiveness. Champagne Perry seemed so common in comparison but at the time she'd loved him too, just as intensely. It was all relative.

Penny continued to daydream as dawn's grey finger delicately inveigled its way in through the chink in Letti's blinds replacing the shaft of street light and gradually emphasising the impassive gilded lips of the Egyptian emperor, prostrate beneath the table top. For a moment Penny thought he was smiling but it was just the effect of the faint movement of the blind as a light breeze blew away the remains of the rainy night.

Penny settled back beneath the quilt. With her mind and her stomach no longer churning, she snatched a few extra hours sleep content in the anticipation of a good breakfast in easy company and with the prospect of soon feeling Jeremy's sensitive hands stroking her hair in that special way exclusive only to him. Those beautiful hands would certainly not be decorated with five wedding rings, she thought. Only one in the foreseeable future if she had her way. Trying to rationalise her dream, Penny slept.

Elizabeth, vaguely aware of Penny moving about on the matching settee, turned over but didn't wake up. For a change her dreams were peaceful and mercifully free of the image of her dead brother Philip, who often appeared to her, mortally wounded and miraculously free of the confines of the well. She'd lost count of the times she'd awakened drenched in perspiration and sobbing with fear.

Usually she dreamt of being hunted down in a decrepit farmyard by a furious and vengeful parody of Philip. Running beside her would be a selection of his pets, eyes wide with fright, tongues lolling, each as eager as herself to escape capture and torture. She always just managed to wake up before he caught her. Sometimes in the background her parents would be standing, watching but never protecting her. She'd see her long-dead father chewing his pipe, leaning on his garden fork, keenly observing the hunt but never lifting a finger. Next to him her mother in her Sunday-best suit and pearls, too preoccupied with her hymn book to hear her daughter's cries for help.

Tonight, however, Elizabeth dreamt of James. They were in the coffee bar where she worked. Outside it was raining and the damp had stained the shoulders of James' trenchcoat. The sound of the real rainstorm against Letti's windows was filtering through to Elizabeth's subconscious. She dreamed she was sitting beside James during her afternoon break. They were sharing a slice of apple pie and drinking cappuccino in companionable silence. The bustle of the other customers around them and the clattering from the kitchens prevented much conversation.

There was something puzzling about James' appearance. Not the familiar olive-green corduroy trousers, the knees of which she shyly caressed with her free hand under the table, but something else. Not the cashmere sweater she had bought him knowing they were saving for a new life but treating him anyway. In her dream he turned slowly towards the coffee bar windows and said, 'The rain has stopped.'

Elizabeth, gazing at him lovingly, suddenly

noticed the minute change in his appearance. Her dream lover was wearing the tiniest emerald stud in his left ear lobe – almost obscured by his hair but clearly visible where he'd swept back his damp locks. Elizabeth found this small concession to vanity so remarkably out of character she was visibly shaken. Neither the country casuals nor the discreet city checks he wore as he went about his business were in keeping with such a frivolous addition to his wardrobe.

'I thought I knew you,' she said dreamily, stupidly.

'You do,' replied James. 'You're only dreaming.'

Elizabeth looked at him again and the earring was gone. The door of the coffee bar swung open and in walked Marjorie, little dead nine-year-old Marjorie wearing the unforgettable red velvet dress. A hole was torn in the skirt of her dress to the exact dimensions of the piece of red velvet which had marked the location of her disappearance.

'Don't trust him, Lizzie,' Marjorie entreated.

Elizabeth wondered dreamily why she herself was an adult and Marjorie remained a child.

'Grown-ups know best,' she replied kindly.

Elizabeth's dream degenerated into a nightmare. Marjorie hung her head, turned and left the coffee bar. She seemed to float gracefully just above the floor despite her plumpness. Her chubby little body seemed not so much covered in puppy fat as bloated, swollen and deathly pale. Her hair was full of earth and dead leaves but still tied with a ribbon that Elizabeth remembered well. Through the rain-streaked glass door Elizabeth saw Marjorie untie a puppy which had been waiting eagerly outside in the rain, tethered to the railings. The puppy pranced around elated to see Marjorie. Except that he couldn't see Marjorie because his eyes had been gouged out. Elizabeth recognised the elated puppy as Buster, one of Philip's long list of childhood pets who met with an inexplicable and nasty accident.

Angela, having the spare bedroom to herself and having missed the best of the rich and generous meal the previous evening, enjoyed a dreamless sleep. Before retiring she'd drawn a deep bath, a luxury she'd missed while locked up in the secure hospital which favoured a brisk regime of supervised showers. Letti had lit the collection of scented bedside candles for her. This was a true gesture of trust. Letti knew Angela had once liked to play with matches but after many sessions of counselling Letti had helped Angela to fight her imaginary fires. She'd also given her an extra pillow so she could recline comfortably propped and write out undisturbed her account of what she would tell them all on the following day.

Angela created her composition leaving nothing out, knowing any remaining demons would be exorcised by her complete honesty in the telling of her tale. Eventually she slept, oblivious to Penny's night-wanderings and the anguished whimpers which punctuated Elizabeth's nightmares.

11

Frog Princes

The rain finally stopped on Saturday morning. Letti, an early riser, had thrown open the dining room window to dissipate the evidence of the excesses of the previous evening. She ignited the wick of a glass lamp which held fragrant oil and the vetiver soon combined with the familiar, sharp green scent of her lilies, restoring sensual harmony to her apartment. Letti didn't smoke but she had wanted Georgia to be completely at ease so had waived her house rules. She wondered if Georgia would have the courage to return this morning for breakfast. Of all of them, Georgia – in Letti's opinion – had shed the most emotional baggage while relating her story and Letti imagined that when she awoke in her own home she'd be feeling much more upbeat and unburdened despite the inevitable hangover.

Last night, as Georgia had turned to leave Letti had seen the tears welling and the hopeless shattered look on her face. Letti was a professional, she knew it always got worse before it got better and she felt Georgia had reached an important turning point. She'd bravely assimilated the worst elements of her relationship with Bruno and laid bare her soul to a group of relative strangers, rationally and articulately. Letti felt extremely proud of her ex-client. She fervently hoped Georgia would come back at some point during the weekend to support and encourage Angela. Of all four women Letti was sure Georgia had spent the longest in hell. Although an excellent counsellor, Letti couldn't work miracles. The best result she could hope for was that Georgia had been hauled back up to a state of limbo out of harm's way. She'd seen and done too much to attain heaven. That would be asking for a lot in the given circumstances. Letti equated heaven with peace of mind and a decent quality of life with no hassle.

While Letti continued to put her ex-client's life and her own apartment in order, her thoughts dwelt on womankind in general. She considered the female of the species, the droves of women from all walks of life one observed milling around every day: squat exhausted mothers pushing buggies full of grubby offspring; elegant protected shopaholics – ladies who lunch; giggling girls with shimmering lip gloss and attitude; elderly womenfolk, bewildered and fragile. All of them going about their business en route to shops, offices, restaurants, universities, home, hospital.

She wondered how some women managed to get from cradle to grave without complicated relationships or tragedy touching them, without temptations, abuse, illness or incarceration – but it did happen. Letti knew that the majority of women led ordinary lives. She imagined them on their deathbeds, suddenly aware of their mortality – recognising in a split second that their particular stint was over. She wondered if they thought – Is this all there is?

Letti preferred to spend her career dealing with the minority: the oddballs and screwballs, the few who because of a freak twist of fate, had been dealt an abnormal life. What Letti, for all her street wisdom and academic ability, couldn't get her head around was that to these, her four guests, their own lives seemed perfectly normal. Execution, disposal or plain undecorated murder was a fact of their lives. Some women took their beatings and accepted the abuse, derision, humility, boredom and dull routine. They denied their deepest questions and their true selves and simply carried on. These four hadn't, this quartet of remarkable rebels. The emaciated Goth, the fanciful country girl, the well-preserved divorcée and the little flame-haired comedienne had each reached flash point. They'd turned and smashed their adversaries straight into four coffins. Letti saw it as her singular and profound mission to coax and cajole them through the aftermath and into the light.

While all this was coursing around Letti's mind, the rest of her body was on autopilot. She'd progressed to her kitchen where she had set the table in the window alcove and partially drawn up the blind to reveal a cold bright morning after the rain. On the street corner below, the bakery looked to be doing a brisk trade. Elizabeth, the first of the guests to emerge and true to her helpful nature, offered to go out for croissants and pastries. She needed fresh air to banish the cobwebs of her nightmare, strands of which still clung stubbornly and creepily.

Elizabeth soon returned clutching a bag of goodies. The aroma reminded her of village life – apples, cinnamon, apricots, cherries and fresh warm buttery pastry. By now Angela, Penny and Letti were assembled cosily at the table in the window alcove, helping each other to English breakfast tea and strong coffee. Penny, used to a genteel lifestyle at one time, drank in the sight – the honey pot, the blackberry conserve, the white serviettes, the huge gold cafetiere and Letti's pristine china. It was all so civilised after prison. Penny had had to tighten her belt upon release and a great deal of her stylish possessions had been sold. She vowed to nudge Jeremy towards the altar. Please God, don't let him have a wife tucked away somewhere, she prayed silently.

Elizabeth had roses in her cheeks from her foray into the cold bright morning. Angela, a shaft of wintry sunlight highlighting her orange hair, wearing a fresh application of bronze-toned make-up and an anticipatory expression, resembled an eager puckish character from a mediaeval fairytale. They all felt delicate after the dinner party but it was nothing a leisurely breakfast wouldn't put right. From the den came melodies from Scott Walker's tamest phase, easy-listening for adoring romantics. Letti preferred his later salutations to whores, itinerants and scarred war veterans. The eloquent anger in some of this later material stirred her causing her to think of her homeland.

She decided the day should start calmly regardless of what Angela was about to reveal. These women needed to make it easy on themselves – breaking skulls and drowning men was very hard to do – she thought mischievously, humming the melody and secretly adapting the lyrics. Letti had a weird and wonderful sense of humour. It had helped her to keep her equilibrium during some very harrowing client confessions.

'We'll eat without Georgia,' said Letti. 'When she left last night I felt she had a lot to mull over but I'm convinced she'll turn up again at some point.'

'I'm positive she's still carrying a torch for

Bruno,' Penny remarked and then added, 'I've progressed since Perry because it was one of those 'sex' things. Because I was forced to share his attentions we weren't able to live together for any length of time. I convinced myself I was in love with him but as soon as I broke the eternal triangle by removing one side the whole thing collapsed. I was then able to see him as he was – a weak greedy opportunist. His wife was probably delighted to have him dealt with. She was a cold fish, or so he said. After I drowned him she wouldn't have had to put up with the messy business of carnal practice. If I hadn't done the deadly deed some other stupid deluded bitch in his harem would have!'

Penny sucked sugar crystals from an immaculate, scarlet-tipped forefinger and then wagged it at Angela. 'What have you got to tell us, Angela? I gather you must have committed a gruesome crime against the male sex to have secured your membership of this exclusive club. Have you been scarred for life like Georgia or are you, after the same style as me, brazenly frolicking with minimal guilt and a nice new lover?'

Angela gulped the remains of her first coffee and on Letti's instructions refilled her cup. 'Are you sitting comfortably, ladies?' she enquired. 'Okay, then I'll begin.' Angela loved an audience, especially an appreciative one. She resolved to share a bit of her history with this particular audience who she thought most appreciative.

'When Prince Charming turns into a frog I'm never surprised, just mildly astonished it took him so long to show his true colours – yellow belly and a black heart. As sure as day follows night every relationship changes. I can see the collapse coming but each time I delude myself it will be different and I hang in there until the bitter end – except for Bill. Bill was just the unlucky one. He copped the full extent of my anger which had been simmering and topped up with each let-down.'

The assembled company murmured in sympathy. Angela, with their full attention, continued.

'Take Antony, the exquisite bisexual Adonis, who began our romance by shyly courting me with tragic tomes by Sylvia Plath in a valiant attempt to feed my soul. To feed my face he'd bring me hand-made chocolates and cook bijou little dinners *à deux* with stuff like quails' eggs and jetoste – Norwegian goats' cheese to the uninitiated. It looked like fudge and tasted like shit actually. Get the picture? Antony was a fawning jester and in the early days always on his best behaviour, a prince among men. It took him a month to turn into a frog. Enjoying the company of a woman but realising, to my cost, that there was no substitute for the real thing, he stole my best silk shirts and the cream of my make-up bag, and hopped off to a greener lily pad. There he tried out

Sylvia Plath on Darwin's great-grand-nephew –
the new boy in town and somewhat of a celebrity
whose tight lightly tanned buttocks were more
than a match for my generous bum. Yes, I had a
male attitude but I was burdoned with tits. My
Adonis preferred androgyny or boys. Years
afterwards I heard Antony had croaked from
AIDS.

'Some princes don't change into frogs for ages
as was the case with Warwick. I met him at work
but he harboured dreams of going to art school.
He'd had three lots of rejections and couldn't get
onto even a very basic foundation course. He could
talk about art and he went on for ages waffling
about "building up a heavy impasto" and "the
quality of light in a Provence field". He knew all
there was to know about the styles and techniques
of the great masters, but when it came to putting
brush to canvas – or even charcoal to sugar paper
– he became creatively constipated. I, like the naive
idiot I was, adoringly painted for him the three set
pieces he needed to get him into college. The self-
portrait I did of him was a dead ringer. All he had
to do was sign it, the slimy bastard – and he did.
And he got on the foundation course on the
strength of it!'

Angela's audience groaned in sympathy.
They'd all bent over backwards and made
sacrifices against their better judgement in their
time for fear of losing the object of their affections

– even Letti. Women are instinctive peacemakers. They refilled their cups, munched their pastries and collectively thought how gullible they'd been – before the four murders of course. Letti, who hadn't killed, reflected that she'd certainly felt like it once or twice. She too had been taken for many a ride.

'Anyway,' said Angela, 'Warwick bluffed his way through his art course. He specialised in photography and film-making and went to countless lectures on the history of art, thus cleverly avoiding dipping his brush. He dipped his dick though, inventing evening classes – glass blowing, calligraphy, batik, anything – to get a pass for an evening with his cronies and art school bimbos. For ages he didn't tell his friends he was living with me. I was too 'square', the breadwinner. I was too busy putting food on our plates to discuss the gloomy comparisons between Nolde and Goya.

'Eventually my presence leaked and he'd bring groups of starving artists back to my flat. I would be brainwashed into posing naked for garrets full of them. They thought he was a cool dude to have a muse, a subservient woman, tucked away.

'He was interested in the 'art' of the bull-fight and I was pressurised into reading everything by Hemingway. He butted me into joining him in a filthy Madrid backstreet with two weird bullfight aficionados. That was our holiday one year, watching animals being goaded to death. He took me around to the back of a bullring to observe procedure. The bull-baiters' horses had gaping holes in their flanks, stuffed with straw to stem the bleeding. Grubby blankets hid their suffering but it showed in the whites of their eyes. At the time I thought the thrill of it all, the buzz as the crowd roared, the colour, the spectacle was stimulating, sexy even – funny how love warps reality.

'I thought Warwick was the bee's knees and couldn't see through his arty patina to his obvious frogness. I was convinced every budding Donatello treated their muse like part of the furniture and I accepted my lot. Eventually, as was the case with Antony, a more attractive diversion turned his head – a lissom blonde textiles heiress who was to be the star of an avant-garde film he was directing at art school. This project looked to me to be a complete rip-off of Fellini but naturally my humble opinion wasn't taken into account.

'It was bye-bye Warwick. He departed in the clothes he stood up in which included my afghan waistcoat – the only warm garment I owned. Clutching his *Playboy* centrefold scrapbook to his tubercular chest – he said it helped him understand the landscape of the female form – he chugged off upon his one concession to materialism, an elderly motorbike, half of which I'd paid for.

'Luckily I met Louis on the rebound, about as

arty as a toilet seat and refreshingly uncomplicated or so I thought at the time. Louis was a big and benevolent old bear – initially. In his paw he clutched fifty pound notes with which to treat me. In the early days of our courtship he would make chivalrous sacrifices, giving me the breast of chicken while he gnawed the leg. He'd bring me bottles of sherry, peaches, bundles of asparagus and joints of gammon. He'd roll up with second-hand jewellery secured from shady deals in bars. All were sprats to catch me, the mackerel. I fell for it all again hook, line and sinker.

'At least before this one started taking me for granted he did me a favour. One starless night he crept stealthily around to the penthouse where Warwick was now living in materialistic splendour with his heiress and took the slimy bastard's motorbike apart, triumphantly bearing back to me my half investment. Revenge was oily, sweet and useless. Shortly after this unusual show of affection Louis lurched off with a barmaid called Lola leaving me with a huge electricity bill and the police hammering on my door in search of fenced jewellery.'

'Poor you,' sympathised Elizabeth, 'but I do envy your style, Angela. You've had a lot of boyfriends. I was too faithful to my brother Philip to gain much experience.'

'Quantity doesn't mean quality,' answered Angela. 'At least you've got James. He sounds perfect for you, Elizabeth. I seem to just attract low-life: lounge-lizards, toads, rats and frogs who never turn into princes. I even married a frog way back when I was seventeen, ages before all these other misjudgements. His habits and personality changed dramatically immediately after the wedding ceremony. This time the frog-husband squatted and it was I who fled Frog Hall losing all my furniture, half the house, custody of the dog and a lot of faith.

'I had to get out quickly. He had a penchant for turning 'funny' when there was a full moon and had a recurring compulsion to place pillows over my face while I slept. The latter settled any rosy ideas I might have entertained about us reaching our first anniversary. Paper, isn't it? I got paper for my first anniversary. A decree absolute citing unreasonable behaviour. I mean – Christ! – all I wanted was to give plasticware parties in domestic bliss and what I got was a psychopath!

'But that was ages ago. Oh, to be seventeen again and know what I know now. Since Warwick – Louis didn't count – there was one more serious romance. I had loved Warwick but I loved Bill the bus driver even more. Maybe because he looked rather like Warwick – tall, green eyes, great cheekbones – but that's where the similarity stopped. Bill was as thick as two short planks.

'I'd seen this particular bus driver manoeuvring through the town every so often over the course of four or five years. Sometimes he drove the bus I took to work but not often. He didn't seem to be allocated a regular route because after he first caught my eye on the number thirty-two I would always scan it but unfortunately the bus would be driven by a driver of lesser charms. Suddenly I'd spy him at the wheel of the number seventy, for instance, and my heart would leap.

'He'd noticed me too and would smile or wink. "Spot the dishy bus driver" became a diversion, a game to lighten my time spent during my journey to and from work. I was quite happy to settle for anonymity. A smile or a wink was enough. I was still raw from the major bust-up with Warwick and had been celibate for eighteen months – a miracle for me. It was very like a story in a teen magazine, you know the scenario, "His green gaze locked with mine and a shiver rippled through my knickers" – that sort of stuff!'

Angela's audience, amused with her tale, giggled in unison. It was pleasingly lighthearted after the conversations of the previous evening. The Walker Brothers added to the easy mood. In the background they were serenading a fresh-faced girl in summer rain.

Elizabeth, the memory of her nightmare still fresh in her mind, was the only one at this stage to see dangerous storm clouds gathering. She'd experienced a sobering reminder of how suddenly a sweet dream could degenerate into a nightmare and had a good idea that Angela's entertaining story might turn chilly. She knew fairytale endings didn't happen but despite her misgivings she, like the others, was absorbing every word. It was the same old story really, only the characters differed.

'In a nutshell,' continued Angela, 'we fancied each other. I'd request "an eighty-five please" in my huskiest voice on the rare occasions he'd be driving my bus and he would look as if he wanted to grab my hand, fare and all, and drag me into the driver's compartment where my covetous gaze would be drawn to the longest pair of male legs and strongest male thighs strained against his regulation trousers.'

'Oh!' groaned Penny reaching for the orange juice in a feigned orgasmic faint, 'I've come over all flushed!' The others told her to shut up, this was better than a soap opera.

Angela smiled, 'I'm a sucker for a uniform – except for coppers of course. I always fancied myself with an airline pilot or a naval officer but never a bus driver. However, stunted bitter broken-hearted working girls can't afford to be picky and I must stress, he was drop-dead gorgeous!'

Penny laughed aloud. Her Arab had worn a uniform which had looked quite fetching on his yacht but that hadn't made him any less of an animal at the end of the day. Penny found Angela's past love life immensely entertaining as did all of them.

Elizabeth, who by now had decided she'd

definitely missed out, sat wide-eyed drinking in every juicy snippet. Secretly she imagined that if it had been her with an equivalent string of men friends she'd have kept her purse and her legs closed. It had taken months for James to seduce her. Odd really that he had been so patient, considering how handsome he was. A shadow passed over the sunny landscape of Elizabeth's daydream. The possibility that James was 'getting it' elsewhere occurred to her. The doubt was fleeting and she dismissed it from her mind as quickly as it had appeared. She thought she would die if he was unfaithful. 'Or he would die if you ever caught him,' came a small voice which had lain silent in her mind since its last instruction – 'Push him down the well, Lizzie, he's bad!' Elizabeth shut out the voice. She recognised it as little Marjorie's.

Letti had been watching the faces of all her guests. She wouldn't intervene but merely keep the coffee flowing and sit back in the knowledge that conversation would flow naturally. She left the kitchen to replenish the background music and returned to applause as Angela took up the threads of her story with the backing of The Crystals who had met their dreamboat on a Monday and his name was Bill.

'I decided the bus driver was a bit young and unsophisticated. Remember girls, I'd been force-fed Hemingway by Warwick and the strategy of

street-wisdom by Louis. Both of them highly
intelligent in their respective fields. Perhaps I
didn't vet him well enough as I was eager to
resume relations after the eighteen celibate months
during which I'd attended small suppers with
equally frustrated divorcées, and my circle of gay
men friends. Occasionally during this period I'd
lunch with older female mentors who, since
retirement, took pleasure in my accounts of goings-
on in the business world. They were able to keep
up with the office gossip and in return offered their
elegant padded shoulders to soak up my tears as
my affairs consecutively crumbled. Those months
were a necessary healing period during which I
licked my emotional wounds.

'Nothing gets a funny-girl down for long,
though. Optimism has to shine through and I felt
ready to set my cap at the bus driver. He was
earmarked as my next conquest because he seemed
so uncomplicated and compliant.

'I remember the evening when it really got
going. I was invited to dine at the stylish table of a
pair of gays. They always ate early so I changed in
the loos at work and launched myself onto a bus
to get to Felix and Greg's soirée in time. They
could be waspish and sulky if their arrangements
were hampered and I was running late. I made it
onto the bus by the skin of my teeth and there sat
'Green eyes'. The conversation went something
like this:

Green eyes: Hello sweetheart, this isn't your usual route, where are you going?

Me: Actually, nosy, I'm going to dine with two gay boys.

Green eyes: Sorry I asked, what a shame.

Me: Is it policy to ask your passengers about their personal arrangements? Brookmeadows please, and I don't know where the stop is.

Green eyes: Seventy pence. I'll show you where to get off but it's a waste of a good woman. You ought to come out with me. I drink in the Golden Galleon every Friday.'

Me (haughtily): Just drive the bus and I'll sort out my own social diary thank you!

Toothless hag occupying the best part of the two front seats who'd been riveted by every word: You tell 'im dear, I'd never trust a fella with 'air that long!

'Over supper I shared my fantasy with Felix and Greg. It was gathered opinion that a mere bus driver was hardly a match for my wit and intellect. If only these two could have seen those thighs and the green eyes they'd have choked on their venison sausages.

'They were condescending enough to tell me the whereabouts of the Golden Galleon, warning me that it was frequented by "plebeian straights and lager louts". It sounded a rather refreshing venue after Warwick's college bar peopled with pseudo-highbrows, or the shabby local famous for horrendous folk evenings where Louis would ply me with Liebfraumilch. The Golden Galleon must be preferable to the backstreet, leopardskin wallpapered club where I was occasionally to be found with Felix and Greg in the role of straight guest of honour. The Golden Galleon sounded normal. Normal was what I craved.

'I agonised for the rest of the week whether I would go along and find him. The thought of yet again getting to know somebody's quirks and foibles, embarking on a new romance, putting my heart at risk after it bore considerable scarring, seemed hardly worth the effort. Friday evening at nine found me glued to the television screen, absorbing nothing. The cat, settling in for the evening, had wrapped himself comfortably around my neck. Should I or shouldn't I?

'By nine forty-five I was showered, spritzed, moisturised, perfumed, simpering and blushing in the public bar of the Golden Galleon surrounded by a trio of assorted bus drivers and chatting away as if I was part of the crew. I hadn't realised how fascinating the various bus routes were, how clever one had to be to calculate change from the fares, or how many different models of double-decker and mini-shuttle existed.

'Somehow I picked up the tab for every round and it seemed only moments before "Time" was called and Bill – I'd learnt his name by now – stood up, all six foot two (hoochey-coo!). I'm a sucker for tall men. He asked if he could walk me home on that first date, while his sidekicks sniggered in the wings. "Certainly not!" I replied, "What sort of a girl do you think I am?" I was going to employ strategy with this one. "Okay," he said indifferently, and then he kissed me.'

Letti smiled. The Crystals were at that very moment singing about an adored Mr America walking his prom queen home while all the stars were shining bright, before kissing her. Hardly life imitating art, but rather appropriate music and excellent timing.

Angela took up her tale again.

'I waited by the phone all the following week and was just about to give up on him. As I made my way dejectedly to work one morning a bus screeched to a halt nearly killing me. It was a message being delivered by one of Bill's minions. Hardly a love sonnet: "Same place, same time, Friday." I stood in a haze of exhaust fumes as if the departed bus was a chariot from the gods. I gazed at the missive pencilled onto an old fag packet as if it was Shakespeare's original love note to Anne Hathaway.

'On Friday I was half an hour early gliding through the gilded doors of the Golden Galleon to be informed by Suggs and Hobgoblin (his mates) that the object of my desires had got fed up and gone off to a disco.

'Why do they snare us with their careless attentions. Why is unreliability so seductive, indifference so desirable? We want what we can't have, don't we, girls? Bill and I, after a few initial hiccups, conducted a hot little affair for six months before he casually dropped into the conversation that he had a wife and 2.4 kids at home in the marital maisonette and did it matter? Now I knew what I suspected all along. His Friday-only availability was dictated by his other commitments to a thick wife plus brats. He was proud of his Ford Granada which drank petrol at an alarming rate necessitating me to take care of the bills for our entertainment. His regular Friday night pass allowed him to bond with his mates, drink lager, talk dirty and pick up stupid, trusting women who were blinded by his languid charms. Stupid women like me.'

Angela glanced at Penny and said bitterly, 'Penny will understand better than most. Every time he stood me up I bristled with the injustice of the situation. I became obsessive. I staked out his home, watching the pregnant wife lumbering to the supermarket, following her as she pushed her trolley, flanked by her kids. I watched her stocking up with family packs of bargain burgers, multi-buy loo rolls, crisps and lurid junk cordial. Little wonder that when I treated Bill to a late meal in a restaurant – as was my habit after the Golden Galleon closed on a Friday night – he'd always order the most exotic, most expensive dish on the menu.

'He had a wife and kids to support. If I wanted

his company then I had to pay for it. I bet she'd never set eyes on a salmon goujon. Bill's complexion was unhealthily pallid, his idea of vegetables being a tin of tomatoes, baked beans or mushy peas. He knew even less than Louis about wine and was bewildered by my criticism of the boxed supply of sweet white the Golden Galleon offered as *vin de maison*.

'His life was pre-planned and bland. He would drive a bus until retirement, get a silver tankard from the company, celebrate his golden wedding and divide his wait for death between the dog track and his allotment. Bill fancied an allotment since I'd introduced him to vegetables. I wondered what the vegetable he'd married thought of his new found penchant for mangetout with almonds!

'I was seen as a necessary evil, nothing serious and nothing to alter the course of his life for. I was just an excuse for him to wash behind his ears and cut his toenails every Friday, the trophy that made him superior to his mates. Bill was Jack the Lad on a Friday night, someone to be envied in bus driver hierarchy.

'And I went along with the charade – the temporary fling to him, the way of life to me. Why? Because he was far less demanding and arrogant than Warwick, less pedantic and a whole lot more attentive to personal toilette than Louis and better looking than all of my previous suitors. It was a visual thing. I'm arty aren't I? I appreciate beauty. Bill's eyes were a hazy grey-green and he used them to full effect to mesmerise me. I was a rabbit in the glare of his double-decker's headlights, ensnared by his passing interest in me.

'He found my randiness flattering – he couldn't believe his luck because "her indoors" was permanently suffering from something or other of a gynaecological nature. And on the subject of gynaecology might I add he made a supreme effort on the rare occasions he was sober enough to shag me, and we all know there's nothing like a great lay to keep us in line – don't we, girls?'

Angela's monologue was relieved by a ripple of embarrassed sniggers. With the sympathies of her fellows she continued.

'When he first told me he was married I stormed back to my retreat and cried all over the cat. A few days later he pulled up next to me in the town centre and with his disarming smile ordered me onto the bus and, lying that his marriage was "open", took about three minutes to persuade me to continue our Friday assignations.

'We were never alone during opening hours. Suggs and Hobgoblin always chaperoned him and our meetings ran to a set pattern. At closing time I would take him for a meal after which we would retire to my place, his beer consumption lending him false bravery. He often overstayed the curfew hour set by his wife. Once he fell asleep and didn't leave until 7 a.m. Somehow he always managed to sweet-talk her out of her anger with excuses to the effect that he'd been too drunk to drive and too broke to take a cab. He'd go off to the depot straight from my bed reeking of woman and Giorgio. I suppose this helped to strengthen his reputation as a lady-killer with his mates.

'Bill was good at excuses and gradually our Fridays became less frequent, maybe fortnightly and then once a month. He justified his neglect of me with, "I've got to play cards with the boys this Friday" or "I'm taking her out, she smells a rat" (or rather my Giorgio!) or "We're going away to a caravan in Yarmouth with the in-laws this weekend."

'You are preaching to the converted, Angela,' Penny chipped in. 'Same old song, different lyrics. My Champagne Perry invented so many trips to Prague I used to call him The Bouncing Czech!'

'I hate to say this,' added Elizabeth, 'but aren't our Jon, James, Jeremy, and probably Jean/Jeanne equally elusive and quite good at disappearing with plausible excuses?'

All the women glared at her. Trust plain-speaking Elizabeth to remind us that even now we're still compromising to some extent. Why the hell don't we learn? thought Letti.

'Carry on, Angela,' she urged, pursing her lips. 'We're all with you.'

'As our times together became less frequent, I became more frantically involved. I cried on the withered bosoms of my older wiser women friends, drooped and snivelled into the gaspacho and Gruyere at Felix and Greg's dinner parties, bored my work colleagues to tears, wrote poetry and drew sombre charcoal sketches of barren landscapes. I'd got it bad. I milked it to the full.

'Months later I was looking Liza Minelli-ish again with a brave little smile and shoulders braced, pretending to enjoy a pub crawl and a blues concert all by myself. During the course of the evening, which happened to be a Friday – I couldn't bear to spend one at home – I met landlords and Turks, polite young men and well-wishing old friends so that by the chime of midnight I was in bed, full of black coffee and almost feeling whole again. I congratulated myself on coming through the mourning period, the aeons since I'd last been invited to the Golden Galleon. I lay like a splendid Czarina, the cat wrapped around my head like a Russian hat as the pair of us drifted companionably towards sleep.

'And then the phone rang. It was Suggs. "Bill's here at my place, he's drunk and he wants you back. He says if you're passing call in." If I'm passing? At midnight? Do we ever do what's best for us, girls? Do we hell! In nanoseconds I was fully repainted and cabbing through the suburbs with black lingerie and diamanté under my raincoat, the collar of which was up-turned like a demented, sex-crazed Mata Hari.

'Suggs' parents were away for the weekend. He lived in the basement of a university lodging house where Mummy and Daddy were caretakers. Suggs although twenty-nine favoured Starwars bedlinen. He'd allocated his bedroom to Bill and I as our reunion love nest. His hobby was model-making. The collection of plastic aircraft soaring over his C3PO and R2D2 duvet cover did little as an aphrodisiac. Further progress to our lovemaking was severely hampered by my paramour's seven pints of German lager for Dutch courage. Brewer's droop and slurred ramblings, translated as "I love my kids" put the tin lid on it. In a red-hot rage I shrugged my raincoat back on and again rang for a cab.

I've no idea why I did what I did next. Leaving Bill and Suggs in an unrousable drunken stupor I gathered an armful of aerosols, glue bottles, toxic paint – all Suggs' stupid model-making stuff. To these I added a bottle of peach liqueur which stood conveniently on Mother Suggs' telephone table. And as I climbed the stairs I sprayed in silver model-aircraft paint the words "Impotent married bastard" all over the cabbage-rose printed wallpaper. Then I systematically dribbled the glue and the flammable alcohol in my wake as I mounted each floral-patterned Wilton-clad stair tread.

'I didn't turn around on reaching the upper landing. The fumes were terrible. I let myself out, gasping lungfuls of cold night air and lit what was supposed to be my post-coital cigarette. This I pushed through the letterbox of the Suggs household and jogged to the waiting taxi. God knows what the cabbie thought. It was about 4.30 a.m. by now and I must have looked like some dwarfish wild-child but I suppose they're used to all sorts of shenanigans. I recall our conversation as clearly as if it was yesterday.

Cabbie: Good party?

Me: Super, not many people though and nowhere to sleep.

Cabbie: Any chance of a coffee when we get to yours?

Me: That depends on whether you're married.

Cabbie: Do I look married?

Me: Well, your shirt's well ironed and you're chauffeuring me around probably because it's preferable to being tucked up with her.

Cabbie: Go on, she'll never know, I'll turn the meter off.

Me: Stuff it, mate!

'Which predictably resulted in the last leg of the journey being a hair-raising gear-crashing experience at a ridiculously inflated price. Men can be so vindictive, can't they, girls? But then so can we. I spent the precarious journey in stubborn silence, imagining the stairwell igniting behind me, flames spreading, billowing like the awful train of a deserted bride fleeing an altar. You never really burned with desire, did you, Bill? I thought.

Burn now!

'And he did – Suggs the sidekick too. They didn't wake up. The noxious fumes from Mr Suggs' lovingly polystyrene-tiled basement ceiling, carefully applied to keep out the damp, did the deed in minutes. The newspapers said the two elder Suggses returned to a very damp home indeed, sodden with the failed efforts of the fire brigade. At the time I wished I'd stayed to watch because I was very keen on men in uniforms then. Not now though.'

The cabbie wasn't happy that night because the little tart had rebuffed his advances. After all, what was a bird like that doing running around the town in the early hours wearing not a lot under that raincoat by the look of it? She'd had on enough bleedin' perfume to gas a bloke. He could smell something else on her too . . . petrol? . . . glue? Yes! That was it. The tart was a bloody solvent-sniffer. God knows what she'd got or where she'd been. His driving had reflected his temper. He'd scared the shit out of her all right, no doubt about it.

Back on the road the cabbie had rummaged under his seat for the girlie magazine he used for kicks when Five bellies – his secret name for his fat wife – turned her fat back on him, and the slags he ferried to and from the nightclubs wouldn't trade a quickie for the fare. He'd go to the gents near the park with his porno picture book, that's what he'd do. Pictures never let you down. That little tart didn't know what she was missing. He was a virile bloke. Where was the soddin' magazine?

He'd only taken his eyes from the road for a few seconds. He was still speeding, still angry. Cabbies were king of the road, they knew it all. Handling a cab came as second nature. He could weave in and out of the traffic on autopilot, a burger in one hand, a plastic cup of the piss they served as coffee at the railway station balanced on the dashboard shelf, chat to his mates over the CB and still cut a smooth path through the rush hour. Not this time. He didn't even see the transit van broken down in an unlit backstreet smack bang ahead of him with two cowboy builders peering helplessly at the smoking engine.

Unlucky cabbie. He'd died with a sneer on his lips and a pudgy hand clutching a well-thumbed centrefold. Lucky Angela. He'd been her only witness as she left the scene of her crime where, fuelled by unrequited passion, she had become an arsonist. Mrs Suggs' rose-patterned wallpaper had curled and crackled in the flames, destroying Angela's spray-painted curse and thus any evidence of the perpetrator's identity.

So the fire-starter was never found. Hobgoblin, the remaining third of the bus-driving trio, had his suspicions but daren't point the finger at Angela because he knew Bill's wife would not be able to stand the knowledge that her beloved was an adulterer. His passing was more than enough to bear without the bitter truth that he had a lady friend. Hobgoblin was a follower, not a leader. He kept quiet fearing he could be the next victim if he made waves. He attended the cremation services and afterwards, as he morosely propped up the bar in the Golden Galleon, pondered that burial might have been more tactful. Still, he thought, there probably hadn't been much left to bury.

In theory Angela got off scot-free. In reality her temporary insanity took a firmer hold. She became introverted and obsessive, performing odd little rituals. She lit small bonfires and held her fingers in the flames. She held her breath until she became puce in the face. She experienced panic attacks at work. Her moods swung the full spectrum from morose and sulky to aggressive. Angela dyed her hair vermilion and dressed herself in every shade of fire from burnt umber to flame red. Her neighbours often heard her howling all night. The few friends who tolerated Angela's radically changed personality nicknamed her Firebird. Her boss together with the company welfare department arranged for her to visit her GP after she failed to return from her lunch break and the firm's accountant saw her jumping up and down in the town centre, snarling and shaking her fists at every double-decker bus that trundled by.

In no time, Angela was dispatched for

psychiatric assessment and closeted in a secure hospital. It was there that she first met Letti who had what appeared at the time the virtually impossible task of extricating the fantasy from the reality. Letti's expertise and patience paid off. It had taken years but Angela was eventually released and attended Letti's out-patient one-to-one sessions where a fuller story emerged but even then Letti hadn't ascertained whether Angela had cast the cigarette through the Suggs' letterbox or not.

Letti thought she had the complete picture but until this calm, factual performance by Angela she had never heard the full story told so lucidly. The atmosphere, the environment, the vibes, the fellow creatures present must have been exactly the right formula for the whole horrendous jigsaw to slot into place. Letti was damned if she was going to break her confidence with Angela and turn her over to the police as a murderess. In her opinion Angela's lengthy incarceration and the catalogue of varied, and often gruelling treatments endured while in hospital had returned Angela to what appeared to be a state of normality – but who knows? Who sets the benchmark of normality? wondered Letti.

12

The Grudge

'I didn't serve time for doing what I did to Bill and Suggs,' said Angela quietly, 'but I served years sectioned in that hospital after I cracked up with guilt. I can't begin to describe the mortification I felt after the full horror of my actions hit me, or the demons that haunted me in the days that followed. I totally lost it. It was only by some incredible fluke that I didn't get caught and punished. Nobody except Hobgoblin knew Bill and I were an item, well, a Friday item. Hobgoblin probably thought a woman, especially a small, love-struck, reasonably intelligent woman would be incapable of such an act. I hardly look as if I'm capable of burning two blokes to death, do I? You're probably surprised that I can speak about the event in such matter-of-fact terms but part of my cure is to be able to tell it how it is.

'Hobgoblin was too concerned for the feelings of Bill's wife and kids to prod a hornet's nest when he wasn't at all sure of the facts, so he didn't let his suspicions be known. I hadn't been seen with Bill for months, had I? And only Suggs was party to the proposed reunion. The police were concentrating on known arsonists, lunatics with a history, criminals with a record, drug-crazed students with axes to grind who'd lodged with the Suggses. It didn't occur to anyone that ordinary unlikely people bear grudges too.

'At the time I was absolutely sure I'd got over the affair but the summons to rekindle it just as my emotional wounds were healing and the subsequent let-down caused something in my brain to snap and swell into a huge anger. I call it 'The Grudge'. I see it as a black mass of evil, some power that lies dormant in everyone and more often than not never has cause to be roused. The Grudge did it, not me. It felt like a separate part of me and its existence was sustained by Bill's indifference and neglect, his casual hold on me. The fact that I was merely a dalliance not vital to his happiness caused The Grudge to shift and rise and finally explode. I was driven, completely taken over. I remember spray-painting the graffiti on Mrs Suggs' walls but I didn't light the match, The Grudge did that.'

Penny found this latest outpouring generated uncomfortably familiar feelings that had been neatly tucked away in her own memory banks. She was in complete sympathy with Angela. The moment she herself had shoved the champagne bottle neck as far as it would go down Perry's gullet had just been perfectly described. Elizabeth too had been jolted back to the past scene of her pushing Philip down the well. She relived the moment when she had stuck her car keys into Philip's neck. She had given free rein to a force she hadn't known she'd possessed, or rather a force that had possessed her for those vital lost seconds.

Georgia wasn't present but Letti was thinking about her and considering the moments when she too had rebelled, hefted the paperweight and cracked open Bruno's skull. They'd all turned a blind eye while jealousy, The Grudge, the ghost of Marjorie – whatever name each woman cared to give their particular motivator – took the wheel and changed their destiny and that of their victims. Letti found these like-moments of unfettered behaviour fascinating. She wondered if everybody bore this capacity deep within them and fate was simply biding time until the wrong set of circumstances presented itself. Absorbed by this theory she asked Angela how she was feeling about it all now.

'Guilty but exonerated!' she confessed.

Penny and Elizabeth glanced at each other in shock. Angela turned her attention to them.

'As I've told you, the only difference between

you and me is that my cell was padded. I've served my sentence exactly as you two have. I'm out now and what's more I've learnt to laugh again.'

'Have you met anyone special since Bill, like we have?' asked Elizabeth. 'I think I would have faded away if I hadn't met James. I owe so much to him.'

'Like I said earlier, I used to be quite the little socialite,' answered Angela. 'Now I'm much more cautious. My very best friends have stood by me, although Felix and Greg were the only ones to visit me in hospital when I was at my worst. Whether their motives were entirely noble I'm not sure. They get off on the strange and the weird. They were practically hammering on the doors to get inside and experience a nut-house.

'They'd bring me tempting little picnics – asparagus and goats' cheese sandwiches with the crusts cut off, miniature bottles of Chablis and flasks of their famous gaspacho. I have vague recollections of sitting with them, laughing and crying and talking gibberish while they ate the food and spoke to me of banalities and platitudes, our conversations peppered with long silences and smiles of indulgence and thinly veiled embarrassment. Others like Elouise kept their distance. She probably agonised about what one should wear to visit a loony bin.

'Of course, you have to take on board that none of my circle knew about the bonfire I'd caused.

Everyone was concerned that I'd had a monumental brainstorm, a nervous collapse and that was the top and bottom of it. None of them knew the truth. It wasn't for a couple of years that I dared admit the truth to myself. It wasn't easy for people to stick around someone showing a series of pretty extreme symptoms of lunacy. Felix and Greg didn't link my breakdown to Bill's death. They'd been so dismissive of our relationship in the early days, commenting on his low intellect and high boredom factor, that I kept quiet about my Friday arrangement. I didn't tell a soul about our affair. Elouise would have been scornful of the hold Bill had over me and my weakness at getting myself into a no-win situation.

'Only Letti, years later, pieced together what led to my mental collapse. Now I've told you because I know you're like me, capable of temporary insanity and if Georgia returns I'll tell her too. We've all been very very bad girls and now we're going to be very good, if not for ourselves, for Letti. She has led us along the crazy paving, coaxing and listening, nursing and supporting us as we found the way out of the maze. I for one am going to get on with my life. I owe it to Letti. And yes, Elizabeth, I've even met somebody with potential. It's happened very recently but dare I say he's lit a little flame in my heart and I'm positive he doesn't drive a bus!'

'You're outrageous!' laughed Penny.

'Do tell,' enthused Elizabeth.

Letti hadn't heard this addendum to the saga and was delighted.

'We'll celebrate with Bucks Fizz and Kir Royale. There's loads of fizz left from last night! Do you realise we're all seeing lovely uncomplicated men. I didn't know Angela had met someone too, I think it's marvellous!' she said, placing four goblets, an armful of Cava bottles and one of cassis on the kitchen table beside the jug of breakfast orange juice. 'Penny, put your skills from the restaurant days to good use as cocktail-mixer, there's a darling – I'm going to change the music.'

What the hell, thought Letti as she sifted through her CDs in the den. Why can't we be a little bit decadent before we resume our roles as dutiful girlfriends and step back into the harsh reality of Monday morning when money has to be earned and codes of behaviour have to be followed and we again, willingly I might add, dedicate great chunks of ourselves to our lovely new men.

Letti had no compulsion to reveal details of her own past amours to her guests. Her romantic history had been considerably less harrowing than theirs but she'd had her share of heartbreak. She could hear Penny gleefully mixing cocktails in the kitchen and instantly had an image of the purple cassis and the brilliant orange sparkling in the sunlit goblets.

She allowed herself a few moment's nostalgia.

The glittering colours reminded her of the Gothic stained-glass windows of the university rooms where she had conducted an intense brief affair with Charles, an outrageously youthful-looking don. His subject was mediaeval music. Charles lived a cosseted life in an academic bell jar. Rarely leaving the environs of the university except to travel in Europe where he conducted his quartet of mediaeval minstrel singers and gave convoluted lectures, Charles led a charmed and privileged life. Letti would sit, cross-legged on the threadbare Persian rug in front of his ornate fireplace, eating black grapes, drinking Rioja and absorbing the ancient music of the Abbess of Bingen emanating from his elderly tape player. The autumn sunlight filtering through the purples and oranges of the fleur-de-lys leaded windows would cast patterns on his face giving her lover an untouchable religious air.

Of course they had touched. Invariably after expounding their theories on life, death, music, art, psychology and literature, the evening would culminate in a gentle romp in the freezing monastic anteroom that served as Charles' bedroom. When he got going he was an enthusiastic lover, distracted at first but a willing participant in the sins of the flesh. Indeed his flesh was cool and white, like a girl's. Charles was not a sun-seeker, a lover of outdoor pursuits. Letti thought that with his bobbed shiny hair, his perfectly regular features and sad eyes he resembled one of the suffering saints depicted in the grander windows of the university chapel. On occasion Charles would visit Letti's home, guiltily instructing his cab driver to return at an appointed time. He didn't drive. Letti was amazed he managed to use planes to get him to and fro when his lecture tours demanded his presence.

Someone else demanded his attention. Charles had a wife tucked away in France, conveniently out of the immediate picture but ever-present. Charles believed in marriage. Without batting an eyelid at his physical betrayal, his self-structured moral code forbade him from divorcing Fleure, as she was called. He was too much of an aesthete, too preoccupied with higher things to tackle the guilt and mental anguish of hurting or ridding himself legally of Fleure. As long as she stayed put in France and kept her visits to the minimum once a trimester he could continue the charade of his marriage.

Letti felt rather like a high-class whore – visited, serviced but never given a dusting off and taken to a wine bar or the theatre or even for a pizza like normal girlfriends. She tolerated this because the whole scenario went in tandem with her strong beliefs that nothing was normal and that the blueprint for acceptable behaviour should be set by the individual. The flaw was that her behaviour wasn't quite matched by that of Charles. Letti compromised hugely and Charles tried to. They had visited a gallery together once but his nervous demeanour at the prospect of possible exposure as an adulterer negated the thrill of being seen with him in public.

Realising that his marriage was sacred to him, strangely barren as it was, Letti resolved to mind her own business and sit back and enjoy her bit of him. She adored his humour. It was very 'sixth-form dorm'. He spoke an entirely different language to her, peppering his conversation with 'jolly good show' and 'Tchaik', which she took to mean his pet name for Tchaikovsky. He would survey her apartment as if it were alien territory. He looked misplaced in her environment, a contemporary continental backdrop at odds with his olde Englishness.

Letti got on with her counselling and accepted her lot. She'd probably have still been with Charles today had it not been for that fateful Saturday afternoon in the public library. As she pored over a reference book in the reading rooms, she witnessed Charles furiously whispering abuse at a meek mousy painfully-thin little woman with a love-struck but mortified expression on her pinched face.

'Read my lips, I never want kids!' hissed Charles.

What shocked Letti most was that 'Read my lips' was one of her own expressions. It sounded ridiculously authoritative and alien coming from

Charles. In his anger he was totally oblivious to Letti's presence. A great tear welled and rolled down the little woman's floridly embarrassed cheek. Letti quietly closed the book and without a backward glance gathered her papers and left, unseen by Charles and unknown to Fleure.

She refused to see Charles again. The articulate and poetic notes penned on university stationery, the cultured bewilderment on her answer-phone, even a visit to her place of work, daring indeed, failed to sway her. Letti rebuffed all his advances which lasted for only a short time. In truth Charles seemed relieved the whole thing between them had been tied up neatly. His protestations stemmed from pride rather than affection. It was this startling insight into Charles' psyche that laid the foundations of Letti's new theory: when the situation called for it women, even strangers, should close ranks ignoring bonds with and loyalty to their lovers, and damned well stick together. Surprisingly in the aftermath of the Charles episode Letti bore no grudge. She did wonder though whether Fleure managed ever to bear children.

Letti selected a familiar Gregorian chant from her CD stack, scrutinised Charles' photograph and name on the cover and with a wry smile replaced it in its slot. She decided to let sleeping dogs – or married dons – lie. Instead she fished out an old well-loved and battered vinyl LP and as Gladys Knight gave her mature heart-wrenching treatment to 'There's more to life than living at the same address' Letti felt a physical tug in her chest, an ache for Jon. It passed. She felt secure in the knowledge that he'd be back. Bending she inhaled the heady scent of the lilies at their most perfect and now completely open. They brought to mind the defencelessness of a woman in love, petals spread wide, creamy white, the stems standing tall against the inevitability of fading, bruising and decay. The dazzling bouquet offering itself, seemed to say, 'Here I am, open and unfurled. Appreciate what I offer while there's time, you'll soon cast me aside when I bow my head, fade and fester.'

Regaining her composure, Letti rejoined her guests. 'Bucks Fizz for me, please! Now Angela, what's all this delicious nonsense about a new boyfriend?' Gladys Knight's deep blue melody wove into the kitchen, her rounded contralto beseeching her vanished Mr Wonderful to help her make it through the night.

Angela addressed her audience.

'When I eventually came out of hospital, Felix and Greg took me to live with them. They kept company with a colourful circle of friends and the presence of a brightly dressed sad midget with a secret sorrow was considered quite run of the mill. Gradually I recovered my strength, my will to live and my sense of humour. I suppose I became their surrogate child, their pet. They chose my clothes, my make-up and weren't a bit embarrassed at having to purchase sanitary towels and ladies' undies. Greg created tempting meals – seafood medleys and home-made chicken soup, lime jelly – the sort of stuff invalids might fancy. Felix played gentle music and lent me wonderful books to get lost in. Fairytales, Rupert Bear annuals from his rosy childhood, sprawling novels about small-town life in mid-America, French classics, anything to fill my mind with new and interesting images and ideas. It worked, they resurrected me.

'The gay bar they frequented became my local. I felt at home where once I'd thought it sleazy and gaudy. Felix told me the two guys who ran it liked me hanging out there because I blended quite well with the leopardskin wallpaper with my fiery jungle colours and my black-ringed eyes. My old boss networked to find me a new job, there was too much gossip to stay in his company. Elouise pulled strings to get me somewhere new to live. A couple of her male devotees moved my stuff in. With more than a little help from my friends I made a fresh start. One legacy of the bad times is that I can't bear to use buses. I'm all right about fire and flames, Letti will confirm this. She allowed me to have candles in my room last night, something that was forbidden in hospital. While I was staring at their flames they helped make my story come together more clearly than ever before.

'I don't see much of Felix and Greg now. Their generosity was boundless while I was peculiar and they liked the attention my ramblings commanded at their gatherings. I was the curiosity, the cabaret. They had little time for normality or straight people but I was the weirdest straight they knew and it gave credibility to their theory that everyone was open to conversion. I don't mean conversion to homosexuality or lesbianism. I mean conversion from an acceptable lifestyle and appearance to one that is different, shocking, unique. I'll be forever in their debt. Who would have taken me in hand at that time? Elouise was and still is a great friend but her social set don't like surprises.

'Once at Felix and Greg's I put a match to a bowl of pot pourri and held my hands over the flames. It was a ritual I needed to perform every so often, an exorcism. I don't need to do it now. Letti knows. The spectators that evening simply carried on sipping their banana daiquiris and nibbling their canapés as if it was 'just something I did', a character trait, odd but not worthy of comment. If you'd seen the guests you'd have understood better.

'There was a man with long needles stuck through his cheeks and ears and also a very old lady with purple contact lenses who was squatting next to the tantalus and reading palms. There was a bald girl, her body crammed into a black rubber dress with two circles cut for her nipples to poke through. Her girlfriend was spreading guacamole on them and lasciviously licking it off to general applause. The goings-on were much too riveting for anyone to give more than a passing glance to a redhead with smouldering fingernails.

'Chez Felix and Greg I was force-fed the crazy, the strange and consequently regaining normality became easy. When I meet them now we go to that leopardskin place. Conversation is a bit stilted and safe because I don't want to dwell on the state I was in and they're both very aware I withheld the root cause of my breakdown from them. I don't blame them for feeling hurt and excluded after all the efforts they put in to nurse me back to health. We've drifted apart.

'I haven't had a relationship since Bill and it's only recently that I've felt drawn towards someone. You know that feeling when you meet someone for the first time and you can instinctively tell they've been through the mill, had similar bad experiences to your own. You look at them and you can sense some buried horror. It's a bit like discovering a long-lost twin. I suppose it's called finding your soul mate. Sounds a bit corny, doesn't it? This whole business is still in the very early stages but I'll tell you about it.

'About three weeks ago I was in the leopardskin bar with Felix and Greg and they had a monumental argument. Greg had confessed to sleeping with some 'rough trade' whom Felix didn't like at all. Don't misunderstand me – they both condoned infidelity. It was a factor I found hard to accept in their lifestyle as they're the closest couple I know. They say they love each other but despite their devotion, they stray occasionally when they feel they've been stereotypically pigeon-paired. They say it's the shock element which helps them keep their feet on the ground and appreciate each other.

'This bewildering arrangement works apparently so long as each tells the other everything that transpires and the other approves of the temporary new partner. But this time Felix was furious at Greg's choice and in front of me called Greg a common cottager and a slapper. Greg slammed down his dry martini onto the bar causing it to splatter the front of Felix's Versace shirt – actually it was hard to see any damage, the pattern was so busy! Greg sailed off haughtily into the night and a drenched Felix, knowing I'd be quite all right by myself – as by now I was as much a part of the furniture as the lilac suedette bar stool I was perched on – ran after his errant lover as fast as his little legs would carry him.

'Drama queen!' commented the beautiful, blue-eyed stranger in the ocelot-print T-shirt who, camouflaged in a recess, sat observing the situation. I knew he was straight like me, but I knew he'd had a very peculiar past. I knew that if he were to stand up he'd be tall and above all I knew with unshakeable conviction that he would become the irresistible drug that would eradicate the final traces of the Bill episode from my blood. At this point we hadn't even spoken to each other. He didn't stand, he stretched like a great big cat and put his hands behind his head, his elbows jutting on either side and for all the world in the fuggy gloom resembled some dark angel.

Johnnie, the most camp of the two proprietors, put down the glass which he'd been nonchalantly polishing, and in a gesture of mock-surrender, raised an immaculately plucked eyebrow heavenward. "Get a load of him, the pretty thing!" he whispered. "And I hear he doesn't bat on my team. He's not on anyone's team by all accounts, my sweet Angelique! (his pet name for me). Methinks you're in with a chance. What an exotic brace of lovebirds you'd make."

'The stranger directed his blue gaze at me. "Join me for a green chartreuse. It will look divine with your hair, it's the opposite end of the spectrum." And I did. I couldn't drink the green liqueur, it tasted like some of the medicine I'd been subjected to in hospital. Johnnie skittered about like Cilla Black conducting *Blind Date*, bringing dishes of olives and bits of cheese on sticks to our table, fawning on us, bestowing upon us a bottle of cold Chardonnay on the house. I couldn't decide whether he was competing for the obvious charms of this mystery customer or crowing because Felix and Greg's oddball protégée had finally scored for herself.

'I suppose the feline stranger was bored. He told me everything yet nothing about himself. There was an aura about him of seclusion, wealth, decadence, complacency. He looked as if he'd done it all and was still unsatisfied. He knew he was a subject of interest and he said it pleased him to grace places like this with his presence and strike up conversation with chosen others just to see what would transpire. It wasn't arrogance. I knew he was simply being truthful.

'From Johnnie's reaction I could tell this man had charisma, glamour in the true sense of the word. Yes, he was glamorous, magical. I wasn't in the least surprised when he told me he performed a drag act in a club on the other side of town just for kicks.

'He said he felt a kindred spirit with women who were victims and I, with my hands covered in burnt tissue and my eyes full of ill-concealed horror, would make a good companion for the evening. He said in general he didn't much like women, or men either and when I asked him if he had family, parents, his generous mouth snarled a response which startled me. "I'm no longer a Mummy's boy!"

'Within moments he reverted to his original teasing mood, leaned down and fixed his beautiful mouth over mine in the longest, slowly-circular, most sensuous kiss I have ever experienced. That one kiss – it was more than a kiss, it was lovemaking – rekindled a dormant fire in me – a fire already built that had lain hissing and smouldering since Bill. That kiss ignited my obsession.

'I knew I was going to see him again. I felt he concealed a madness just as I did. He said he was going to Amsterdam for a time to conduct some business and also to seek some pleasure. He looked as if he did exactly as he pleased. I can't stop thinking about him. Johnnie says he'd visited the leopardskin bar several times before but had never spoken until that night, he says he would usually just observe and absorb the covetous looks of the punters. Johnnie says he puts him in mind of a vampire but Johnnie watches too many movies.

'Anyway he must have gone to Amsterdam, I haven't seen him since. I've returned to the bar a lot since then, just in case. He didn't make a firm arrangement, just said he'd catch up with me at the bar when he returned. That night when Johnnie called "Time" mystery-man called me a cab, paid for it and the last I saw of him was this tall broad-shouldered figure with the collar of his leather jacket turned up, loping off into the night.

'I've even wondered since if I dreamt him. Johnnie says no and that two bottles of Chardonnay is enough to make us all see the first person who chats us up in ages as mystical and alluring.

'Just before he slammed the door of my cab he told me his name was Paris – quite a name, romantic isn't it?'

Letti who had been listening very carefully didn't think it was romantic at all. She had registered Angela's description of Paris, this asexual paragon, this new love-interest and potential saviour and meticulously noted all the facts: his part-time diversion as a drag artiste, his haunts, his appearance, his kindred feelings towards 'women who were victims'. Now she was uncomfortable with the knowledge. An annoying insect of doubt buzzed at the periphery of her thoughts, needling, jabbing, forcing her to work while outwardly her expression remained impassive as she calmly sipped her drink.

The inevitable stung her as swiftly and surely as a wasp. Paris was Georgia's Jean/Jeanne. The lovely louche man/woman currently courting her was now focusing his attention on Angela. Paris and Jean/Jeanne were one and the same man. And now he had the arrogance to entertain aspirations of becoming Angela's 'new best friend' instead.

The women (all except Angela, that is) had heard Georgia's excited account of her deep friendship with Jean/Jeanne. Over dinner they'd drunkenly complimented her, registering mild surprise at his habit of cross-dressing and they vaguely remembered he performed a drag act. Amid the catalogue of confessions, a lot of information had failed to register. Each had been obsessed with her own sad history and recovery so only Letti possessed the expertise and freedom to stand outside the circle, log the facts and assimilate the overall picture. Letti didn't think it was a very pretty picture.

Angela continued to sing Paris' praises. Elizabeth and Penny continued to listen and encourage but only Letti had guessed that Georgia – the most wounded and perhaps the most vulnerable of the bunch, Georgia who couldn't bear to stay overnight and who needed to scuttle away to recharge her strength before resuming the weekend, Georgia who'd been shyly proud to share her new peace, almost boasting of the new life she'd begun to discover with Jean/Jeanne, was tangled in duplicity with a self-obsessed creature whose callous charms far outshone Bruno's animal attraction.

Oblivious, the others partied on, licking pastry crumbs from fingers, mixing and consuming their colourful cocktails, heads together giggling and exchanging snippets and anecdotes about their new boyfriends: Elizabeth's James, the coffee bar charmer; Penny's Jeremy, the gallant gallery owner and now Angela's Paris – or rather Angela's Paris and Georgia's Jean/Jeanne.

Letti observed her pupils, the result of her labours. Three highly strung clients chilling out and laughing like schoolgirls. The last thing Letti was going to do was burst the bubble. She kept her doubts to herself but in her heart, she nurtured the first stirrings, a primeval almost indiscernible embryonic shift but it nudged her a step towards joining the rare category that was the nature of the others. The cancerous little concept presented itself again and Letti found herself despising, almost hating Paris, Jean/Jeanne or whoever he purported to be. As yet Letti hadn't put a name to the uncomfortable irritating little feeling. Had she described the symptoms to her guests they might have enlightened her. Letti was bearing a grudge.

Gladys Knight's final plaintive track swelled into Letti's kitchen. Her anguish directed this time at her Los Angeles dream boy and his imminent departure 'On a midnight train to Georgia'. Sod this for coincidence! thought Letti angrily as she imagined the likely scenario of Georgia and Angela pining for their mutual dream boy, each unaware they were sharing his affections, each probably wondering of his whereabouts when he was with the other.

Letti stomped off down the hallway to change the tune. Penny, Elizabeth and Angela, engrossed in their conversation and enlivened by the cocktails, hardly registered her absence and were completely oblivious to her change of mood. Letti had wanted to meet Jean/Jeanne after hearing Georgia's intriguing account of his appearance and his lifestyle. Now that she'd discovered he fancied himself as a serial lover and was about to put the metaphorical cat amongst her cherished pigeons she felt an even stronger desire to make his acquaintance.

13

Archangel to Dark Angel

Late on Saturday morning under a rumpled duvet in a darkened bedroom Georgia jolted awake. She felt surprisingly light-hearted after the previous evening's morose journey homeward. Her hangover was minimal and she couldn't recall her dreams. Dead Bruno and little lost Luke were the last thing on her mind as she drew back the curtains and saw the heavy rains had given way to watery sunshine.

Georgia felt almost strong, more positive now than she'd felt in ages. The previous evening with all the caring, sharing, comparison and discussion together with the delicious and extravagant meal must have strengthened her and laid a few ghosts. She showered while Meatloaf melodically reminded her 'Two Out of Three ain't Bad'.

Georgia disagreed. In her book, wanting and needing someone was no good without the third – loving someone. And she felt that she was now ready to love Jean/Jeanne. Humming to herself she also decided she was a step nearer to loving herself after all Letti's hard work with her.

While drying and spiking up her blue-black hair in the mirror she reprimanded her reflection for being weak to cut and run from Letti's gathering. Her eyes now purple-lidded and emphasised by black liner stared back at her, dark and knowing and full of the conviction that she would return to Letti's apartment that afternoon, rejoin the others, get to know Angela the late-comer a little better and apologise for her nervous departure.

Georgia took a long swig of black coffee laced with Scotch. This normally served as breakfast; whisky was a staple of her diet. The generous nightcap last night had worked its usual alchemy and induced a deep sleep untroubled by nightmares. Hugging the mug to her thin chest Georgia wondered if Jean/Jeanne would come calling today. She left all the arrangements to him. In fact she'd never been invited to his place. On the one occasion she'd suggested his house as an alternative venue to her small dark flat his mood had changed alarmingly. He'd adopted a shuttered obstinate demeanour, not meeting her eyes but instead staring studiously down at his elegant suede boots and like a sullen boy he'd quietly insisted, 'Mother wouldn't like it.'

Georgia thought his mother was dead but she wasn't sure. She accepted his decision because she rather liked his aura of mystery. Visually he was extremely exotic but his shrouded past added to his glamour. In any case Georgia relished the freedom their relationship afforded her. She herself became nervous if too many plans were laid for her or restrictions imposed – the previous evening for instance. The invitation to stay overnight had been spontaneous but nevertheless Georgia had felt captured, trapped and so she had bolted. Now feeling rather ashamed at her low threshold of tolerance she was determined to go back. Letti had encouraged her to return without prior notice just when it suited her and now it suited her.

Georgia danced around to Meatloaf pumped up to full volume and hurriedly gathered things together in an overnight bag. If Letti was inclined to continue her party until Sunday, Georgia wanted some of the action. She'd discovered an elite group who understood: posh Penny; wary-but-wise Elizabeth and puckish flame-haired Angela with the orange clothes and bright warpaint.

It was with Angela she identified the most. Angela's off-beat sense of humour, her punky colour sense and her chaotic past love life all appealed to Georgia. She'd liked Angela on sight from the moment she'd burst in on the company, the white rabbit late for the mad hatter's tea party. Georgia thought Angela was also right up Jean/Jeanne's street. She felt sure that if they met they'd get on like a house on fire.

Meatloaf roaring their testimony to 'Midnight at the Lost and Found' almost drowned out the sound of the doorbell. Bruno was long dead but Georgia still took a while to unchain her door and admit her visitor. Out of habit she kept enough ironmongery around her locks to keep out Attila the Hun. Jean/Jeanne, a bottle of Scotch in one hand and a sheaf of flowers and a Prada bag in the other, leaned elegantly in her doorway. Georgia didn't have a clue who he was at first, until he spoke. Today he was one of the girls.

Georgia dragged him in, squealing with admiration and collapsing with delight in the centre of the small room, scattering the bouquet. Jean/Jeanne performed an exaggerated twirl. On his head was a soft shiny jet-black wig which must have cost the earth. Covering his usually bright blue irises were brown contact lenses. He wore his own black jeans and polo sweater and a full-length black leather trenchcoat.

'Come to the cabaret, my friend!' he urged pouting and blowing a kiss knowing full well he looked drop-dead gorgeous.

Georgia inhaled his fragrance, a heady combination of Paloma Picasso and Johnnie

Walker. She hardly recognised this catwalk beauty stalking around posing and preening. Jean/Jeanne whether in male or female mode and with his vast collection of guises had always previously appeared as a blonde. This was his supreme effort, his best one yet.

'Today I've decided blondes don't have more fun, lend me more make-up, Georgia. Let's play around and paint my eyes like yours and then we'll go out and seek amusement. What a pair of black-haired beauties we'll be!'

Georgia couldn't take her eyes from him. He was achingly beautiful, angular and androgynous. She wished she looked half as good. He was the sister she'd never had, her best friend, her lover and her saviour from the horrors of Bruno.

'Your own mother wouldn't recognise you,' she said.

It was out before she could curb it. It was taboo to mention Jean/Jeanne's mother. He didn't seem to notice her slip, though. Today he was in a playful daring outrageous mood.

Georgia and Jean/Jeanne installed themselves in front of the mirror working amid a clutter of make-up and perfume bottles, refilling their tumblers of Scotch and ginger and having a ball while in the background The Kinks sang their cynical homage to 'Lola, Lo-Lo-Lo-Lo-Lola' – the crème de la crème of cross-dressers.

Jean/Jeanne with his wig and lenses and

Georgia's deft touch with the lip brush and mascara wand was completely transformed from his usual brand of handsome flaxen-haired persona into a new striking brown-eyed beauty. Georgia was amazed at his versatility, his chameleon quality. The number of different characters he was able to shrug on and shed as comfortably as clothing, was almost scary. It didn't take long to complete his transformation from Archangel to Dark Angel.

When he was completely satisfied with his appearance and there was only a couple of fingers of Scotch remaining in the bottle he took Georgia by the hand, led her to her still-unmade bed and made love to her. It wasn't the rough indifferent act that had been Bruno's unimaginative style, but feminine tactile sensuous love, all fragrance and whisky-induced abandon. He was Narcissus and Georgia his weaker more fragile reflection.

When she dared to consider their relationship Georgia admitted to herself that Jean/Jeanne took from her, his generous lips sucking and suckling in an erotic vampiric manner, draining all her emotions. Yes, Jean/Jeanne took but Georgia was more than willing to give. After the barren waste of her years under Bruno's command and the painful time shut away, she craved sensuality, intimacy and peace despite her skittish reluctance to be physically closed in. She depended on him for her equilibrium, her sanity. Without him she knew she could easily become unbalanced again.

Ray Davies on full blast through the speakers was observantly remarking on 'a dedicated follower of fashion' as Jean/Jeanne repaired his lipstick and Georgia gathered up and arranged her flowers, burying her face amongst their creamy heads. What was it with lilies? There must be a glut at the moment. All the men in all the world seemed to be giving them to their women.

Their scent transported Georgia back to the previous evening in Letti's apartment. She now had to choose between going back or hanging out with Jean/Jeanne – or did she? A crazy idea occurred to her. Rather than forfeit his company when she rejoined the women's group why not take him with her in his female get-up? He wouldn't be surprised by their revelations. She'd kept no secrets from him although she suspected he had a whole Pandora's box full. He knew all about Bruno, or he should have known had he listened properly. Jean/Jeanne was rather self-obsessed and Georgia thought he tended not to believe her account of her past exploits. It all sounded too far-fetched. He probably thought she was a bit of a fantasist.

Jean/Jeanne was Georgia's trump card against adversity, her best asset in life. She was so proud of him and she wanted to take him and show him off, to present him as her prize to Letti, Elizabeth, Penny and Angela as a proud cat exhibits a mouse.

Georgia considered him a good catch. Letti had expressed a desire to meet him, so why not? And he would bolster her courage when once more she was ensconced in Letti's environment. She could lean on him, trust him to give her strength.

Georgia thought it best not to tell him much in case he wouldn't play her game. She resolved to tell him only that they were going to meet an amazing woman, very dear to Georgia's heart. The others she would keep as a surprise but she had a pretty good idea that he'd like them, especially Angela. Georgia fancied taking the lead for a change. It would be a sophisticated game of blind man's buff. Besides Jean/Jeanne always craved newer more amusing adventures, more stimulating company, fresh fields, new audiences. If she could pull off this meeting she would definitely earn 'Brownie points' from her hero.

'Let's go to the The Sphinx and Lynx for the afternoon, drink malt whisky and knock 'em dead. The whole place will be lusting after us and I want to see if Johnnie realises who I am,' suggested Jean/Jeanne.

Georgia had never been to The Sphinx and Lynx. She didn't know Johnnie the proprietor and she certainly had no idea that this was one of Angela's haunts, or that Jean/Jeanne had spent an evening there recently wooing Angela with his golden hair and vivid blue eyes, using his charms as Paris the pretty boy to hypnotic effect.

Jean/Jeanne loved a game of dare, bending the rules and testing his abilities. He half hoped his latest conquest, Angela, would be at the bar. He felt sure she wouldn't know him as a dark-haired brown-eyed woman. He felt almost nauseous at the thrill of such a delicious deception.

'Let's not go anywhere new,' said Georgia. 'You know I get nervous when I have to go into new places. Sometimes I see Bruno in a crowd, actually hear his voice, his husky laugh. He raises his pint glass to me across a crowded room. I look away and then he's gone. His ghost haunts me in bars and clubs. I think the smell of the beer and the cigarette smoke weave a spell in my imagination and trigger my memories of him. Let me decide where we go today. I've cooked up a little magical mystery tour for you. You'll be so impressed with my wit and imagination, and I'm desperate for you to meet someone who has had as much input as you into saving my life. The pair of you are just about the most important people in my world.'

'Well then what are we waiting for?' said Jean/Jeanne amiably.

Out in the street the two head-turners earned appreciative whistles from a couple of beefy blokes who'd been arguing outside a pub. Georgia and Jean/Jeanne grinned at each other, both wondering what the outcome would have been if they'd accepted the men's offer of a drink. Georgia expected Jean/Jeanne would have fooled them, his voice was husky but not overtly male. She would have liked to have gone along with the charade but was determined not to be diverted from her plan. And besides, the two blokes although quite handsome, looked as if they wouldn't tolerate being taken for mugs. Georgia had first-hand knowledge of being on the receiving end of a fist if she tried to be too clever and so was happy to give them a wide berth.

Jean/Jeanne was pleased to see their route took them past The Sphinx and Lynx and while Georgia queued in an off-licence to buy wine for Letti, he slipped inside. Jean/Jeanne couldn't bring himself to pass the ornate double doors without entering. Inside it was impossible to discern whether it was day or night. Lunchtime lounge-lizards and beer-swilling bar-flies swarmed around Johnnie. He swatted them off, eyes glittering at the prospect of fresh meat on the premises and turned all his attention to serving the newly arrived tall, black-haired woman who was either a model or a gender-change. Johnnie liked what he saw. There wasn't an ounce of extra fat on her elegant bones. She was stunning.

The newcomer stayed only long enough to drink down in one a glass of malt whisky. As she threw back a graceful head to toss down the golden liquid, Johnnie saw an Adam's apple ripple on the smooth, kissable throat. With a little frisson of excitement he realised his customer was a man, which interested him even more. A drooling predatory Johnnie finished serving and made a move along the bar to treat his prey to a drink on the house. But the stranger had gone, mission accomplished. Johnnie hadn't recognised Paris from Adam. As Georgia had ventured to say earlier, Paris' own mother wouldn't have recognised him.

Georgia hadn't had time to miss Jean/Jeanne and was just emerging with her tissue-wrapped wine when he rejoined her. Knowing his weakness for drifting off to window-shop, she didn't even ask where he'd been. Jean/Jeanne liked this aspect of Georgia's character. She let him be free, trusted him.

As predicted Jean/Jeanne kept pausing to window-shop or dive into shoe shops or jewellers. He loved pretty things. Georgia considered his bottomless wallet and wondered what he actually did for a real living. Surely the Sunday drag act wasn't sufficient to finance his extravagant and self-indulgent lifestyle. She remembered him saying something once about being abandoned by his father who'd settled a great deal of guilt-money on his furious wife who had eventually died of a broken heart. Jean/Jeanne made reference to his mother quite a lot, not enough for Georgia to build up a picture of his background, but she assumed at times the woman might still be alive because disjointed comments on her tastes, looks and mannerisms cropped up often in Jean/Jeanne's diatribes, especially when he'd been hitting the Johnnie Walker. In fact he rambled on about quite a lot of topics, situations, locations, odd occasions and colourful people but because these were usually monologues and very disjointed, none of it seemed real. Georgia wasn't allowed to mention Mother, neither did Jean/Jeanne tolerate questions relating to his own comments about her. He simply referred to her a lot in relation to most of what he did which led Georgia to believe that although Mother was dead she had never stopped pulling his strings and continued to influence his actions.

Georgia's inner thoughts had left her with a clouded expression, which was misinterpreted by Jean/Jeanne as tiredness. He raised a graceful leather-clad arm to hail a cab. In seconds one screeched over, the driver nearly falling over himself to settle such a gorgeous pair of women into his vehicle.

'Your chariot, madam!' said Jean/Jeanne theatrically. 'Well, go on, tell the poor bloke the destination, you're the one with all the secrets, Honeybunny!'

Georgia gave the cabbie the name of Letti's street. She omitted the actual address because she wanted to be dropped at the end of the street giving her time to gather her thoughts while the pair of them walked for a few minutes. It was beginning to dawn on her now the whisky was losing its effect that Letti and the others might not be too delighted with having an extra 'woman' sprung on them. But it was too late to bottle-out now. She foraged for her hip flask, shared a nip with her companion and nestled back into the comfortable depths of the big rear seat.

The cabbie, glancing surreptitiously in the mirror, was getting quietly turned on. All he usually got in the way of punters on a Saturday afternoon was a cab full of mothers, kids, buggies and shopping or the occasional incoherent lunch time drunk. Alleluia! Here on a plate to feed his fantasies were a couple of great-looking dark-haired dykes, done up to the nines sharing kisses and swigs from a silver flask. They kept hugging and caressing each other's designer-clad knees. Blimey! thought the cabbie, this is better than *Knave* or *Fiesta*!

He used to get his girlie magazines, well-thumbed and second-hand, from his best mate, the one who used to drive the graveyard shift. The cabbie thought about his best mate who, a good few years ago now, had smashed into a broken-down transit van in an unlit backstreet one terrible night. The cabbie remembered the night well because it was the same night there'd been a bad house fire. Two bus drivers had copped it. Yes, his mate and those bus drivers had certainly been on the graveyard shift that night, no doubt about it. He missed his mate and with him dead and gone he had to buy his own magazines. From that day onwards he'd resolved to only work the day shift, it was safer.

The cabbie shook himself back to the present, it didn't do to take your eyes from the road. There was plenty of action on the back seat. The tall one with all the make-up looked a bit butch, she must be the bull dyke of the two. He bet she was a model. The slighter one with the shadows under her eyes, the purple lipstick and not much in the tit department looked like some sort of a junkie – bloody good looking though, both of them. Christ! it was difficult driving this thing with a hard on.

Jean/Jeanne wished he hadn't heard the name of their destination correctly. But it was a long street, surely there couldn't be such a coincidence. He continued to stroke Georgia's leg while he rationalised his thoughts and planned his strategy. I've been lucky so far, I'm invincible, charmed. This isn't going to spoil things. If by some remote twist of fate it is the same address, I'm sure I won't be recognised. Johnnie didn't know me in The Sphinx and Lynx, even Georgia didn't know me as I stood in her doorway. The other one has no idea whatsoever that I cross dress. She wouldn't believe it of me in a million years. I'll go, yes I will, I'll see it through. What have I got to lose? I don't give a shit about any of the bitches. Mother knows, they're nothing but strumpets.

Jean/Jeanne bent and kissed Georgia on the

mouth. The cabbie surreptitiously eased himself, having trouble negotiating a bend. Despite the distraction they all arrived safely. The cabbie, one hand clutching a handsome tip, the other on his trousers, watched the couple retreating down the elegant avenue, the taller one resting her arm loosely across the shoulders of the pale thin one who clutched a bottle of wine. Must be going to some party, thought the cabbie . . . all done up like a dog's dinner on a Saturday afternoon . . . posh area too . . . bloody amazing how the other half live.

As they approached Letti's building Jean/Jeanne felt the familiar surge of adrenalin, the same buzz he always got when he was about to realise one of his elaborate dreams. Women who were victims were ideal playthings and he loved manipulating them. He was Jean/Jeanne, he was Paris the puppeteer, he was who the hell he fancied being at any given time. There was a tiny beat of fear in his heart. This was going to be a big kick but what if it all went pear-shaped? No, he'd be okay, he was omnipotent. Since Mother had let him down, nothing could touch him. Patting his hair he got out his mirror to check his disguise. It was more than a disguise – he was a completely different person to his usual repertoire.

As he and Georgia reached the marbled entrance to Letti's apartment building Georgia strode straight past! Thank God, Jean/Jeanne offered up a prayer. It's not her place after all, I wonder where the hell she's taking me? A few yards further on Georgia suddenly stopped and retraced her steps, Jean/Jeanne in her wake. Georgia had only been to Letti's place on the one occasion – yesterday. Letti counselled her clients in a stark office with tinted windows and no distractions, miles away from her private habitat because until the previous evening, Letti had never liked to mix business with pleasure.

'We've gone past it. Oh! here it is, these flash doorways all look the same to me,' stated Georgia with conviction as, taking Jean/Jeanne's damp hand and oblivious to his horrified expression, she led him up to the outer door and pressed the intercom buzzer.

14

Spectre at the Feast

Letti's door buzzer sounded, competing with the thud, thud, thud of Bowie's homage to 'Jean Genie' and the occasional laughter and clinking of glasses. 'Sits like a man but he smiles like a reptile,' crowed the thin white duke. Georgia at last, thought Letti, I knew she'd find the nerve to come back. Letti invited her guest up, throwing wide the door of her apartment to be confronted by two women, posing in black, painted and sleek, like a fashion spread from *Harpers & Queen*.

'This is Jean/Jeanne,' Georgia breathlessly explained. 'Jean/Jeanne this is Letti. Don't be cross, will you Letti? You did say how much you wanted to meet him and now he can tell us all how he's made me happy again. Look, I know it's women only but he's made a very special effort to fit in and I think he's the prettiest of all of us, don't you?'

Christ! thought Letti as she took in details of the lean exotic creature whose brown spaniel eyes winningly implored her not to leave him . . . her? . . . out on the doorstep. Letti's mind went into overdrive. Whoever Georgia's boyfriend was today he certainly wasn't the fair Adonis known to Angela who called himself Paris. Oh, what the hell, her guests were all big girls – all murderesses to be technically correct. If there was going to be an emotional clash it might as well be under her jurisdiction. Letti had set herself up as mentor and who else but she had the expertise to handle rage, insanity, shock . . . all the ingredients were here on a plate at her doorstep and her intrinsic inquisitiveness for investigating the human mind's forbidden corridors guided her to make a decision.

'Do come in and join the party both of you. We're mixing cocktails and talking about everybody's Mr Wonderful so what more appropriate than to have a live example of one of our new men in our midst! You'll have to earn your keep though Jean/Jeanne. Join in and bare your soul.'

Bloody hell! thought Jean/Jeanne as he thanked her, not really surprised but considerably relieved that Letti hadn't the faintest idea of his true identity or at least not for the moment. He felt the familiar thrill of superiority. He still had the ability to deceive, to manipulate. God, women were so vulnerable, so blinkered, so bovine!

Letti led Georgia and Jean/Jeanne into the den where, in the interest of comfort and intimacy, she'd suggested they relocate. Angela had lit candles. The now-familiar gargoyles held them aloft, grimacing evilly. Letti had laid out a cheese board, parma ham and peaches. Elizabeth had gone out again to the corner bakery and bought warm baguettes. There was a bowl of mackerel mashed with thinly sliced red onion and garlic paste, next to which stood a bottle of slivovitz, forming a meal traditionally enjoyed on high days and holidays in Letti's homeland. The pungent aroma transported her back sharply to happy occasions in her early teens.

She and her brothers used to enjoy the fish mixture heaped onto thick country bread. After their meal they tossed back the fiery slivovitz liqueur one shot after the other in excitement, laughing, squabbling and competing with each other to see who could drink the most without passing out. They would beg their father to drive them into the nearest town which they'd proceed to paint red with all the carefree determination of youth unhampered by a preordained future. In those days Letti had thought she would stay forever in the area where she was born and probably marry one of the eligible friends of her brothers. She didn't. Letti missed her brothers. Her parents were long dead, her family scattered by a series of bloody political uprisings.

Penny was still presiding over the wine and cocktails while David Bowie warned them of a post-holocaust famine with an articulate rendition of 'Diamond Dogs'.

The sun had gone in, the blinds were drawn and the Moroccan lamp, slowly swivelling by its own heat, stencilled everything and everyone in the room with a moving pattern. Thus lit, the women took on the appearance of a pack of leopards, lounging on the long low settees like big cats sunning themselves along dappled branches. In this dimly-lit den Jean/Jeanne's disguise was incredibly convincing. He stood on the threshold flanked by Georgia and his diminutive hostess who announced, 'Here's Georgia back again and this is Jean/Jeanne. We feel we know him quite well already don't we girls? Jean/Jeanne meet Angela, Penny and Elizabeth.'

Jean/Jeanne playing it for all he was worth, accepted a flute of white wine and, confident in his disguise, pushed it even further by plonking his elegant self down beside Angela. She, knowing from Georgia's earlier description this beautiful stranger to be male, had quite a problem equating the actuality with the description. Trying not to appear rude she scrutinised Jean/Jeanne's androgynous figure and immaculate make-up and felt warmth, envy and admiration – anything other than recognition. Angela didn't get it. She had no idea that this was the blond, charismatic dreamboat from her leopardskin bar who'd crept right under her skin, kissed her senseless and then vanished off to Amsterdam. Her Paris!

Letti was a little more disturbed and a lot more intrigued by Jean/Jeanne. She was sure she had met him before. The feeling was almost indefinable, nevertheless she felt a small tug, a familiar chemistry, a tiny, tenuous link but as much as she observed his mannerisms she couldn't quite come up with an answer. Perhaps he'd been a client at some time. Maybe she'd come across him in his other guise – his Paris garb and visage. She couldn't make the connection having never seen him as the blond boulevardier so beloved of Angela. Letti tried hard to imagine this dark shiny-bobbed 'woman' as a fair-haired male but the make-up was too much of a masque and yet . . . her confusion cleared slightly, she almost had it, the key. In a vague flash of recognition it was almost a certainty and then it slithered away like a silver-fish, leaving her infuriated.

Jean/Jeanne was thinking fast. Outwardly he was smiling at Angela, Georgia on his right clinging possessively, her arm entwined in his. He was doing what he did best: commanding attention, generating fascination. Inwardly he was well aware of the shrink watching him, like the beady-eyed, clever little hawk that she was. This

221

was his supreme thrill. Letti was looking puzzled and perplexed. She disliked jigsaw puzzles with missing pieces, machinery with lost components. Letti was a perfectionist. This was her party, the guests her creation and Jean/Jeanne knew he was without doubt the cat amongst her pigeons. He knew her so well and what gave him the biggest buzz was that Letti didn't know him from Adam, or Paris . . . or Jon.

'We've brought liquid refreshment,' said Georgia, her rare upbeat mood obviously due to her pride in being able to introduce her lover to the others.

She playfully slid the bottle along the low table towards Penny like a rhinestone cowboy to his barroom queen. Beneath the heavy plate-glass table top the Egyptian king stared fixedly upwards as if the food and wine above him, in the light of the shrine-like candles, were a ritual offering, homage from these handmaidens who gathered around his gold and lapis lazuli mock tomb. Jean/Jeanne noticed the fake sarcophagus and remarked what a brilliant idea it was as a table base. Of course he'd seen it before but he wasn't saying.

As Jon he'd made love to Letti on the low settee by the light of candles held by those same gargoyles, whispered his false desires into her attentive little ear, stripped away her intellectual, analytical patina and found the core of the woman. He had made her his slave before donning his pin-striped business suit and his tortoiseshell glasses, straightening his silk tie, picking up his crocodile-skin briefcase and palmtop computer and vanishing off, charmingly apologetic, to one of his imaginary European seminars. For a counsellor she was pretty damned gullible – they all were. Strumpets, all of them.

Penny didn't much like drag queens. She was a man's woman. In her view a robust straightforward shag took a lot of beating. Of course she'd dressed up for Champagne Perry, donned the silk teddie and the crotchless knickers which were just about the only gifts he'd been happy to open his wallet for. And with Jeremy she'd turned a few cartwheels and kissed him in all the right places, more willingly of course because he was so generous. He bought her gifts from his gallery, gave her Italian shoes from his art-buying forays. Little presents of rare perfume, old brandy and antique jewellery came as standard with Jeremy. Penny would rather have her Jeremy any day than Georgia's Jean/Jeanne. Jeremy was one hundred per cent straight. His flamboyant hand-painted silk waistcoats and longish slickly-gelled dark-blond hair were a testament to his artiness, not a symptom of questionable gender or bizarre feminine proclivities.

In a mellow haze at the end of the settee, Penny sipped her wine and leaning her head back, rested against Letti's embroidered cushions. She closed her eyes and listened to Jean/Jeanne chatting to Georgia and Angela. His voice was attractive, husky and medium-pitched, neither a masculine baritone nor feminine. Jean/Jeanne had probably pitched his voice higher than normal in keeping with the role he was playing for them today. Penny admired his nerve but didn't particularly wish to look at him. In truth what rankled her most was that he was more glamorous than any of the assembled company. She felt uncomfortable when eclipsed in the beauty stakes by other women let alone a man! Penny didn't really want to look at his clothing, his endless legs or the wig. But his voice was attractive, she thought as she relaxed, eyes closed, and listened to him. There was a soothing and familiar quality to his voice. It bothered her slightly but not enough to cause her to dwell on it.

Elizabeth of all of them resented the intruder but was also strangely attracted to him. She felt it was an injustice that Georgia was to be allowed the privilege of flaunting her new trophy-love whereas the rest of them only had words to offer while the objects of their affections were unavailable. It wasn't fair. She wished her James could be here in the den with them, sitting beside her, his arm slung nonchalantly over her shoulders in that casual way he adopted that made her feel so special, so singled out, so chosen. James wasn't overtly tactile but each time he touched her hand she felt needed, the other half of a couple.

She wondered how he was spending his time during this weekend's visit to his parents. Suffolk wasn't the end of the earth but she could never contact him at their cottage. James said his mother was phobic about telephones and refused to have one in the house, said they always brought bad news. The old folk relied on a neighbour's telephone for necessary emergency calls, otherwise they kept themselves to themselves according to James. As much as Elizabeth wanted to phone the neighbours to simply tell James she was missing him and looking forward to 'their Wednesday' she didn't even know the neighbour's name, and besides James might think she was pushing for too much attention. He was a very busy man, a very private man. Elizabeth daren't rock the boat. She resolved to loosen up a bit more this Wednesday, reveal a bit more about herself and then perhaps James would be more forthcoming. It takes two, she thought.

This soul-baring weekend was doing her a power of good. She'd tasted the potent slivovitz and politely rejected it in favour of Cointreau. Elizabeth squinted at the square bottle and noted the alarming dip in the original level. It was rather like fruit cordial and went down a treat. It also dulled her pain, made her more receptive to the others' company and it certainly helped her warm towards this strange character Jean/Jeanne. For some obscure reason, Elizabeth felt an odd sensation, a feeling of love/hatred towards this man/woman. Funny how strong liquor freed the senses. These feelings made Elizabeth feel vaguely guilty. On one level she quite fancied Jean/Jeanne. It was extraordinary, she felt as if she'd known him for ages. How could that be?

Jean/Jeanne held court. He had them all mesmerised – all the strumpets. As the liquor flowed so did the conversation. His confidence grew by the minute. He was invincible, perfect, the puppet master. He was principal boy, he was Paris . . . Jean/Jeanne . . . Jon . . . all the stars of the show.

Oh yes, Jean/Jeanne was magnanimous enough to play the bit-parts as well as take on an extra role if his warped script demanded it. Every superstar needed to get into character as an extra or two to keep his hand in, sharpen his skills. It didn't trouble Jean/Jeanne at all to remove his trademark emerald ear stud and browse the huge mahogany-doored dressing room in the town house mother had conveniently bequeathed him. There he would bring out all the costumes that were the tools of his trade, his deception.

The conservative discreetly checked suits, corduroy jackets and brogues clothed James, the sales representative. James, who was only available on Wednesdays (elderly parents permitting), would weave ridiculous pipe dreams with Elizabeth, the country girl.

The James persona didn't particularly stimulate him creatively. He preferred himself as Jeremy. Jeremy was more like himself – if there was a 'himself' – affluent, cultured, artistic and prone to taking exotic trips and performing acts of generosity. Mother's art collection and wine cellar, as well as her perfume and jewellery coffret were a constant source of trinkets and love tokens. He would gel back his blond mane to accentuate his fine profile and wear grey lenses to lessen the tell-tale brilliance of his baby blues. How his mother had loved to match the ribbon trim on his party dresses to the exact shade of his eyes. It was easy to become Jeremy, bragging about art and travel, gracing Penny – the classy strumpet – with his occasional presence, promising the earth and weaving dreams, giving nothing except yet another command performance. Mother commanded this crazy cabaret. Mother knew best.

All this ran through Jean/Jeanne's mind as he pouted and posed making Georgia proud and all the others a little in love with him. Jean/Jeanne was now one of the girls.

What bothered him was how the hell these four women all came to be together at this party of Letti's? Jean/Jeanne was a creature who thrived on strategy and calculation. Careful planning, rehearsal and a perfect performance was his thing. Coincidence was an unconsidered factor, a quotient lacking in his dealings. He had a taste, a blood-lust for women who were victims but he underestimated the inevitable which through history has never been measurable, containable. Coincidence can suddenly occur to shatter the best-laid plans of mice and men, completely wiping out plot, map or reason and changing the course of things in a few horrifying seconds of revelation.

There was no answer to why all his women had assembled in Jean/Jeanne's company at that given time. The wounded seek each other out, sniffing out those similarly afflicted yet often not recognising each other's similarities. They continue to crop up in the same locations together, forming their various communities, their sub-cultures, their nameless underground clubs, their leper colonies and their communes. Disease-ridden conclaves, feminist movements, ghettos, fan clubs, working men's clubs, women's institutes, animal rights activists, veggies, vegans and vampires, the innocuous or the heavy mob. As much as people are designed to integrate and dance a multi-racial many-faceted pattern over the surface of the earth they invariably close ranks and seek out their own kind – by rote or by coincidence or by all being linked by one dividing factor, a catalyst.

Here high up in a stylish apartment sat Letti the catalyst. She was the reason they were gathered together sharing their horrors, their capacities to murder and their attraction for one man, the same man – a mockery-monogamy.

This meeting had occurred naturally, evolving from Letti's desire to say a last goodbye to her ex-clients. From the outside, unlike a school for the blind or a yacht club, it was impossible to detect visually what these guests had in common. The normal naked eye would never have deduced this was a symposium for murderesses, purposely invited to dine together but all blissfully unaware of a much more vital common ground, their individual passion for the latest addition to the coterie – Jean/Jeanne, Paris, Jon, James, Jeremy. It was a fluke, pure coincidence.

Jean/Jeanne couldn't see past their insecurities, their pain. He'd heard each tale, all the ramblings about pushing siblings down wells, shoving champagne bottles down fat gullets in Victorian bathrooms. He'd listened to Georgia who, in his view, was the craziest of the lot. She'd slotted a cut-glass paperweight into the head of some thug, or so she said. He had dismissed it all as fantasy. Only recently he had met Angela, the one with the red hair who liked to play with matches. She seemed to have some obsession with fire. It was laughable, piss-talk, the stuff most insecure tarts and fag hags hanging around gay bars brag about to make themselves seem interesting.

All the strumpets were deluded weak victims, rejected man-haters. However absurd their confessions, these elaborate tales of misdemeanours came nowhere near Jean/Jeanne's own disturbed, erotic, kinky and colourful past. He'd listened to each of them in turn, feigning patience but in reality he was complacent and bored, absorbing little and grunting during all the right pauses. Because his life to date had been such a warped and weird carry-on he found their stories trivial. Nothing compared to his own experiences, nothing matched his vanity, nothing and nobody compared.

'Nothing Compares 2 U,' mourned Sinéad O'Connor from the speakers, sad and shaven, her lyrics epitomising the collective agonies of Georgia, Elizabeth, Penny and Angela. Penny sang along. She thought of Champagne Perry and compared her long-dead lover with Jeremy. She decided they'd both been a bit elusive and wondered where Jeremy was at the moment – probably completing a sale in the gallery, caressing a smooth piece of sculpture with his wonderful sensitive touch.

Angela liked Georgia's new friend very much. Life with Felix and Greg and their gay and gregarious entourage had left her not in the least censorious. She too envied Georgia and wished Paris would show up. Love at first sight was possible. She'd loved Bill the bus driver on sight. But Angela was the first to admit to a tendency to obsession and she was obsessed with Paris.

She resolved to stake out that leopardskin bar on a regular basis in the hope of seeing him again soon. Angela was convinced he'd return, fonder for his absence, and seek her out. She imagined herself out for the evening with him, making up a foursome with Georgia and Jean/Jeanne. What a beautiful quartet they'd make! Unbiased and incorrigibly extrovert. Yes, thought Angela, as she listened to Jean/Jeanne wittily relating his adventures in Berlin, Prague and Amsterdam, here was a man very like Paris. They'd get on, they had Amsterdam in common and they both needed to bend the rules. She couldn't wait to arrange a date. It would be much more satisfactory than those clandestine meetings she had endured with Bill, Suggs and Hobgoblin in the Golden Galleon.

Angela continued to observe Jean/Jeanne as he spoke. He had fascinating eyes – alert and expressive – and had a certain way of making whoever he engaged in conversation with seem the most vital person on earth. Those eyes reminded her of someone and that mocking wisdom in his expression seemed very familiar despite the expertly applied make-up. That was it! Jean/Jeanne's eyes were exactly like Paris' eyes – but how stupid, Angela reprimanded herself, I must be more pissed and besotted than I thought. Of course his eyes aren't anything like my Paris' eyes.

Paris' eyes were indeed quite different to Jean/Jeanne's brown eyes, spaniel's eyes which were eyes to be trusted. Paris' eyes were an icy sapphire blue. Cold, glittering Nordic eyes . . . angel's eyes.

15

The Nickname

Letti allowed herself to relax slightly. Jean/Jeanne's female guise was incredible and certainly foolproof enough for Angela not to twig that Jean/Jeanne and Paris were one and the same man. She left them all to it for a while, quietly slipping away towards the kitchen to assemble a casserole for dinner that would need minimal attention. The conversation was too good to miss and Letti was a hostess not a martyr. The dinner party had evolved into a weekend as she'd hoped and she didn't want to miss a thing. Popping off into her bedroom she admired her lilies. Jon was so thoughtful and generous. There were enough blooms to spread all through the apartment but the arrangement in her bedroom was the best because it bore his special message, written in his elegant italic scrawl, 'See you soon, Honeybunny. Yours, J.'

Progressing to her kitchen Letti assembled the ingredients of the meal, took out her chef's knives and set to work. While planning last night's gathering, and trusting her guests, Letti had made a conscious decision to leave all sharp objects, paperweights, champagne bottles and matches within full view of, and easy access to, her guests. She knew from the many counselling sessions that certain objects held fetish fears for each of the women. Angela and matches; Georgia and paperweights or cranberry-coloured glass; Penny and bubble baths; and Elizabeth and cruelty to animals. Letti had encouraged them to confront and live with their individual bêtes noires. She was very proud of how far each had come back along the twisted path to normality.

A small figure in her trademark black, Letti diced vegetables, boned chicken, sprinkled herbs and sloshed wine into her cookpot – taking pleasure in preparing the concoction like a busy little witch, a modern-day alchemist.

In the den somebody had switched the music. 'I put a spell on you,' Geordie-boy Alan Price proudly boasted, 'because you're mine.' Letti hummed along with him, enjoying the volume. There were no near neighbours to complain, the entire development seemed to be peopled with faceless wealthy absentees. Letti liked it that way. Her job revolved around people and their problems, so she wasn't at all interested in her neighbours having a say in how she conducted her private life. The flat below was empty most of the time. Letti imagined it was the town love nest of a prominent dignitary who used it to get his very important end away on rare occasions. Middle Eastern gentlemen and visiting Japanese made up the remaining tenancies.

The basement had been boarded up since squatters with a taste for luxury had been forcibly evicted. Letti doubted if anyone in the entire street knew her name or even of her existence. The Gold Blend style of neighbourliness was an ad-man's cosy myth. If she'd knocked on the door of any of the nearby homes for a cup of sugar after she moved in Letti knew she'd have been answered by echoing silence or greeted by some dubious man in a jellaba.

'I put a spell on you' . . . the music was loud, insistent and still as mesmerising as it had been in the sixties. Letti believed the past was important to recall, however painful. One's journey through life with its wrong moves, mistakes, regrets and achievements, buzzes and highs should be revisited and considered occasionally to remind oneself how incredibly complex and unique each individual is. Letti believed in taking stock, unlocking doors hitherto bolted shut and giving the past an airing. Her ethos was such that she truly believed that this was the key to harnessing the strength to go onwards and grow, thus learning that should fate choose to throw a further set of crazy circumstances, and the dice were again loaded with a terrible choice, it would be second nature to grasp what was on offer, make a measured decision from remembered behaviour and swiftly deal with the adversary. Suppose Penny, for example, was again emotionally abused but this time by Jeremy, the arty consort who was a touch too noble to be true, Letti hoped Penny would be able to recognise the makings of a love-rat before she got hurt.

As counsellor-turned-hostess, she had listened to her ex-clients as they'd shared details of their new men. Indeed she was delighted to see animation in once-blank faces. Hardened murderesses, bright-eyed and blushing like breathless schoolgirls, swapping anecdotes of better times with new loves – it was a gratifying sight. But now Letti had deduced that two of her precious pigeons, Angela and Georgia, were being two-timed by the deceitful self-obsessed chameleon who at this precise moment was keeping his deluded harem spellbound right here in Letti's own private space, her holy of holies, her den.

At that moment in time, however, Jean/Jeanne wasn't actually where the den-mother thought he was. He had decided to feign a gig at the gay bar and take his leave of the ladies just as soon as was opportune. But vanity had taken the upper hand and he'd felt confident enough to offer to freshen the ice bucket first. Unobserved by Letti, he leaned, framed in the kitchen doorway watching her work, her back to him, capable hands assembling supper. Her shining helmet of hair bobbed from side to side as she sang along with Sting, 'Every move you make, every breath you take, I'll be watching you.' Clearing his throat and practising his female voice he asked Letti for ice.

'I'll be watching you,' menaced Sting . . .

Letti whirled round mid-chop and faced this black-haired beauty, yellow pepper in one hand, paring knife glittering in the other. She didn't mince her words.

'Have a glass of something and a girly chat out here for a while, will you Jean/Jeanne? Or shall I call you Paris? I'm sure Angela's busy telling Georgia how much she misses her blond deity who's supposedly in Amsterdam, and I'm positive Georgia's taking her mind off things with more chit-chat about what a paragon you are. Love is blind Jean/Jeanne but I am not, so I suggest you cook up a hot date and get the hell out of here and away from the pair of them before you open up the biggest can of worms even a reptile like you couldn't contend with!'

Jean/Jeanne sank down into the alcove seat, grabbed a bottle of Fitou, filled a goblet and drank down the contents like a cowboy builder downing a pint of lager tops. Beneath his matte foundation he had visibly paled.

The pinball wizard, imagined options of undetected escape and exposure ricocheted around his mind. So, Letti knew he was Paris and Jean/Jeanne but the supercilious bitch still hadn't a clue he was her Jon. Ha! he thought, as he swilled down his second helping of red wine, she's warning me off. I'll go, it's no hassle to dump them all. I've won in any case and I'm bored. She's sussed me out but she'd wet her sensible panties if she realised I was her very own Jon not to mention Jeremy and James! It's time to go – I quite fancy Morocco. I like this brand new black-haired bombshell guise. I'll develop it, I'll use it and I will get the hell out of here . . . Mother was right, I should have left the strumpets alone but they chase me, put it on a plate so I take.

Once Jean/Jeanne had decided to take Letti's advice and bow out unseen as requested, he felt slightly better, a little less cornered and accused. He didn't blame Letti for wanting to be rid of him. These women were obviously her pet project. Never in his romancing with her as Jon had she once mentioned them. What a professional she was! She'd no doubt invested a lot of work in them and knowing her stubborn character wouldn't want anything to threaten the progress.

He realised with relief that he was out of the woods if he discreetly left. He was sure she wouldn't tell on him. She'd make excuses for his departure and, fiercely protective of Georgia and Angela, would keep to herself her rather clever discovery that Jean/Jeanne or Paris was not what he seemed, not the answer to their prayers, the true love whom they fully expected to live with happily ever after.

They had already rid themselves of their pathetic partners in the most extraordinary circumstances, each disposing neatly of their respective King Rat. How droll then that in their hearts and in their beds, and tonight right under their noses was Emperor Rat. Letti was going to move mountains to make sure this outrageous duplicity remained a secret between her and Jean/Jeanne and while she was busy moving mountains for others he was convinced she'd fail to recognise him as Jon.

After basking in the initial glory of showing off her new best friend, Georgia wondered where he'd got to with the ice bucket. Georgia didn't want Letti to feel imposed upon. She knew full well how Jean/Jeanne needed to win the undivided attention of anybody new and interesting who crossed his path and it was obvious he was intrigued by Letti and her lifestyle. What Georgia didn't want was for Jean/Jeanne to bulldoze proceedings into a scenario where he was the star. Letti had been gracious enough to let him into the company but she didn't know the extent of his vanity. Jean/Jeanne liked to be the prime mover and the whole point of this weekend as Georgia saw it was to establish equality, harmony – everyone having their say, taking their turn. Georgia worried that there could soon be an imbalance unless she kept a tight rein on her lover.

Penny, Angela and Elizabeth were enjoying a lively debate on the pros and cons of having a live-in partner as opposed to one who preferred to play away matches. It had reached the stage where opinion swung in favour of occasional visitations, unavailability making the cherished one so much more maddeningly attractive. As the conversation progressed an element of wistfulness was evident. Georgia saw that they all secretly craved more than was their allotted slice of the action and felt that this was the best juncture at which to go and powder her nose and then haul Jean/Jeanne away from Letti. She knew however much she pined for him to make a commitment he was only ever going to see her to suit himself. She'd learnt compromise very early on in their relationship, she knew the score.

Shutting herself in Letti's chrome and white bathroom Georgia ran both wrists under the full blast of the cold tap to sober herself up, one of the more useful habits she'd learnt from Bruno. Georgia scrutinised her reflection – large dark eyes in a white face, purple-painted lips, gaunt body sinuous and prepared like a taut spring. Prepared for what? She was safe here. She helped herself to a spritz of Letti's perfume, envying her the surroundings, the minimalist luxury. She knew a few fragmented details about Letti fleeing some foreign country years ago amid uprising and death, sole custodian of the family fortune. Little wonder her counsellor had chosen the psychiatric field as her profession. Still, it made Letti more like the rest of them. None of them had anything much to do with their families now, after the acts they'd committed. Georgia thought it was for the best. She imagined how her cousin Clive would have introduced her to his partner, Steven, over dinner.

'Steven, this is cousin Georgia, she's been in a secure prison for a while – pass the cranberry jelly please – Georgia cracked her boyfriend's head open with a paperweight because he smashed up our grandmother's china doll – is the pheasant cooked in the middle? It looks a bit bloody – Poor old Bruno bled all over the Axminster. Georgia, this is Steven. He's been dying to meet you.'

It just wouldn't do, thought Georgia. Nice families didn't go a bundle on having murderesses in their midst, even after they'd served their time. So she hadn't contacted hers and they hadn't contacted her – not that they knew where she was nowadays. Pity all the same, she'd got on with Clive. His front door was the exact shade of her purple lipstick and his mind was as broad as his intellect. He'd probably have been delighted to welcome her back into society but it was Georgia's choice. She'd wanted a fresh start, anonymity, a blank sheet. Now Jean/Jeanne was scribbling all over it.

Georgia stared at her reflection and challenged herself to get on with her life, drink less whisky, make more of herself and her time. Letti had given her the key to survival. She owed it to Letti to make progress. Georgia knew Jean/Jeanne was a dangerous influence. She did adore him, but as she stood alone, locked in the small bathroom a revelation struck her. She'd had flashes of realisation while locked in her cell, perhaps the confinement allowed her to channel her thoughts. Jean/Jeanne was a wonderful diversion, a great companion, avant-garde, daring and beautiful to hang out with but she knew he would never possess her one hundred per cent. Perhaps she didn't love him. It would never be like Bruno. Georgia, in those few private moments, cool and calculating, temporarily sober and reflective, reached a decision. She could take him or leave him. She was in control.

The hallway was redolent with the fragrance of lilies, like the lilies Jean/Jeanne had brought to her earlier today. From the kitchen doorway Georgia could see Letti preparing vegetables and engaged in earnest conversation with Jean/Jeanne who sat silhouetted in the alcove repeatedly raising a glass to his lips. They both had their backs to Georgia.

The kitchen smelt invitingly of fresh vegetables, wine and herbs. On the marbled worktop, just inside the doorway stood a black onyx pestle and mortar holding the pungent crushed garlic cloves. Georgia looked at it and marvelled at what a complex mix Letti was: efficient home-maker, professional businesswoman, friend, exile and style-guru. It was formidable how she was able to juggle her roles. Georgia thought it little wonder that Letti and Jean/Jeanne had so much to discuss in the kitchen. They were both people with many strings to their respective bows. Georgia waited for a suitable moment to walk up and interrupt what appeared to be an animated discussion.

'Go piss off!' Letti's voice rose angrily. Georgia backed into the shadowy hallway, listening horrified. 'If Georgia or Angela ever find out you're promising them both the earth, playing one against the other as Jean/Jeanne or Paris while keeping God knows how many other fans pining by the telephone, champing at the bit, I'll kill you!' she threatened feistily, drawing her small frame up to its full height of five foot two and looking more than a little bit crazed, one hand waving the paring knife, the other crushing a pepper.

'Okay, stay cool, I'm out of here, Honeybunny.' placated Jean/Jeanne in one of his deeper voices, forgetting momentarily who he was supposed to be.

Letti's face changed dramatically, the furious flush gave way to an ashen pallor. Not so much because it was her Jon's voice coming from the strangely familiar beauty's perfectly painted lips, addressing her by the private nickname she thought was their shared and cherished secret – but more because of the shocking swiftness with which Georgia, mascara tears coursing down her white cheeks, slid silently into the room. Without hesitation Georgia took the onyx mortar, garlic and all, hefted it and smacked her false idol accurately across the back of his bewigged skull causing him to collapse in front of Letti in graceful slow motion before the word 'Honeybunny' had faded on his lips. This type of behaviour came easily to Georgia, thought Letti abstractedly – and why not? Been there, done that, got the blood-spattered T-shirt.

Elizabeth, Angela and Penny, upon hearing the thump of Paris ricocheting against the kitchen table, causing Letti's casserole dish to smash onto the slate floor, immediately downed glasses and took to their feet like racehorses, appearing a few seconds later, screeching and open-mouthed in the kitchen doorway like the three witches from *Macbeth*. The tableau confronting them stunned them to silence. Jean/Jeanne lay face downwards on the floor, still alive but not kicking. He'd lost his dark wig and his long, Paris-blond hair was clearly visible. Angela recoiled in horrified recognition.

Letti, kneeling in a ratatouille of olive oil,

vegetables, red wine and Jean/Jeanne's blood, slowly turned him over. His eyes were open but unfocused and he'd lost one brown contact lens. Georgia, reeking of garlic and shaking violently, had seated herself and was weighing the weapon from hand to hand. 'My death is like an open door,' blithely sang Scott Walker from the den, 'a patient girl who knows the score.'

Very fucking apt, thought Letti, reverting from wronged girlfriend to analytical counsellor as she rose from the floor like a phoenix from the ashes and faced her gasping guests.

'Don't touch him yet, he's hardly going to move far is he? Yes Angela, this is Paris. Yes Georgia, he's also your Jean/Jeanne and what causes me the greatest grief, although my professional training has supposedly equipped me with an immunity to the unbelievable, I'm astonished to inform you all that here also lies my Jon . . . My not-very-often-available, eligible Mr Wonderful. So it seems we're in this together girls.'

'More than you know, Letti,' contributed Penny, dangerously drunk and doubly disappointed. 'I claim the right to give this bastard a bubble bath, something we all know I'm incredibly good at. Should it be my pleasure to remove his make-up and clothing it will become patently obvious that we also have my Jeremy lying here before us. My gorgeous, gallery owner, the man who calls me Honeybunny. Of course I didn't recognise him at first without his trademark half-tub of hair gel or his precious silk waistcoat . . . well, well, well, and to think only last night I dreamt my faithful but not-easy-to-pin-down lover was wearing five bloody wedding rings!'

Elizabeth wasn't saying anything at all. She had retreated further back down the hallway and was busily throwing up over the cloying and now wilting lilies. James, she mourned, how could you pretend to be in Suffolk with your parents every weekend? They probably don't even exist.

James wasn't reading her thoughts, however. He lay supine, like a big, golden run-over cat. One blurred unfocused brown eye, one dull blue one staring at nothing. He looked for all the world like a wise and fine tom cat who'd used up his ninth life and now lay twitching and helpless, at the mercy of the next vehicle to happen by. A bit like one of my brother Philip's tortured pets really, considered Elizabeth, suppressing the urge to put her injured James out of his misery – well that's what she'd had to do scores of times after Philip's abominations, hadn't she? She pulled herself together and felt that familiar jolt of fury and self-preservation.

'Pity there's not a water well here Letti,' she said as she rejoined the chaos in the kitchen, 'because whoever you think this is on the floor, he is also my 'Wednesday man', my James, and it may surprise you to know that I'm not going to drip and droop about in the expected village-girl manner à la 'I heard a maiden singing – Oh don't deceive me' style of behaviour. Oh no, I fancy playing nasty with this James or Jeremy or Jon or Jean/Jeanne or Paris or whatever he sodding well calls himself because I'm angry, very angry! If there was a well right outside in your communal gardens, I promise that I would have no hesitation in pushing this fake bastard down it!'

Thank God there isn't, thought Letti. The others remained silent. Elizabeth wasn't prone to using strong language. They let her continue.

'I dreamt about James last night. In my dream he was wearing a tiny emerald earring. I woke up puzzled at such an out-of-character aspect of my fine, tweedy travelling salesman, my false fiancé. Now look at him, earrings in both ears, full make-up and drag. Boy! This load of shit I've been dealt that masquerades as life never fails to surprise me.' Her voice altered and became childish and sing-song. 'You were right all along, Marjorie-down-the-well . . . you spoke to me in my head, tried to warn me.'

Oh Christ! groaned Letti inwardly, she's reverting, becoming unravelled. They probably all are. I feel like sodding well joining them. After all it's me who's spent an entire career expounding my theory that insanity is invincible.

16

Comeuppance

On the kitchen floor, Paris regained consciousness and tested his senses one by one. He could smell red wine and garlic. He could hear a child chattering in a sing-song voice about someone called 'Marjorie-down-the-well'. He could taste blood in his mouth where he'd bitten into his tongue at the moment of impact. He couldn't see very clearly because one of his coloured contact lenses had lodged under an eyelid. He was sure he could speak but in the present circumstances thought it prudent to keep silent until he'd developed a strategy.

Something was bothering him, an aspect of his situation that caused a groan of despair to escape his lipstick-smeared lips. He couldn't feel or move his legs! Pressing his perfectly manicured fingernails into his palms and clenching both fists, relief washed through his clouded mind in a brief moment of respite. From the waist downward he could feel nothing but he still had sensations in both hands. Don't panic Paris, stay cool, he chanted to himself. It's only temporary. You've had a nasty crack on the head. He addressed himself as Paris, his given name, because when he wasn't in the mood for theatre he settled for his original self and he certainly wasn't feeling up to play-acting at the moment.

To celebrate his name, Paris had been bundled off at the age of four to Cornwall by Mother and her clique of upper-crust pseudo-hippie kaftan-draped female support group for some sort of pagan christening. He could still recall being dunked into a freezing pool beside a waterfall then being clutched to various patchouli-scented breasts while somebody chanted mumbo jumbo poetry, after which he'd been divested of his favourite party dress while four naked women danced around him in a voluptuous pink and white parody of 'The Farmer Wants a Wife'.

Nothing surprised Paris. Back at nursery school he'd yearned to be called something solid and British like Jon, Jeremy or James. He liked those names and he'd certainly compensated for it in later life – compensated too well.

Paris tried to move his legs again. Nothing. He decided to play dead until he recuperated. I'm in shock, that's all, he thought. Yes that's it. One of the strumpets has hit me with something heavy. They'll start panicking soon and look after me – they love me don't they? One major aspect of his personality remained untouched: his misplaced vanity.

'I'm going to give him a bath as I promised. Are you going to stop me, Letti?' enquired Penny, back in control of herself, vengeful and imperious.

Letti won't let this happen, thought Paris as the fingers of his left hand began to tingle and numbness slowly claimed more of him.

'Feel free,' answered Letti indifferently from her new position. Letti had entered the no-man's-land of indecision and emerged on the other side of the fence with the wicked minority. She experienced an alien emotion and allowed it to flourish. Letti felt murderous.

'Here, take these matches, Angela. Go and light the candles in the bathroom and draw a lovely deep bath for our special guest. Leave the choice of scented bath oil to Penny, I know she's into aromatherapy, or she used to be until Champagne Perry spoilt it all for her. Perhaps our gentleman caller might be able to revive her interest.'

Angela performed the task. She felt strong as she pocketed the matches; they were a familiar weapon. Paris, who'd been drifting in and out of consciousness came to as he was unceremoniously deposited up to his chest in ylang-ylang scented bubbles by all five of them. He could barely turn his head. The small candle-lit steam-filled bathroom seemed overcrowded. They all peered down at him like witches round a cauldron, smiling. Paris didn't smile back. Neither did he speak, he couldn't, but he could still think clearly and smell the overpowering scent of the musky bath oil. Four of them left, quietly shutting the door behind them, leaving him alone with Penny.

Paris realised with embarrassed fury that at some point he'd been stripped of his clothes and wig. Since Mother he'd allowed no one to mess around with him until he gave permission. During his affairs with women he'd always taken the lead and now here he lay, head propped between the taps, helpless and immobile, watching Penny divest herself of her clothing, tying up her hair in a knot and thus raising her still-beautiful and generous breasts before matter-of-factly climbing in with him – a ball of cotton wool in one hand, a bottle of something indefinable in the other. Oh God! She's got chloroform or something! he panicked. She's going to put me out, kill me.

Penny read his mind.

'Oh don't be so silly, Jeremy. I'm just going to remove Jean/Jeanne's make-up, it's spoilt anyway and then we're going to play a lovely game called Champagne Perry!'

Letti tapped on the door and entered carrying a black lacquered tray bearing a bottle of champagne and one crystal flute. The women didn't speak to each other, merely nodded as if every action was pre-rehearsed. Paris had trouble seeing clearly because several of the candles had been extinguished by the steam which swirled around Penny. Her oily body glistened in the half-light causing her to appear quite beautiful. Ruthlessly beautiful. But Paris was powerless to respond as, straddling him, she languorously soaped her breasts with circular caresses as if she had all the time in the world. Time to indulge oneself was considered a precious commodity by those who had done time.

Penny leaned over and poured herself a glass of champagne.

'As there's only one glass you'll be drinking yours out of the bottle, Jeremy. That's the way we play this game,' she explained.

Paris was in watery hell. Time and time again she inserted the bottle between his clenched teeth, chipping them and forcing him to swallow until he almost, but not quite, choked to death. Again and again she grasped handfuls of his soaking, blond hair and ducked him beneath the bath water before hauling him upwards just in time, each time at the very last moment before his lungs exploded. She clasped his rigid, powerless torso against her own slippery, writhing one before ducking him again until he almost drowned – but not quite. Penny was christening him again. It was much worse than with Mother. Whatever she'd done to him during their many bizarre bathtime rituals, Mother had never harmed him – physically.

Penny was much more careful this time. She knew what to do, had done it all before, got the wet T-shirt.

'Bend me, shape me any way you want me,' sang Penny at the top of her voice.

Paris couldn't feel his body but he was soon aware that he was being hauled out of the bath and dragged along Letti's hallway where the women propped him in a sitting position next to a huge vase of wilting lilies, his gift to Letti when everything had been all right. Now everything was not all right. Paris could see the door which led to the outer communal hall and freedom. He coughed up soapy water. Naked and livid he stared at his captors, held their collective mocking gaze with his ice-blue one. Both brown contact lenses were long gone down the plughole as had a lot of his self-assurance.

Then they had the good grace to dress him again in his black sweater and jeans. This Paris found much more humiliating than Penny's enforced champagne bath. Convinced that he'd been about to drown, Paris clutched at the smallest straw – perhaps now they'd had their silly bit of wronged-female revenge they'd get him to a hospital. They brought him to the outer door. Maybe they intended to put him into the hall outside where he could call for one of the other residents to help him – if he could call.

Are you putting me outside? asked Paris.

His brain formulated the question, his mouth opened but all his vocal chords would produce was an incoherent series of grunts. As the effect of Georgia's mortar attack took hold of Paris' brain the various vital functions were shutting down. He felt as if he was an empty house where someone within was methodically traversing each room, pulling the window blinds down firmly and shutting each door for ever, preparing to depart. Paris held on to the redeeming factors that he could still see and hear and that his intelligence and awareness remained intact. But what good was this with a paralysed body? He seethed with fury, his sapphire stare locking with the triumphant gaze of each of the women in turn. Unabashed they stared back.

Penny, bright-eyed and elated now she'd laid her ghost, done what she'd originally meant to do to Champagne Perry – given him a good fright without killing him.

Georgia, black eyes full of disappointment and contempt, disgusted with herself for falling for such a charade after the street wisdom learned from Bruno.

Angela, his latest flame, eyes filled with relief and self-preservation, delighted they'd only just begun their association, euphoric that she'd escaped to a greater degree the torture the others must be going through. Even though she'd been his latest acquisition she had loved him. Love at first sight. Angela was an obsessive.

Letti, whose eyes he searched for a rational conclusion to all this madness. Letti, the one who hadn't committed a crime of passion. Surely he'd find a shred of compassion there, but no such luck. Of all of them, Letti's eyes held the most vitriol and hatred.

Finally Elizabeth, the one who in Paris' considered opinion adored him the most, would do anything for her James, her tweedy dependable 'Wednesday man'. She would surely save him. But her expression was blank and shuttered. Paris' gaze bore into hers but Elizabeth's eyes were as dead as those of the little girl at the bottom of a well. Paris continued to stare. The lights were on but there was no one at home. And as he stared at her she moved towards him, opened the outer door, bent and put her strong country-bred arms under his armpits and dragged his limp body down the echoing passage which led from Letti's front door.

The passageway was shadowy in the fading light of the winter afternoon. From his new position propped against the metal doors of the communal rubbish chute Paris could see the remaining quartet of women standing just outside Letti's door, hands on hips, waiting and watching.

Bear baiters, cock fighters, he hissed inwardly. Fucking vulture, he fumed as with the same strength she'd employed to help Uncle Bernard handle bales of hay at harvest time, Elizabeth swung open the doors to the chute, hefted and tipped Paris forward and downwards into its sour-smelling maw.

'Ding-dong-bell, Paris-down-the-well,' the adult Elizabeth chanted in the nine-year-old Elizabeth's voice. Paris fell downwards, paralysed and powerless.

Letti's apartment was situated towards the top of the building. It seemed a very long time before Paris hit the sparse amount of bin bags lying at the bottom which did little to break his fall. He wished people wouldn't put bottles into their bin bags. What the hell did they think bottle banks were for? Mercifully he couldn't feel his shattered legs but his brain logged the crunch as they fractured. Unlike Philip's muddy and bloody demise, Paris' wounds appeared minimal when observed by the five women who'd flocked into the lift and travelled in considerably more comfort than he had to his present location. Elizabeth was pleased with herself. She'd exacted a very satisfactory revenge and this one hadn't died like Philip. Her brother Philip's death seemed somehow less horrific now – more of a rehearsal that had gone wrong.

There wasn't a soul about to rescue him. Paris

couldn't believe his misfortune. Every resident's door remained firmly closed as five pairs of hands lifted him. His jeans from the knees downwards were sodden with the blood from his useless legs. Letti took two heavy-duty black plastic bin bags from the neat stack stored at the chute exit and manoeuvred Paris' feet into one, taping it at his waist. Had he been able to register pain he'd have screamed blue murder. Had he been able to speak someone might have heard him, had someone been around to hear. The other bag she placed over his head. Between them the women rolled him along the floor until he was tightly wrapped in his black plastic shroud. To the casual observer he might have been a six foot wide roll of carpet. Thus packaged it was a piece of cake to bundle him into the waiting lift and up again to the door of Letti's apartment.

Paris could barely breathe but he could still hear. Just as Letti was turning her key in the lock to regain access he heard one of the neighbouring doors open. Paris tried to writhe. His dead muscles refused to function. He attempted to call out, a mouthful of inhaled black plastic stifled his feeble grunts. But his hearing seemed more acute, compensated for by his terrible disabilities.

'Good evening, ladies,' said what sounded to Paris like a male with an Arabic accent. 'May I help you with your heavy burden?'

'Thank you, but the five of us are quite capable

and you look well loaded with luggage yourself,' replied Letti, cool, calm and collected. 'It's a new rug for my home,' she elaborated, warming to the theme of her inventiveness.

'Very well. I bid you a happy time, ladies,' answered the portly potentate. 'I leave England now. I return to my country which is famous for its beautiful carpets. I am sure yours is as fine. I hope it brings you many pleasures.'

Will he ever shut up and piss off? thought Georgia. He bowed and picked up two bulging suitcases.

'Oh yes, this parcel brings us many pleasures!' whispered one of the murderesses out of hearing of the anonymous arms dealer as he retreated into the lift.

No! Please no! a mute Paris screamed in his head, struggling for breath. He couldn't stand the chemical, toxic stink of the plastic bag confining him. There was something else unpleasant, another smell combining with this to close his throat and clog his nostrils . . . blood. The bottom of the bag securing his lower half was filling slowly with blood oozing from his shattered legs. Paris could feel neither the pain nor the stickiness lining the bag but he felt fear. It replaced his anger as he heard the lift departing and with it his chance of salvation.

They were taking him back inside Letti's flat, they weren't taking him off the premises after all.

The bitches had stood back and let Elizabeth push him down the chute. They had indulged her insane fantasy, her crazy idea of revenge. It was some sick re-enactment of what Elizabeth had done to her brother many years ago and now they were going to play more vengeful, dangerous games with him. They were animals. It was preposterous, unthinkable!

Paris had always been the ringmaster, allocating his time to these biddable baser beings, controlling them, coaxing them to perform, devising elaborate acts in his exclusive personal circus. He'd thought he could proudly mingle incognito amongst them in a grand finale, pull off his greatest stunt yet but now he was the stooge, the entertainment. It had degenerated into a freak show.

Divesting him of his plastic wrapping they placed him full length along one of the settees in the den, head supported by Letti's sequined cushions. He looked like an exotic captive animal, tethered by his paralysis, eyes wild and alert. 'Making him comfortable' hardly applied. The blood from his damaged legs seeped into the fabric beneath him though mercifully he felt no pain.

'We ought to put a bin bag under him, Letti,' suggested Elizabeth.

They were a tidy-minded bunch sharing a need to snip off loose ends. It came from being involuntarily incarcerated – an untidy interlude in anybody's life. None of the women liked things to be out of place. All had forfeited possessions. They thought Letti would be horrified at having her upholstery ruined. They misjudged Letti's frame of mind.

'No! Leave him be,' she said. 'This pleasant environment and the *objets d'art* I've so lovingly collected which you see displayed around you have come to mean nothing to me. It all became irrelevant from the moment I met Jon. I was so in love. I'd have set up home in a cowshed with him if the situation had allowed. He was perfect for me – unmarried, handsome, bright, respectful of the confidentiality imposed by my work, independently wealthy, the lot. Jon was everything a woman imagines her white knight to be. He had a great sense of fun, would tease me about my serious demeanour, my theories and beliefs. Often, whether going away on business or for no reason at all, he'd send me lilies – flowers for his Honeybunny.

'Stylish possessions ceased to matter, eclipsed by the blaze of my mistaken misplaced affection. I've been very fond of someone before – Charles, an academic, a very married academic. But I've never loved, or received love in return for that matter. I honestly believed Jon loved me. Call it vanity, self-assurance, whatever. I had no earlier experience of love with which to compare the depth of his affection.

'Unfortunately I overlooked small details, glossed over the many discrepancies in Jon's explanations. I'm not one to need explanations. Having been a free spirit myself for so long I respected his need for a degree of private space, secrecy if you like. He made statements and I believed. Statements regarding his love for me, his intentions, his whereabouts . . . I questioned nothing, accepted all. What a mistake! I neglected to keep something of myself harboured for a rainy day. I should have secreted away a slush fund of emotions just in case. Now it's raining cats and dogs – wild cats and rabid dogs!'

Angela was listening to Letti as she sat cross-legged amongst her hostess's music collection, browsing and brooding. 'My ship is coming in,' Scott Walker's towering voice soared triumphantly through the apartment. There were no neighbours to complain.

'Yes, that's about the measure of it,' continued Letti. 'Just imagine . . . I am at the peak of my career in private practice, plus I hold an enviable consultancy in a renowned hospital. I have sole access to family wealth, amassed through generations of hard work and prudent investment – and now safely squirrelled away in an offshore account. My ship had certainly come in with Jon the charismatic captain on the bridge. I boarded and believed we'd sail our dream boat off into the sunset. And what am I left with? Debris, flotsam, a monumental shipwreck.

'Believe me ladies, a bloodstained settee is the least of my concerns! Now I truly know what it was like for you to be rejected and deceived, what made you dangerously furious. But you four have been dealt a double hand of losing cards. This is my first major heartbreak. My dreams have shattered, my cosy, ordered little world's exploded but I've hit the ground running and I feel very much inclined to keep running, back down the rocky road to my humble beginnings. Climbing the ladder of material and emotional success has got me absolutely nowhere. I'm left with a fifth share of the booby prize and just look at him! Here he lies, on the very same settee where he first seduced me – if seduced is the word, for I was more than willing. As we all were I suppose.'

'Weren't we just!' spat Penny. 'But he was so deliciously sensuous and irresistible. After vowing never again to co-habit with a man until he married me what did I do? Bump into a man so apparently suitable that I took short cuts without doing any groundwork or wondering about his circumstances. He was so truly the man of the moment that I happily built a house of straw, castles in the sky, dreams of domesticity on thin ice. It's just like a story my mother used to tell me about a bird settling comfortably on a warm chimney pot, thinking it will stay warm forever when all its little friends are flying off to sunny places. When the frost sets in, the bird sits there freezing to death in its stupidity, not daring to move.

'To give him his due Jeremy never actually promised anything concrete. He said every gift and trinket was a token of our engagement. He didn't seem married but I suspected he might have been because he was so dismissive of the subject of his domestic arrangements. I mean, for God's sake, how could I think I had a solid future with a man and not even know his address? After all the sordid business with Champagne Perry I hid my head in the sand for self-preservation. What fifty-something woman with a history like mine wouldn't? It's quite simple. I dared not ask in case the bubble burst. I made excuses to myself for him and ignorance was bliss. It wasn't until I got together here last night with you girls and listened to myself singing his praises that the doubts already lying dormant were awakened. We think we've ensnared the fake lover who conned us don't we? But what we have lying here is nobody at all.'

'What do you mean?' asked Elizabeth.

Penny enlightened her.

'This beautiful battered bastard who's probably bleeding to death as we sit here affords us only a Pyrrhic victory. He isn't Jeremy, he was only Jeremy in my eyes. Yes, I've got rid of a great deal of pent-up fury by half-drowning him but in effect

I wasn't getting revenge on Jeremy was I, because Jeremy was imagined. He's not Jon, neither is he your James, Elizabeth, steady old tweedy James with a face too pretty to be a travelling salesman, who doted on his parents, who loved an ex-con and who wanted nothing more than to set up a tearoom. It just doesn't fit now does it?

'He was only ever Jean/Jeanne on his own terms too. Georgia, had the privilege of knowing him when he wasn't in drag. Just for part of his time with her he was the Byronic and rather secretive tall blond bloke who wasn't anyone in particular. Georgia must have been the most confused of the lot of us because she had access to two of him! Angela knew him as Paris in probably this same disguise.

'Now if we all try and look impartially at the man over there on Letti's settee, search the familiar yet unfamiliar features, scan the expressionless face cleansed of make-up and full of fear, fury and pain, who do we see? Mr Nobody, a stranger.'

The women all nodded. Penny warmed to her theme and spoke with fervour.

'Because our separate impressions were a fabrication, his fabrication bolstered by our wishful thinking, we'll never catch our prey will we? This isn't my Jeremy because Jeremy was an invention and I breathed life into him, conspired in his creation.'

'It kills me to admit it but I know you're right,

Penny,' said a remorseful Elizabeth. 'When James walked into the coffee bar and bothered to listen to my dreams, my hoped-for reconciliation with my mother, my desire to return to my village, my fantasies about starting up tearooms of my own, he absorbed this information and simply embroidered the basic 'if onlys', elaborated on the desires and turned them into 'why not' and 'we can do it together'. James wove a rainbow through my grey world. Who wouldn't have accepted him at face value if they'd been in the same boat as me at the time? If you're offered angel cake when you're on a diet of bread and margarine you'd spring at it just to break the monotony, even if you didn't have a sweet tooth. I was okay in my post-prison world, had a reasonable job, enough to eat, and a good counsellor who'd shored up the gaping holes in my self-esteem. 'Okay' isn't a patch on 'in love' or 'in love with a possible rosy future' is it?

'On one level I trusted him implicitly, as Penny trusted Jeremy, as Letti trusted Jon, Georgia and Angela likewise with their new best friends. Dad always taught me not to accept sweets from strangers and to watch out for the big bad wolf. Philip was a big enough, bad enough wolf, torturing small defenceless animals but what we have here is the worst type of werewolf, not just Jekyll and Hyde but a scary composite of extra personalities, disguised in the clothing of five different sheep!'

Elizabeth, drained by her outburst addressed the man she knew as James.

'What big white teeth you have, Grandma! What a clever boy you thought you were, but you didn't count on bumping into five Little Red Riding Hoods all in the same place at the same time, did you? It doesn't look much like a fairy-tale ending for you now, does it?'

She's mad. The thought crystallised in Paris' agile mind, trapped in his broken and immobile body. She was always the weirdest of the five of them. The seeds of insanity were sown when she did whatever she did to her brother. My false promises have fed and cultivated her madness in the same way she cultivated the myth that was James. Now it's all out of control. Paris remembered the empty gaze Elizabeth had granted him before hoisting him bodily down the rubbish chute. If any of them is going to kill me, cast the final stone, it's going to be her. I know these things, I know women, Mother taught me

How wrong he was.

17

Decisions

Georgia and Angela left Letti, Penny and Elizabeth sitting opposite Paris comparing broken hearts and debating his future. Returning to the kitchen and ignoring the mess on the once immaculate floor they drew the blinds against the Saturday evening winter sky. They both reflected on how time had flown and events taken so many twists and turns since Letti had placed the perfectly halved and garnished avocados before her guests only the previous evening. There didn't seem much point in removing the debris from the floor.

In the back of their minds Angela and Georgia knew they'd have to leave this place at some point before Monday morning. Neither had a clue about what to do with Paris. A state of limbo reigned in the apartment as each woman came to her decision

– that she had no intention whatsoever of trying to save her lover, tend his wounds, summon a doctor

Had Paris not been rendered incapable of utilising his acting skills he might have had a cat in hell's chance of drawing an ally, a saviour from amongst the five of them. He would have quickly assessed the one who in his opinion loved him the most, the most malleable, and switched into character to draw on her compassion. He would have given the greatest performance of his life as James maybe, if Elizabeth had been his chosen victim. He would soon have turned her around against the others, gained her sympathies and at least extricated himself from their clutches. But Paris was paralysed, grievously wounded by Georgia's blow, wounded more than he knew. Reclining on Letti's settee, lucid but unable to move, he listened intently to the women's conversation as Eric Burdon screamed in the background, 'We gotta get out of this place if it's the last thing we ever do!'

Paris wasn't going anywhere.

In the kitchen Angela and Georgia took alternate swigs from Georgia's hip flask.

'It might appear,' said Angela, 'that I am the least involved. You hit him, Penny half-drowned him, Elizabeth was responsible for smashing up his legs and this whole nightmare has taken place on Letti's premises with her blessing. I just want you to know that I'm not going to be the one to take his side and try to save him, although by the look of him I don't think he's got long even if the entire cast of *ER* turned up for supper!'

Georgia marvelled at Angela's natural gift for humorous remarks considering the dire circumstances they shared.

'I was as involved emotionally with Paris as you were,' continued Angela. 'I latch on to a man instantly if I like the look of him, that's my style. That's why I've got through so many men, gained so much experience – as Elizabeth rightly remarked on Friday when I was talking about my life. Poor Elizabeth seemed to envy my track record, but if you go solely for looks, the gift wrapping, you usually get stuck with a bloke with a monumental ego, or some man who can't bond with you because he's always been paraded about like a Ken doll by his women. Blokes like Paris are usually flawed. Of everyone I should have spotted it and probably would have cottoned on quite soon, except for the fact that I only spent one night with him.

'That night was enough though for me to become as deeply involved as any of you. I felt exactly the same helpless abandon as when I first clapped eyes on Bill in his double-decker bus. Long courtships and fannying around until you finally get your kit off leave me cold. I was determined to get into Paris' jeans the minute he touched base from Amsterdam. I would have found him, haunted the leopardskin bar, as I call it, every night to wait for my prey. I know myself. At least my time with Letti and being locked up in that hospital taught me honesty. I'm an obsessive, a repeater. So after my one-night stand I'm in just as deep as you four. I love Paris, or the Paris that was, not that thing soiling the settee in there.'

Georgia understood. They were quite alike, Angela and herself, two painted ladies with a taste for Scotch who bore a grudge.

'I know you can't stand blokes, Georgia, since all that stuff with the hard man, but Paris was different, wasn't he?' continued Angela passing back the empty hip flask. 'Why am I talking about him in the past tense? He's still here, just not the man or woman we thought he was. Surely he won't last long with those injuries. Bizarre isn't it? We ought to be horrified at our actions. It might just as well have been me who clouted him with the mortar, or Letti could have gone for him with that cook's knife. I'm surprised she didn't. I've never seen her let go before but she doesn't care now, does she? Her world's gone tits-up too, hasn't it?'

Angela didn't expect Georgia to answer this series of questions because she believed them to be facts. She was simply making observations but her drinking partner in any case agreed with her views, was completely in tune.

Georgia was drunk but not disorderly. The

whisky expanded her perceptions, crystallised reality yet removed her from it or appeared to. Every object was bright-edged and super-clear – Angela's vivid orange hair, the blood on the floor, the yellow pepper lying on the kitchen table. She poured the remains of the discarded Fitou and pushed a goblet towards Angela who was fidgeting and full of energy now that she'd articulated her reasoning to Georgia, told it how it was.

They'd both loved Paris but they'd both loved two completely different characters and therefore neither jealousy nor competitiveness was a factor in their joint relationship. The harem would not, as Paris had hoped, split into various camps, bickering and raging amongst themselves about who'd had the best of him, been his favourite. There would be no ugly scene comparable to that of a wife and a series of mistresses squabbling at a wake over their man, the same man. Paris' five dalliances could only recognise one fifth of him, their particular lot. The James bit allocated to Elizabeth, the Jon bit that was Letti's temporary pleasure to have known, the Jeremy character adored by Penny, Georgia's Jean/Jeanne and Angela's Paris.

Thus in the aftermath of the incomprehensibly shocking unveiling of their demigod as a shared lover their reactions were not at all as they might have been. They became like five widows pacing a storm-lashed quayside, mutually mourning their drowned fishermen, five different fishermen. Their shared loss and combined assaults strengthened them as a whole rather than split them. Whatever they decided, and a decision was going to have to be made soon, they'd be in absolute unison. There had been five of Paris and because of this his prey were now as one.

Angela was restless, hyped up, preparing for something. To run? She didn't know yet. They all had 'the buzz' if her own feelings were anything to go by, adrenalin was kicking in and The Grudge was very evident in the apartment, weaving through their minds like the sinuous source of raw energy that it was.

'In theory we ought to be at each other's throats,' rationalised Georgia. 'But he wasn't such a genius after all. He was so good at what he did, so believable, that we're treating him as separate men and we all know what we did to our original separate men when the going got tough! He was a very silly boy not to listen to me when I tried to talk it through with him. I honestly don't think he believed me when I told him about Bruno and the paperweight. I'll bet Penny tried to confess how she sent Champagne Perry to a watery grave, Elizabeth too. She loved her brother but didn't hesitate to push him down that well. Christ! Wasn't it a revelation to watch her shove Paris down the rubbish chute? He underestimated her capabilities big time! It was very remiss of him not to listen. Blokes are usually too in love with themselves to read the signs.

'Listen, Angela, someone in the den is having a nostalgia attack.'

Letti had fished out a rave from the grave, a scratched single by Shirley Bassey. 'Natalie' implored Bassey muzzily, the wear and tear on the vinyl causing the tragic lyric to appear even more scarred and wounded than was originally intended. 'You are young, you are free.'

None of them were young but now they'd lost their five Mr Wonderfuls they had nothing to lose but their freedom. The four murderesses were damned if Paris' imminent death was going to result in a second stretch. What did he think they were – crazy? Doing time for a crime of passion had been bad enough but being banged up for jointly killing off someone who had never existed was just too much.

'Can you believe this, Angela?' said Georgia. 'He could do stuff most blokes wouldn't dream of. It's as if he could get right inside a woman's head and know exactly what rang her bell. He could pull all the right strings, press the right buttons to get me aroused and I'd still be desperate for a re-match. That's why he got to me. I thought I'd never make love with a man after Bruno. Jean/Jeanne won me over by knowing as much about my desires as I did. That was his secret, his skill. But while he was pulling this soft, sensuous veil over my eyes in reality he was taking all and giving nothing, or appearing to give all physically but keeping back the essence of himself, his soul, his heart. I'm beginning to realise that he probably didn't have a heart or soul to give.

'Remove the character portrayals and at the end of the day when the curtain goes down, the actor – Jeremy, Jon or whoever he'd been, ceases to exist but there is nobody to take his place. When he takes off his wig, creams off his warpaint, pops out his contact lenses or kicks off his high heels there's nothing left except a faceless husk, a dummy, a male mannequin and that's what we've got in the other room.

'Here, finish this and we'll go and see what's going on in the den.' Georgia and Angela clinked goblets and, opinions aired and theories shared, they linked arms and walked purposefully down the hall. As they brushed past the vast flower arrangement, the lilies bowed their heads in further decay.

'Shame about our casserole,' remarked Letti as Georgia and Angela rejoined the group in her den. 'I'll go and rustle up a picnic. We'll eat in the dining room while we have a board meeting. We don't need an agenda do we? There's little doubt about our top priority,' she added appraising Paris with cold indifference.

Paris shuddered, or rather he felt a creepy

tingling at the back of his neck. From the neck downwards he might as well have been a corpse.

'How can we be hungry?' asked Penny. 'But then, what's happened here this afternoon is just about run-of-the-mill stuff to us considering what we got up to once, isn't it ladies? I wonder how we dared hope our lives would revert to normal once we'd been let out. Poor old Jeremy is probably clinging to the delusion that I feel remorse for what I've just done but drowning comes as standard with good old Penny, doesn't it? Bye-bye sweetie, don't get up,' she mocked as she rose from the settee opposite Paris, followed by Angela, Georgia and Elizabeth.

Letti bent and replaced a sputtering candle, absent-mindedly caressing the wings of the gargoyle which held it and equally absent-mindedly planting a kiss on the crown of Paris' head. While doing so she inhaled the scent of his hair, free of blood since Penny had bathed him. It was a preoccupied gesture, a goodbye kiss.

She kissed me! It's going to be all right now, they're going to open a few more bottles, make themselves a sandwich and discuss how to get me to a hospital without incriminating themselves. Letti's still calling the shots, they'll do as she says, she's not a murderess.

Letti ceremoniously changed the music, selecting one of her favourites for Paris to listen to while his fate was decided. 'She whispers oh such pretty lies, don't believe her,' warned The Walker Brothers urgently pressing their anthem. 'The female of the species is deadlier than the male.' Leaving Paris alone with the music swirling around him, candlelight enhancing his ruined blond head, Letti quietly clicked shut the door of her den.

Disregarding the mess in the kitchen Penny and Elizabeth were assembling brie and cranberry rolls, deftly slicing tomatoes and cutting feta. Standing with their feet in the drying puddle of wine and blood, knives glittering in their hands, they looked like a couple of surgeons performing a swift life-saving procedure. Elizabeth smiled to herself – there wasn't going to be any life-saving in this household tonight!

Angela and Letti were preparing the dining room. As Letti drew out the chairs Angela produced her precious box of matches and lit the candles and incense burner. Letti regarded the tall vase of dying lilies, some of the surplus from Jon's generous bouquet which had allowed her to decorate every room. The patchouli emanating from the brass burner fought to override their over-sweet odour of decay. Letti reminded herself she'd soon be out of here so why bother to remove the flowers? If her apartment smelt like a graveyard then surely that was appropriate.

Georgia, still fighting her claustrophobia, had offered to go down to the off-licence. Her hip flask was dry and so was Letti's wine rack. General consensus of opinion concluded it a little silly to sober up while there was difficult work to be done, nasty work, and there was nothing nicer than a designer sandwich and an elegant Bohemian glass of full-bodied red wine to bolster a girl with a distasteful task to perform. We might be mad, bad and dangerous, thought Georgia as she galloped down the stairs, but we have our principles.

The street was quite deserted it being the limbo hour after those who worked on Saturdays had gone home to an early supper and the lottery and before the party animals emerged in their finery to continue the age-old quest for a life, a laugh and if they were lucky, love. Love! thought Georgia cynically as she trudged towards her destination. I suppose I loved Bruno, though he had a strange way of loving me back. A beaten dog hangs around waiting for its master to make everything all right again, more out of inquisitiveness than faithfulness. I probably stuck it with Bruno for so long for precisely the same reason. I was pathetic, obsessed with the high motive of making good out of bad, refusing to let him go and then when I eventually wised up and shipped out I was able to see that I was the strong one. I made the decisions, called the shots. I left the relationship and when he followed me because his tiny egotistical mind couldn't accept rejection, I turned nasty because his hunting wasn't in my script. There was no alternative but to strike out, eliminate him, draw a neat line through my mistake.

And I paid for it, paid in full, did my time. When I came out I had nothing to lose. What was the point looking for another relationship? I now knew my powers. My tolerance would be such that if a bloke so much as raised a hand against me or messed with my emotions I'd kill him. I knew how, I had the secret. So I played a different game, danced to an alternative tune and when Jean/Jeanne cropped up I recognised someone as empty inside as me. I didn't even bother to ask where he lived because I didn't give a damn. He was beautiful and quite attentive. He'd go missing for days at a time. But this was more suitable than he could ever guess. It prevented me from forming too close a bond. We were two great pretenders, empty-hearted lovers, a couple of fakes.

I owe Jean/Jeanne nothing, neither compassion nor mercy. It's just his bloody bad luck that he tried to make me part of his harem. He picked someone with a soul as empty as his. Oh, I was flattered to dance to his tune, be his best girlfriend and physically he soothed me and coaxed me through some pretty rigid hang-ups that were the legacy of Bruno's lovemaking. Lovemaking! Huh!

Georgia browsed the off-licence shelves, made her purchases and teetered on the doorstep surveying the street. She had choices. She could turn right and keep walking away from it all. It would be no big deal to leave this town and go where nobody knew her. Nobody much knew her here for that matter. Her work colleagues knew only what she allowed them to know which was a fraction of the whole. Georgia had perfected her anonymity.

A left turn would take her back to Letti's flat and the fantastic charade unfolding within. Georgia had cast the first stone, whacked Jean/Jeanne with Letti's mortar for being a very silly boy, lashed out instinctively like an impatient teased cat. Now she wanted to see the end result, wrap up this distasteful package of rubbish, put a final nail into the coffin, lay her ghost. Fed up with running she turned left. The crowded breathless feelings she occasionally felt when in a lift or an enclosed space with others or when she had a big decision to make receded.

Letti buzzed her back into the stairwell and as she climbed upwards again to the apartment she paused, refilled her hip flask, took a long burning draught and toasted herself for not bolting. Letti had taught her to face the music and this was music for which she definitely knew the score. Jean/Jeanne shouldn't have reminded her of what love was supposed to be like. Jean/Jeanne had got under her skin and found a huge festering wound. Tough luck Jean/Jeanne.

Given the opportunity to run Letti was pleased Georgia had decided to return. Not only had this tested Georgia's resilience, it had exercised Letti's own powers of analysis and confirmed them to be in excellent working order. She had behaved exactly as Letti expected.

Georgia found all the women seated around Letti's dining table, empty glasses at the ready, supper tastefully laid before them. Had the helpless man with appalling injuries not been lying out of sight in the den awaiting his fate, the scene could have been mistaken for an old girls' reunion, a jewellery or lingerie party, a hen night. Penny poured the wine.

'How very apt,' she remarked, spearing a forkful of feta, greenery and olives. 'Greek salad for our Greek tragedy. Well he does look remarkably like a felled Greek god, doesn't he?'

Letti raised her glass and announced, 'You expect me to be chairperson, to direct us to a unanimous decision and steer this group through to a suitable conclusion, don't you? It's because you've been used to sitting at my feet listening to the oracle, happy to experience my unique brand of calm counselling.

'Actually I'd made up my mind to wind up my illustrious career in exchange for one of stylish subservience after Jon declared his love for me. Silly me, I had dreams of becoming a supportive and stylish wife to my handsome eligible businessman. I was going to announce my decision to you all over supper last night but as your stories unfolded parallels were becoming increasingly obvious. During supper my doubts emerged and I was able to share them with you. The maze as it untangled led us all to the central point at which stood Paris, the empty shell, my Jon unmasked.

'Of course now there'll be no rosy sunset-kissed future with Jon and I'm supposed to get on with things, continue my life in the same vein. But the revelation of our mutual boyfriend has unleashed a secret stash of insanity. Quite honestly I'm powerless to direct my actions and I don't want to. I shall join with you, collaborate in whatever has to be done without the remotest wish to lead, and then I may very well never return to my office or the hospital. How can I? I'm driven by a new set of motives: fury, disappointment, a huge grudge and admiration for you lot.

'Who knows what I'm going to do next? I certainly don't. But we're surely adamant that we're not going to be put away for anything we've collectively done recently nor the task we have no option but to complete before this weekend is over.'

'What are we going to do with him?' queried Elizabeth. 'And what'll happen to me? I injured him the most. Now that James doesn't exist I've got nothing to live for. There'll be no tearoom, no cottage with roses round the door, no babies, which means no bargaining power by which I might have got back on speaking terms with my mother, nothing. I suggest you all hot-foot it out of here as soon as possible. I'm more than happy to stay and carry the can. I don't like life on the outside any better than life on the inside. Since my release the only nice thing that has happened to me is James and look what a nasty mess that turns out to be. Lies, deceit, bullshit. I'm empty, dead inside. You saw me dump him down the rubbish chute. That's what he is – rubbish. That's what my dreams are – rotten decayed illusions. Let me sit here alone with him tonight. I'll call the police tomorrow morning and you'll all be long gone. I want to give myself up.'

She stared through them, a glazed resigned look in her eyes.

'No, Elizabeth!' said Georgia. 'We're equally to blame. Whoever finds what's left of him will never know who afflicted which wounds, who set the ball rolling – anyway it was me wasn't it? If any of us should take the rap I should, but I'm damned well not going to and neither are you, Elizabeth, Read my lips, not guilty! You're not guilty! When we leave, you leave. There's no question about it.'

Georgia smacked Elizabeth smartly across her cheek. Elizabeth snapped back into a more alert attitude, eyes refocusing, a degree of awareness returning to her expression.

'Not guilty,' she echoed back from a dark secret vault of her mind, which was her regular bolthole when things got too hot to handle.

Penny, taking advantage of the ensuing silence, raised an elegant hand and wagged a scarlet-tipped finger accusingly in the general direction of the closed door to the den. 'If none of us lays a finger on him from now onwards, individually we can hardly be held responsible for his death. Georgia didn't mean to injure him so badly when she hit him. She was just lashing out more in spite than anything else. It was an instant reaction on realising he was an impostor, a serial lover. She did it for all of us.

'Elizabeth and I have probably aggravated his condition. I'm not totally sure what Elizabeth's motives were but I merely intended to have a little sport with him while he was incapacitated. The reality of drowning him was the last thing on my mind. I suppose I wanted to toy with him to avenge his playing with me, with us all. How dare he mess around with our minds!

'I for one don't give a damn what becomes of him but I certainly do care that none of us gets put away for a bit of justifiable revenge that's gone too far. What I'm trying to say is that I propose we take him somewhere miles away when it's dark tonight, dump him like the rubbish he is, come back here, clear up Letti's flat and then get the hell out of her life and attempt to get on with the travesties that are our lives.'

'Great in theory, Liz,' considered ever-cynical Angela out loud, 'but how on earth do you think we're going to get a six-foot parcel from the heart of the town out to some remote location without being captured? We were bloody lucky to fend off that Arab bloke. What shall we do, dismember him? Oh silly me, he'll probably still be alive since we've just decided to refrain from injuring him further. Cabbies can be pretty stupid but I think one might query our cargo. Or should we lay my own particular ghost to rest and take a bus? If the driver's as thick as my Bill was he'll be too busy ogling our legs to notice us hauling a twelve-stone utility-size bin bag dripping with blood up to the top deck.

'Let's get real, I know we're pissed but this isn't an episode of *Morse*. How we spend the rest of our lives hinges on getting out of this – dare I say – minor bit of trouble compared to what we got saddled with before. It ought to be like falling off a log the second time around. Come on girls, get a grip!'

'I don't care if I never see this place again,' said Letti. 'Don't you realise how painful it is to sit at this very dining table where Jon and I have finger-fed each other asparagus, clinked these same goblets and toasted our future together. The settee he's bleeding all over was where we first made love, the bath he so recently shared with Penny is where I used to sit marinading in perfumed foam while he lovingly massaged body lotion into my work-tensed shoulders. I can't bear to recount what intimacies and precious secrets were absorbed by my bedroom walls. I'll never be able to enter my kitchen without picturing him, idly playing around on his palmtop computer, a glass of wine at his side, swapping ideas and lovers' banter while I, the stupid gullible idiot, conjured up tempting little suppers *à deux*.

'And the lilies, the lilies for Honeybunny, I never want to smell or set eyes on lilies ever again except at his funeral but of course none of us will be at his funeral, will we? Who'll arrange his funeral, does he have a family, a partner, a genuine wife, a mother?'

'Jean/Jeanne rambled on quite often about his mother,' recalled Georgia. 'I got a very disjointed account of his relationship with her. Sometimes he'd explode if I dared to question him. Then at other times, completely out of context of the subject we had been discussing, he would make throwaway remarks alluding to her. It seemed as though she and her opinions were always hovering in his mind. I'm pretty sure she's dead but he would speak about her as if she were still alive, still pulling his strings and influencing him. I think she was fat. He couldn't bear fat women. Look at me, look at us all, not an extra ounce on any of us, so we were all his type in that respect. Mother, I think, must have vetted his girlfriends in the early years and I'm pretty sure she influenced his appearance. He did say he was an only child and he and Mother used to dress up together a lot. Hence the outrageous dressing-up sessions he indulged in and insisted on repeating with me. It was almost ritualistic. He gave me little-used bottles of attar of roses, Joy, Rochas, Taboo ... and stuff you can't buy anymore like Emeraude and Evening in Paris. That's how I got the impression he was plundering a legacy, a stash of goodies from a dusty treasure trove in some grand town house. I didn't ask where he lived. It was an out-of-bounds, taboo subject.'

'So are we to presume he lives alone, this wounded man we have here?' asked Penny. 'Letti tell us all how you see this situation.'

'Go on, Letti,' added Angela eagerly. 'You're good at cutting the crap. I remember after every counselling session you'd weed out the salient points, the crucial progress we'd made and the bad bits that still needed a lot of attention. You'd lean forward in your chair, in your lovely cool office and tell me the absolute truth in a few sentences, economically but wonderfully precise. Each time I left I would be a little better, a little improved, less screwed up, more whole.'

'You're so right Angela, I'd quite forgotten how strong Letti made me feel at my blackest time. The feeling of strength has stayed with me, so much so that I tend to take my cure for granted. I never want to feel like I did when Letti first set eyes on me, none of us do. Let's remember how beaten down and hopeless we were. Let's beware of putting ourselves at any further risk.'

Letti smiled self-deprecatingly, leaned forward in her familiar counsellor pose and gave her guests what they wanted.

'Right! His name as far as we know is Paris. He's wealthy, probably lives alone in his dead mother's house. There's been no mention of a father or siblings and our fears that he has a wife are probably groundless. He isn't into computers, neither is he a gallery owner or a travelling salesman. We've all had first-hand evidence this afternoon of what a plausible drag artiste he is and so what he's told Georgia and Angela is probably true, or at least this is how he occupies part of his time and it's likely to be an area in which he may be missed.

'He's a plausible liar, articulate, well educated, undeniably handsome and has no moral code whatsoever, at least in his dealings with women. I'd go so far as to say he hates women, all women because of some strong influence, physical or mental, exerted over him by his mother. This is a man bent on evening the score, already damaged and scarred far beyond anything we five have inflicted upon him.

'He appears to possess an arrogance, a self-absorption that renders him invincible to pain. He is unaware that he is mortally injured. He believes nothing and nobody can touch him. I can see in his eyes that he still searches for a solution to his predicament in one of us, believing us to be vulnerable to his charms despite the fact that we are now aware of his duplicity, his multiplicity! He can't believe his bad luck.'

'Never mind a thumbnail sketch, tell all. This is fascinating, Letti,' observed Georgia. 'What else?'

Letti coolly reached for the slivovitz, tossed back a generous shot and resumed her account.

'We didn't lure him here to seek revenge. His arrival was purely due to a random set of circumstances. I admit that after hearing Georgia's and then Angela's description of their new heart-throbs I had them marked as one and the same. Not in a thousand years did I expect one of his invented characters to be my Jon, the only man I'd let myself truly love, the only man I've been close to or have let into my life as the hoped-for permanent fixture.

'Georgia witnessed my shock when Paris in the role of her Jean/Jeanne made a bad mistake and addressed me as Honeybunny, his pet name for me. She absorbed my rage. If she hadn't struck him with the mortar I would have carved him up with my paring knife as surely as I was slicing into that pepper. All the feeling was there, the white-hot crazy, forbidden, wild, grudge-led impromptu hatred. Does this describe it? You've each experienced it. That moment was my turn to experience the same as you. It must be like dying after a terminal illness, you suddenly fall in and know the answer to a forbidden question.

'Georgia got to him first otherwise it would have been me. Elizabeth and Penny had a little necessary sport with him, as would Angela given the chance. It was purely random, all of it. Paris has met with an unfortunate accident. This accident happens to have occurred on my premises. My premises are temporary, they and their contents mean nothing to me. I could just walk away and never look back. I could leave my career and never bat an eyelash.

'I've told you, my decision was made to chuck it all in for Jon. I have no reason to change my thinking, rather I'm going to adapt it. I'm still going to give it all up. I no longer feel equipped to make evaluations on the many-layered subject of insanity or rare and abnormal behaviour because now I too have exhibited extreme and rare behaviour. The oracle has been hoist with her own petard.

'So ladies, Paris as far as we're all concerned, now that his aliases have been blown, is in effect unknown to us. He bears injuries which are the result of random circumstances leading to an accident and he lies on premises which can be and will be shortly evacuated forever. Four of the women who are witness to his predicament belong nowhere in particular, having severed close family connections or having been ostracised by friends and family due to their previous record of unacceptable behaviour. I, the fifth witness, fully intend to keep running when I exit this apartment and this situation and not touch ground until I'm on home soil.

'There'll be a brother or a cousin somewhere in my shattered and ruined homeland to welcome the prodigal shrink plus what's left of the family fortune back into the fold. I might just marry the local dentist. He was the prime feature of my parents' blueprint for my future before I flew the nest! By now he'll be pot-bellied, balding and endearingly reliable, the complete antithesis of Jon. I'll bake bread and we'll guzzle slivovitz and exchange domestic banalities until our diamond wedding after which I'll die peacefully having requested any flowers except lilies at my funeral.

'In truth wishful scenario and happy ending aside I will go home and I will seek out any remaining relatives but I expect the war and present dictatorship have rendered both my town and my kin unrecognisable and impossible to locate.

'I think we should leave Paris alone and walk out of this apartment under cover of night, all of us – including Elizabeth who we will not allow to weaken. None of us must weaken!'

'Where will we go?' asked Elizabeth. 'Nobody knows we're here do they. Did any of you tell anybody at all where you were going on Friday evening?' The realisation and irony struck the group of women almost simultaneously.

'I told Jeremy before he went off on his buying trip,' Penny stated.

'I told James before he went to Suffolk to see his parents,' said Elizabeth.

'Before he went off to his mythical computer symposium I told Jon I was entertaining some ex-clients.'

'I told Elouise in Hades wine bar that I couldn't stay and chat with her upwardly-mobile friends because I wanted an early night. Elouise isn't the type of friend you pass over in favour of a prior arrangement. She always has to be top kiddie. Even if I had told her the truth she wouldn't have been listening. Elouise is only really concerned with herself and she was the centre of attention as usual, swigging cocktails, the sycophantic satellites homing in when I left. I don't think she even said goodbye.

'If I'd been able to locate the recent object of my desires, Paris, I suppose I would have told him. Huh! Amsterdam. It's amazing how we believe what we want to hear, isn't it?' remarked Angela bitterly.

Georgia smiled ruefully. 'At lunchtime today I told Jean/Jeanne I'd been to a great dinner party last night. Then I invited him to meet someone as special to me as him. I didn't name Letti or any of you. It was going to be a brilliant diversion to amuse him, a game where he could really be one of the girls. It was also going to be a bit of a cabaret for you, a chance for you to meet my 'new best friend'.

'He obviously realised at the last minute that we were heading for Letti's flat, but because he was so bloody arrogant and sure of himself in his disguise he took a risk and gambled on Letti not knowing him as her Jon. He'd been such a pillar of strength to Letti, so male, so blond, normal and suitable he banked on her being oblivious to his charade. It was feasible. After all, when he knocked on my door and stood there with an armful of lilies, looking incredibly plausible in full drag complete with black wig, coloured contact lenses and flawless make-up, I didn't know him. I had a great deal of difficulty equating him with Jean/Jeanne, the look I'm used to – the blond blue-eyed bloke and part-time entertainer in The Sphinx and Lynx – your leopardskin bar, Angela. I was fooled although I was well aware of his habit of cross-dressing. But, Letti, you didn't know, it's the last thing you would have expected of Jon so I suppose he thought he could fool you for as long as it took to fabricate an excuse leading to a sharp exit.

Angela was fuming. 'He called us all Honeybunny, even me who he'd just met. Bye, Honeybunny, he said as he put me in a cab and went off to whoever's turn it was to be duped. We all believed the Honeybunny nickname was an individual and precious name, shared solely between our lover and ourself. We thought it was intensely private, his endearment for his pet. All he was doing was labelling us identically to make it easy for himself. He knew he might slip up and call Letti Georgia or Angela Penny, or Elizabeth Letti. Bastard! I bet there's a florist somewhere in this town who considers Paris his best customer. Wow! They must have thought Honeybunny was quite a girl if every bloody bouquet he ordered was multiplied by five. Honeybunny got showered with a hell of a lot of lilies didn't she?

They all turned and looked at the lilies in the dining room. Like those in the hall the stems were flaccid in their greenish, slimy water, necks bowed as if weeping. The heads were cast down towards the table top, shrivelled petals browning and beginning to curl.

In the den Paris' once sensitive hands, now with fingernails broken and dirtied from his trip down the rubbish chute, were starting to curl and stiffen in creeping paralysis like the claws of a crab, beached on its back waiting in supplication for five keen-eyed gulls.

18

The Last Supper

Paris lay listening to The Animals beseeching a nameless woman to change her mind about leaving them behind – raw hopeless lyrics. He too felt raw and hopeless. It was an alien, almost forgotten emotion. He'd never yearned for anything or anyone since his youth. At six he'd wished his father had changed his mind about leaving him behind. At sixteen he'd yearned to leave his mother and her suffocating attentions. But since Mother's death he'd possessed everything he desired. If he became bored with a woman, a city, a book or a diversion, he would reject what irritated him and move on. The world had been his oyster which he'd swallowed eagerly, gleaning its aphrodisiac properties. Listening, learning, laughing, taking, but never loving, never giving.

Not usually one for reflecting on his actions, he now wished he'd given a bit more of himself to any one of his five Honeybunnies but the simple reality of time management meant that to fit them all in and keep them reasonably happy he could only usually manage a fortnightly, or, if he was feeling particularly devious and energetic, weekly visit to any one of them. Juggling these women had given him a big buzz.

He'd nearly blown it when he bumped into Georgia in the early hours of Saturday morning but he'd been wearing his 'Jeremy' hair gel, 'Jon' spectacles and 'James' jacket. He'd been an amalgam of everyone that evening. He usually threw anything on in the run-up to one of his great performances, the debut of a new character. Having decided to be the new black beauty who was to stun Georgia later that day he'd been aimlessly walking the rain-lashed streets at 2 a.m. working out how to shed the Jeremy and James personae and the two women who loved them.

He'd recruited a new potential harem member called Angela in recent weeks. Surprising himself he'd told her his christened name – Paris. Angela interested him. She wore orange clothes and had scar tissue on her hands. She'd told him she'd once played with fire. She was probably a fag hag because it looked as if the bar stool she occupied in The Sphinx and Lynx was her exclusive perch and the camp couple who had been with her up until they'd had some sort of lovers' tiff and flounced out, seemed to be part of her set. Because of the company she kept Paris concluded Angela would not be adverse to his penchant for wearing drag. Besides she reminded him a bit of Georgia. Both women had alluded to getting rid of the love of their life by suspect means and being punished for it. Now, as he lay incapacitated, disjointed memories reeling through his injured head, Paris fervently wished that he'd listened when his conquests had granted him the odd insight to their history.

Adding Angela to his harem necessitated a cull, a killing off of the cloying attentions of a couple of the women with whom he'd become bored. Paris, before getting into this present predicament, had made a measured decision to shed Penny who was getting a bit long in the tooth, not fat like Mother but dangerously near the age at which Mother had become most troublesome and demanding. Elizabeth would have had to have gone too because she was making noises about tearooms and moving to the country and having children – a fantasy he'd readily fed, but it was getting dangerously near the moment when he'd have to put his money where his mouth was. Pity really, Elizabeth was the least trouble of the bunch, very low maintenance but marriage – ha! Paris laughed at the ridiculous idea, or tried to. His vocal chords only produced a strangled grunt.

He had intended to keep Letti – she was the

cleverest, the most astute. She was also the plainest but he forgave her that because her brain was so attractive. They'd indulged in pillow talk about travelling to Letti's homeland. She wanted a career change, a complete life shift and Paris was tempted. He adored travel and he was confident he'd be able to dump her if she proved too clingy once she'd introduced him to enough eastern European contacts for him to go on from there.

Paris knew himself too well. He invariably went on from 'there' – the point where he had elicited as much interest and information from his conquests as desired then sated he would up sticks and vanish without a backward glance. Paris knew himself well but nobody else did. Those who crossed his path were granted a complete fabrication or a cameo insight to the real man. Friends and relationships were meaningless to Paris – he feasted and moved on. Paris really was 'Mr Nobody'.

Johnnie, the proprietor of The Sphinx and Lynx, knew him best of all. He had merely covetously admired Paris on the occasions they spoke yet astutely he described him to Angela as a vampire figure.

Paris could still move his neck slightly. From his position on the settee, out of the corner of one blue eye he studied the frozen stare of the painted Pharaoh bearing the weight of the long glass table top directly next to him. The golden lips of the effigy seemed to smirk by the light of the flickering candles.

It's okay for you, Paris directed his anger at the decorative bulk lying in state beside him. In your lifetime it was considered normal for you to pose and preen, up to your eyebrows in turquoise eye shadow and black kohl. And a string of biddable adoring women who pandered to your every whim came as standard, didn't it? Paris raised his blue gaze and followed the kaleidoscopic fretwork patterns cast onto the dark ceiling of Letti's den as the Moroccan lamp slowly turned. The combined effect of the light, the gargoyles and the papier-mâché mock mummy's tomb planted an uncomfortable thought in his mind. I am a sacrifice lying on an altar waiting for the women who once worshipped me to decide my fate.

He was beginning to get some peculiar ideas as vital areas of his damaged brain gently shut down. He felt he was losing his grip on reality but – brain damage apart – Paris in his entire life had never once managed to maintain a grip on reality.

The last supper had progressed to the Dutch courage stage. Letti had cunningly tanked Elizabeth up on the last of her Cointreau. Elizabeth now seemed resigned to whatever task or decision lay before her. There was no longer an aura of guilt and regret about her. Georgia's well-timed slap had snapped her back into line. Georgia had a habit of smacking people around the head, thought Letti. This time the desired result had been achieved.

Georgia swigged from her hip flask, occasionally passing it to Angela. Penny rolled a brandy balloon between flattened palms and gazed into the amber contents as a fortune teller searches for a vision of the future. Her eyes never strayed from whatever she may or may not have seen working its alchemy in the bottom of the glass. She tapped the table top sharply with a silver fork and, having gained everyone's attention, stated with perfect clarity their plan for Paris.

The quintet stood and tossed back their drinks in a toast to – agreement, sisterhood, freedom? They weren't sure, probably they were saluting the complexity of the female of the species. Whatever the small ritual represented there was absolutely no doubt that it marked five becoming one against the one who pretended to be five.

The last Animals track had just finished and Paris lay in silence. He heard the five chairs scraping back as the women rose in the dining room and clinked crystal against crystal. No longer calling the shots for the first time in his life, he wanted his mother. She would have seen off these strumpets, bathed his wounds, stroked his golden hair and called him her Honeybunny.

Wounds. His excruciatingly slow brain asked his neck muscles to move. With tremendous effort

Paris lifted his head and looked down at his shattered legs. What he saw confirmed the insidious creeping worm of doubt that up until then he'd fenced off and filed away under 'impossible' in his mind. I'm trapped, I can't walk away. They always wanted me, they have me now, he thought.

He heard their whispers as they walked purposefully down the hallway. He watched as the den door opened and his ex-girlfriends filed in. They noted his fine profile, the curve of his cheekbone, his sensuous lips, the eye that was visible to them wide with fear and a trace of anger, glittering bright as a sapphire by the light of the gargoyles' candles. His thick golden hair, free of gel and wig and newly washed by Penny, flopped naturally over his perfect forehead. Paris looked exactly as he was – indefinable, asexual, a creature of immense beauty more so because he was trapped by his injuries. Just like the palest ice-blue stare of a magnificent silver wolf, leg clamped in the iron jaws of a trap, fixed on approaching hunters, Paris' gaze contained an element of refusal to accept his fate.

In this wounded man's company Letti, Elizabeth, Penny, Georgia and Angela felt an acute sadness at the shattering of their dreams. In exposing their lover they had gained no victory. Each had shot themselves in the foot, effectively devastating their individual imagined futures.

They would have preferred to continue unawares, living a lie, seeing Paris on a regular basis and deluding themselves. Paris would have made it all better, given them back their dignity, and they might have had the strength by then to go onwards, eventually leaving him before he left them. They'd have been able to recognise the signs of his boredom and given up on the relationship in a normal manner, without doing anything so drastic as drowning him, smashing his skull with a paperweight, pushing him down a well, or incinerating him. They might have cried a bit, been eternally grateful for the pleasant time they'd enjoyed with him, before parting in a polite and ladylike way.

But a lethal cocktail of fate, coincidence and the still-open wounds of past misdemeanours had blown sky high whatever bridges had been rebuilt. It was too early. They weren't ready to leave him neither were they ready for him to leave them. Elizabeth and Penny would have been mortified had they known Paris was preparing to pension them off. Either of them might have reacted with violence but as things were they'd been drawn into a wider ring of shock and anger – shock and anger multiplied by five. And now Paris' lifeblood was seeping into Letti's settee in tandem with the colour draining from their rosy dreams.

The hatred and contempt the quintet initially experienced on finding out the truth was replaced by a sense of unbearable loss. It was a bleak mourning, a yearning to turn back the clock to only a day ago when things were so different, when five excited tipsy women clung to a dream, hardly believing their luck. Flushed and gaining courage under Letti's calming tutelage the four clients had taken turns to relate anecdotes and list the attributes of their Prince Charming. Of the five guises Paris was the only one who existed to any extent and even he would soon cease to exist.

Paris managed to turn his head slightly to look at them as they slowly, like a line of pallbearers, took their places beside him. Little maids all in a row, thought Paris. Elizabeth was nearest to his head. Not so little, she was the tallest of the five. Elizabeth, his country girl who worked part time in a coffee bar, wore minimal make-up and faded florals and abhorred cruelty to animals. The latter had something to do with her brother but again Paris had been too wrapped up in his own dramas to listen. She obviously didn't have an aversion to cruelty to men considering how she'd hoisted him over the side of the rubbish chute showing no mercy. Very cruel, thought Paris. But then James, tweedy salesman James, had been very cruel to her by suddenly ceasing to be real.

Next to Elizabeth stood Angela, his petite, flame-haired newest acquisition. She watched him wide-eyed as if taking a last look at him in case he metamorphosed into someone else. He didn't blame her. Firebird Angela. He could have had endless sport inveigling his way into this one's heart. She remained motionless, a box of matches clasped in one scarred hand. His latest flame.

Next was Penny wearing Mother's earrings, one of the many gifts from groomed generous arty and utterly fake Jeremy The old master that wasn't. Good old well-preserved Penny who was going to have to go. She'll get over Jeremy, thought Paris, she's a survivor.

Then Letti, who'd studied the cases of four women with a grudge, empathised, learnt the rules and defected after being led up the garden path by the counterfeit computer buff, Jon. Paris was very disappointed in Letti, his plain Jane with a brain. She had joined the ranks of the naughty girls.

Lastly, beside his blood-soaked feet stood Georgia. Her candlelit pallor, blue-black hair, damson lips and violet-lidded eyes held him spellbound. She was the one Paris most wanted to be, if he couldn't be Mother – in her youth of course. He wanted to dress up as Georgia. Lovemaking with the other four had been robotic, a necessary function which allowed him to continue courting them. With Georgia he had almost experienced what it was like to be a woman. In his wigs and lingerie, paint and pearls, he'd got closer to Georgia than Bruno, the thug she sometimes screamed for in her sleep and as she thrashed and clung and sighed and wept in her coming.

He would have hung around Georgia for much longer. She complemented him visually and could outdrink him. She didn't want to marry him and thanks to him her self-esteem had begun to return. He had encouraged her to invent new games to play, find new venues in which to flaunt their show-stopping potential as a couple of decadent Gothic drama queens.

Unfortunately her enthusiasm for a new audience to bear witness to her new best friend had landed him in this mega-shit. Why the hell had he let himself be led over Letti's threshold? He was a fool. He had expected to dupe Letti until he could make his apologies and leave. He certainly didn't expect the others to be there. But Paris in bolstering Georgia's self-esteem had bred a monster. He wasn't sure but he thought it had been Georgia who'd hit him. She hadn't hesitated at clobbering Bruno the Brute, had she?

Paris could now believe everything Georgia had confessed to him on the many occasions they'd drunk themselves into oblivion – Paris pining for Mother, Georgia pining for the hulk she'd murdered. Murdered! Paris turned the word over in his clouding mind. These witches were out of control, it came easy to them, they'd done it all before. Letti hadn't – yet, but he could see she was more than delighted to be an accessory.

Elizabeth and Angela moved out of his line of vision. For the moment he couldn't see what they were doing. The others filed anti-clockwise round the great oblong glass top of the coffee table so that Georgia, Letti and Penny were at the far end near his feet facing Elizabeth and Angela. Letti broke away from the group briefly to move the two gargoyle-held candles to the side-cabinet where her music collection was set out. While she was there she selected her favourite CD and held it near to the candle flame to scan the cover. Apparently satisfied she programmed the player but did not press 'play'. Shock had replaced Paris' fear. He lay rigid and mute helplessly observing the silver CD shining in Letti's hand. His brain now awash with blood tricked him. He thought she was holding a star.

Silence reigned in the den until Letti, who had returned to join the others, commanded 'Lift!' Between them they raised the huge slab of plate glass and managed to heft it onto the other empty settee. The Pharaoh depicted on the sarcophagus lid was now fully visible in all his majestic gilded glory. For a papier-mâché and wooden impostor he looked pretty damned authentic. But then so had Paris. Elizabeth at one end and Georgia at the other lifted the lid and swung it open. Paris had known where he was going from the moment Letti had removed the candlesticks.

Suddenly Georgia gave a cry and ran out of the room. She loves me! She's going for help! Paris observed weakly. But she soon returned, arms full of dripping dying lilies, every lily she could find in the apartment. She threw most of them into the mummy case so that they lined its floor making a bed of festering flora. Paris when buying this generous floral tribute for Letti had also bought his own funeral flowers.

The five women lifted their dark angel, then lowered him into the casket. Letti crossed his arms over his chest and before closing the lid she placed a final bunch of dead lilies on him. It was the largest, the once cherished bouquet from her bedroom, still bearing Jon's' label of love and now a fitting epitaph to Paris, 'See you very soon, Honeybunny. Yours J.'

His sapphire eyes continued to gaze upwards in the growing darkness as the lid swung shut. Loss of vision seemed to hone Paris' one remaining unimpaired sense. He heard the heavy glass table top being replaced and the stony clunk-clunk as Letti replaced the pair of gargoyles and lit two new candles.

'Bye bye Mummy's boy!' said one of the strumpets. Paris thought it was Georgia.

He heard the women whispering amongst themselves, making arrangements and comparing strategies. After dark on Saturday night and before dawn on Sunday morning, leaving suitably long intervals between each departure, they left the apartment one by one. Letti was the last to leave. He felt her presence as she stood for a while at the head of his prison. She didn't say goodbye but before closing the door of her den she sighed and pressed 'play' on the sound system. A cathedral organ preceded Scott Walker's dark angel solo 'Archangel'. His voice as awe-inspiring as the voice of Azrael, as pure as the voice of Abdiel, soared powerfully through the rooms. Singing from his soul he taunted death. 'Silence, to hear once more, her footsteps down the lonely corridor.'

Just before dawn there were footsteps down the lonely corridor to Letti's apartment as one of the women returned. The lone figure stood in the shadows for a while as if considering a decision. She was small, flame-haired and carried a box of matches and an outdated newspaper. She suddenly extracted and struck a match and after cupping one scarred hand around it to nurture the flame ignited the newspaper. Ignoring the fresh burns the action caused to her hands, she pushed the flaming torch through Letti's letterbox, turned and fled agilely – a firebird, flash of orange and blurred bronze, vanishing into the dark stairwell.